A Divine Life

ଞଓଔ

Book Two
of
The Divine Trilogy

ଞଓଔ

by
R.E. Hargrave

xoxo
REH

R.E. Hargrave

Praise for A Divine Life

A Divine Live... Hmm... Well I can honestly say that I've just finished reading the most amazing book that has graced my kindle in a long time. This is an awesome author who can create a world so real you hate to leave it when the book ends. With a writing skill that can only be described as sexy, gritty, sharp, and sinfully stunning; she creates a sensual story line decorated with addictive characters.

~author **Sapphire Kande**
Claiming Celyse

The author pulled no punches in her delivery and amazed me at how she pulled a straight up no sharing newbie like me into her tale and made me see that through this experience they both discovered what was in front of their eyes. That the love they shared was pure and strong. Honest and with so much trust that it made me long for a master of my own.

~ author **Elena M. Reyes**
Ardor

I said it with the first book of the trilogy, To Serve Is Divine, and I'll say the same with this installment: BDSM is not my genre. "Then why did you bother to read this book?" I hear you ask. Well, simply because Hargrave has a writing style that sucked me in from the first sentence. Not only that, but she keeps up with the plot of the story instead of relying on just the intimate scenes between her characters. I'm a sucker for a good plot, and Hargrave's stories always leave me wanting more.

~ author **N. Wood**
Waves of Healing

Table of Contents

Table of Contents continued

Acknowledgements

Reaching the second leg of the Divine journey has been hard won, and daunting at times. It wouldn't have been possible without several key people.

With my warmest, heartfelt thanks, I dedicate this installment to:

My husband and children, thank you for your patience, love, and support.
Anyone who ever enjoyed the offerings of my alter ego texasbella.
Massy, for picking me up whenever I wasn't sure I could keep going. I owe you, baby girl.
Kelly and Malin, you ladies know what you mean to me.
Sapphire Kande, your support has been phenomenal and I can't thank you enough for all you've done.
Michelle, there's a special chapter in here just for you, because you asked for it!
Special thanks to:
Elizabeth M. Lawrence for making this jewel shine.

JC Clarke, you are so many things to me. A fabulous prereader, an amazing cover designer, and sounding board, but most of all, you're my best friend. Thank you for always being there for me.

R.E. Hargrave

ଞୀଔଔ

CHAPTER ONE

ଞୀଔଔ

Catherine raised her freckle-dusted face up to the spray of wet warmth flowing from the shower head. She took her time, turning around and letting the water soak into her wavy, red hair. Leaning forward, she let the water massage her back, and she breathed deep to inhale the steamy air. What lay in store for her today remained unknown leaving Catherine nervous and excited.

One year ago today, Catherine had earned the privilege to call her Sir, Jayden Masterson, Master when he'd enclosed her neck in her beloved black pearl collar. When they played over the last few weekends, he'd hinted that he had a series of challenges in store to celebrate the anniversary. It had been hard to stop herself from guessing at what they might be. He was her Master, and she knew that whatever he had planned would be exquisite and just what she needed. Master always knew what was best for her.

Reaching for the shampoo, Catherine recalled the reason behind her nervousness. She would be spending the day with unknown people, rather than with her Master like she'd first thought. Her hand tightened around the bottle, and she squeezed a generous dollop onto her palm, working the sweet-smelling shampoo through her thick tresses.

Catherine closed her eyes and remembered the night before. She could hear Master's hypnotic voice describing the new experiences the sunrise would bring.

"My precious jewel, you have done so well in the last year with me. Kneel."

Catherine lowered to the ground, positioning herself in front of him on her knees so that her naked bottom was resting against her heels, and clasped her hands behind her back, which caused her bare breasts to thrust toward Master.

"Perfect. Now, crawl to me and release my cock with your mouth."

Sir's instructions were followed with precision; the submissive crawled to where her Master reclined in his favorite chair. Resting her hands on his thighs, Catherine leaned forward and used her teeth to pull the string on the loose pants he'd worn into the playroom. With her nose, Catherine pushed the strings apart before gripping the edge of the pants with her teeth, and then pulling them down over his large erection.

Master assisted by lifting his ass just enough for her to tug the pants down to his thighs.

"Now, suck my cock nice and slow while you listen to me."

He didn't have to repeat himself. Catherine moved forward and kissed his balls before running her tongue from the base of his long cock up to the tip. She sucked off the salty drop of pre-come that had appeared on the swollen head, and then opened her mouth to descend over him. Her measured pace was languid while she established a rhythm: up, swirl her tongue around the head, and then back down. His taste and scent were still fresh from his morning shower.

Catherine rinsed the shampoo from her hair and filled her hand with conditioner, working it in like she had with the shampoo. She rinsed again, and then applied another handful of conditioner.

Working it in slower this time, she left it to soak while she squeezed body wash onto her puff. On her first pass, she made quick work of washing her body. Once she had rinsed herself, she loaded the puff up again. This time, following Master's instructions, she worked the soap into her skin in slow, tight circles across her breasts, over her arms and legs, and then across her ass, before settling the puff into a gentle rubbing motion over her sex while she continued to remember the previous night.

"You will not be receiving any release this evening, slut. Trust me that the abstinence from coming I've imposed on you since last weekend will be well worth it, come tomorrow. You're to set your alarm for seven o'clock, and then get up and fix yourself a bowl of oatmeal, a small bowl of berries, and a glass of orange juice. Once you've eaten, go shower. I want you to wash your hair and use the conditioner twice. While the second application . . . Oh, fuck, that feels good . . . is soaking in your hair, you're to use the cherry and bamboo cream body wash on yourself twice. Make sure you scrub that pussy of mine until you are on the edge of orgasm, but do not come!"

At his edict, Catherine whimpered around his cock.

"Once you've rinsed the soap and conditioner from your body, shave your legs and underarms before you get out. Do your makeup. Dry your hair, and style it in a high ponytail. Dress in the brown trench coat and matching

high heels you purchased last weekend on our shopping trip, but nothing else. After a glass of water, you're to head out to the parking lot. Micah will be picking you up at eight-thirty to drive you to your destination. Upon arrival, you're to check in under the name Jayden's Slut. Suck a little faster, slut."

Hollowing out her cheeks, she started moving up and down his cock with more speed.

"Mm, very nice, Catherine. Once you've arrived at the location, you have my permission to come when needed as the day progresses. However, you are required to achieve at least one orgasm during each . . . procedure."

Catherine's sucking slowed while what he'd said sank in. Master was asking her to be naked and orgasming with strangers. This was going to be humiliating, and oh, so much fun.

A sharp pinch on her nipple brought her back to focus on the task at hand.

She realized at that point that she was on the verge of orgasming and needed to stop. With a sigh, Catherine removed the puff from between her legs and washed the remaining soap off while she recalled the rest of Master's instructions.

"Stop, Catherine. Assume your ready position." Master's voice didn't waiver; in fact, it seemed almost indifferent.

Allowing Master's thick cock to fall from her mouth, she returned to her kneeling stance, worried that she was now in trouble. He reached forward and pinched her nipples between his thumbs and forefingers and began to pull. Catherine offered herself to him by not fighting against the tug. Instead, she delighted in the sting that radiated up into her breasts from his tight pinches—so much that she arched her back.

"I don't want any hesitation from you, slut. Tomorrow is all about pushing your limits. I've gone to great lengths to set up this anniversary day. You will experience humiliation and pain, but most of all, I promise you'll experience great pleasure."

Catherine couldn't suppress the shudder that ran through her body at Master's words. It prompted him to pull harder on her nipples.

"Your attendants have been given permission to play with your body in any way they want – respecting your limits, of course – with the exception that the males cannot put their cocks into My pussy. You will follow their instructions, and you will thank them properly for their sessions with you. Everyone has been asked to record their session with you and email it to me at my office afterward. Do you understand my requirements for tomorrow, Catherine? You may speak."

She nodded her head and whispered, "Aye, Master."

"Very good. Now, finish sucking me off, and swallow all I give you. Then you need to get to bed; you have a busy day tomorrow."

It didn't take long until Catherine felt the warm jets of his come splashing across her tongue and down her throat while she swallowed with greed.

Hurrying to finish her shower, Catherine shaved, and then hopped out. Once she'd toweled off, she did her hair and makeup. Last was getting dressed—if you could call putting on nothing but a coat and shoes being dressed.

Stopping in the kitchen, she drank her required glass of water, and then washed up her breakfast dishes. A glance at the clock told her it was time to go. She used the bathroom one last time and tidied up, before checking her coat sash to ensure that she wouldn't display anything indecent to the neighbors.

With a final, cleansing breath, Catherine made her way down to the curb, holding her head high and her shoulders back. It was 8:29 a.m., and Micah was just pulling up to where she waited. A gust of wind blew one side of Catherine's coat back, giving him a peek at what was underneath.

Micah came around to open the door for her, and she didn't miss the adjustment he made to the crotch of his trousers.

"G'morning, Catherine. Ready for an exciting day?" he asked with a shy smile.

"Aye, Micah, I am. Thank you." Catherine shot him a wink and climbed in, and he closed the door behind her.

∞

Jayden watched her beautiful green eyes blink while they adjusted to the dim interior of the car. He chuckled at her quiet gasp when she saw him.

"Master, you startled this girl," she whispered.

"Good morning, Catherine. I trust you followed all of my instructions this morning?"

She nodded her assent.

"Very good, Jewel. I have a gift for you, but first I want to play."

Her breath hitched, and Jayden delighted in Catherine's reaction. The privacy window began to rise, but Jayden was quick to halt its progress. "Micah, please leave it down today."

Over the last two years that Micah had been Jayden's driver and errand boy, his submissive tendencies had come to the surface. He'd become Jayden's pretty, frosted-hair, blue-eyed boy toy, joining Catherine and Jayden's secretary, Samantha. Micah was aware of Jayden's lifestyle – his kinks, as it were – and his loyalty would be hard to replace.

However, Jayden knew that getting Micah involved with a new Dom would be best for both of them, even if that meant he might have to give up a dedicated employee. He had already spoken with his friend, Shawn Carpenter, about the possibility of him taking on Micah as his own submissive. Shawn was looking forward to the meeting.

"Micah, did you enjoy Catherine's little peep show just now?" Jayden held eye contact with Micah in the rear view mirror, but he could still see Catherine in his peripheral vision. She squirmed in her seat at this verbal acknowledgement that he'd seen her wardrobe malfunction.

"Yes, Sir," Micah answered with no shame.

"Thank you for your honesty, Micah." Jayden moved to the seat by the divider window, sitting with his back to his driver. "Unzip your pants, take your cock out, and stroke it," Jayden ordered. When he heard Catherine's sharp intake of breath, he knew this was going to be fun.

"Thank you, Sir." The sound of his zipper going down filled the car, followed by a low moan when Micah began stroking himself.

"Do you need some lube, Micah?" Jayden asked. It was time to put his plan into action, and let the chips fall where they may.

One way or another, his relationship with Catherine would be changing today. He knew what he was setting out to do would surprise her. However, that was what today was all about: surprising her and pushing her.

Jayden had decided to ease her into the intense day by being present for her first push.

"Please, Sir," Micah answered.

Turning his head to watch Catherine, Jayden gave his next command. "Put your hand through the window, Micah. Catherine, moisten it."

When she hesitated, Jayden grabbed her and pulled her over his lap. He pushed the trench coat up to her waist, revealing her glorious, naked ass. With a quick strike of his hand, he began to chastise her. "When I tell you to do something, slut," he popped her bottom again, "you are not," her reddening rump clenched with the next smack, "to hesitate!" The Dom wrapped up the speedy punishment with two more strikes, one to each cheek.

"This girl is sorry, Master," she moaned with a whimper.

Jayden knew that Catherine was desperate for the release he had denied her all week and that her pussy would be wet from the small spanking. This was one reason why she was his favorite and collared submissive: she was a pain slut. He liked to be rough with his girls as long as they got off on it, and there was no denying that she did. Jayden had never come across a wetter cunt than what he found after cracking his toys over Catherine's delicate flesh or clamping those perfect, pain-loving nipples.

When he shoved two fingers into Catherine, Jayden found a wet pussy, like he'd expected. He wiggled his fingers around for a minute, and her breathing picked up. When her thighs parted to allow him better access, Jayden pulled away and slipped his index finger into his mouth.

"Delicious," he taunted while sucking his finger clean. "Open," he ordered Micah, pushing his coated middle finger into the sub's mouth. "Isn't she?" he asked once Micah's lips had closed on his finger. While Micah licked and sucked, Jayden pushed his finger in and out of his mouth.

"Mm, mm-hmm," Micah agreed.

"Micah, I'd like you to join us back here."

When Micah started to zip up his pants, Jayden stopped him. "No. You need to remove your clothes before you step out of the car."

ഇറങ്ങ

CHAPTER TWO

ഇറങ്ങ

Moments later, Micah sat across from Jayden and Catherine in the back of the car in all his naked glory. His impressive dick looked to be about eight inches long and quite thick, but it was hard to tell for certain, since it curved toward Micah's body. Jayden doubted that Catherine's tiny hand would be able to close around it. They would be testing that theory soon.

"You have my permission to lube your hand with Catherine's cunt juices. Take your time scooping them from her pussy." When her thighs started to close at his words, Jayden gave her ass a firm smack, eliciting a moan from her, and her legs fell back open. "Let me explain, slut. Micah, you may kneel next to us."

Obeying, Micah knelt on the floor of the car and reached forward. Sliding his right hand down to Catherine's core, he slipped a finger into her, pulled it out, and licked it.

Jayden smirked, amused by Micah's eagerness.

Micah repeated his previous action with two fingers. When he came back with three fingers, Jayden's hand came down on Catherine's ass in time with Micah's fingers pushing in.

Jayden could smell the surge of arousal that came off of her at their combined attention.

"Holy shit, Sir! I felt her get wetter!" Micah exclaimed in awe, pulling his fingers out to grasp his dick.

With a bemused chuckle, Jayden returned his attention to the Irish beauty in his lap who was raising her ass in the air much like a cat in heat and whimpering. In random patterns, he applied light but firm smacks over her rounded rump, never hitting the same spot twice in a row.

"Now, Catherine, as I explained last night, you will have several of your soft limits pushed today. I'm not going to tell you which ones, because that would spoil the surprise."

Micah's strokes picked up, but Jayden didn't want him to come yet. "Micah, re-lube and slow down."

His fingers slipped back into Catherine while Jayden's hand landed on the part of her ass that was spread open just above where Micah's fingers were buried deep.

"Oh, fuck. Thank you, Master," fell from Catherine's lips with a moan.

"You're doing splendid with this first push, Jewel. You didn't think you could share your Master with another at the same time. Judging by your wet cunt, I'd say you are quite enjoying sharing my attentions."

Catherine let out a contented sigh, and her thighs relaxed, opening further, which pleased Jayden.

Stunning.

"Micah, I want you to sit on the seat now and spread your legs. It's your turn to kneel, Catherine, in front of Micah with your knees apart. I want to see your glistening cunt while you swallow Micah's cock."

They got into position, and fuck if Jayden's cock didn't come to full attention at the sight. When her head lowered to take Micah into her mouth, Jayden reached around his submissive and untied her coat, sliding it off her arms and leaving her just as naked as Micah—except for the shoes. Slipping the belt free from the loops on the coat, Jayden pulled both of Catherine's hands behind her back and tied them together at the wrists.

The belt was just long enough that Jayden could hold it from his seat across from Catherine and Micah. On each down-stroke of her head, the tug from the belt in his hand went straight to his cock.

Micah's head was thrown back against the headrest while Catherine sucked his cock in earnest. Her pussy lips were puffy, and Jayden could see her arousal running down her inner thighs from her slick folds. It was time to take this up another notch.

"Micah, reach down and pinch Catherine's nipples—you're not to release them until I tell you."

Both subs groaned when Micah obeyed, and his fingers closed over her rock hard nubs.

Jayden pulled the belt tighter, forcing Catherine's arms to straighten behind her back, which in turn forced her tits to thrust into Micah's grip. She was making delightful whimpering noises, despite her full mouth.

When Micah's eyes slammed shut and his shoulders tensed, Jayden knew their time was almost up.

"Slut, your mouth is about to be filled with Micah's jizz. Do not swallow—hold it."

He was unable to get any further before Micah was keening and grunting; his hips thrust into her mouth three times, and then stilled. When Micah shuddered, Jayden pulled on the belt until he heard the pop of Micah's spent dick releasing from Catherine's mouth, and she moved to kneel upright.

Afterward, he untied her hands and ordered his two playthings to switch places. To their credit, they maneuvered the change in positions without Catherine spilling a drop of the come in her mouth, and Micah never let go of her now cherry-red nipples.

"Micah, eat your come out of my slut's mouth."

Their mouths connected, and he could hear Micah lapping his own jizz from Catherine's mouth. Lucky for Jayden and his aching cock, he knew Catherine was going to come soon. Then he would get his release.

"Micah, pinch her nipples harder while you pull them. I want her tits stretched out from her body."

Catherine hissed out a throaty, "Aye, so good," while Micah followed Jayden's instructions.

"Now, eat her pussy well. When she starts squirting – and trust me, she will – release her tits and drink her down. In case that wasn't clear, Catherine, you now have permission to come at will for the remainder of the day."

Four minutes later, Catherine was thrashing and screaming: "Oh, God! Oh, fuck! Oh, Master!" over and over, while Micah did his best to drink the nectar she was spraying all over him.

It was beautiful to watch and erotic as fuck.

Jayden knew he was a bit sadistic, but he liked to deny Catherine her orgasms for long periods of time because she would always squirt, spraying what seemed like gallons of come, once he allowed it. *Sexy. As. Hell.*

Keeping an eye on Catherine, Jayden opened the car door and stepped out, before extending his hand back to help her. "Stand in the ready position."

Without a word, she stepped out, her hands went behind her head, and her feet spread shoulder-width apart. With her back straightened, breasts pushed forward at him, and chin high, her eyes went to the ground in respectful submission. She didn't seem to notice, or care, that she was standing in her apartment parking lot naked.

Jayden knew he needed to hurry this along before they got caught. "Micah, step out here and kneel next to Catherine."

The Dom circled his jewel with slow, calculated steps, taking in the sight of her. Clad in nothing but her brown stilettos, her calves had sharp definition, and her backside was lifted. His fingers grazed over her pink ass cheeks when he came back around to stand in front of her. Unable to resist, he leaned forward and licked her hardened left nipple. Closing his mouth around the bud, he bit down while his hand came up to pinch the right one at the same time.

Her eyelashes fluttered, and Catherine sighed into the pain.

Beautiful.

Reaching into his pocket, Jayden removed the special collar he'd had made for today. "Catherine, look at me."

She raised her eyes, and Jayden saw nothing but contentment in them.

"I told you I had a gift for you," he began, extending his hand so she could see the heavy, braided-leather choker he held. Hanging from the front was a sterling silver paddle, engraved with the words: Jayden's Slut. "Lift your hair for me."

When she complied, Jayden leaned in and fastened the choker around her neck after collecting her pearl collar for safekeeping. He then began the exchange of words they'd taken to using whenever he placed a collar on her: "Your servitude is surreal, Jewel."

To which she responded, "To serve you is divine, Master." Then she added in a whisper, "Thank you, Master. This girl thinks it is beautiful."

Taking a step back, Jayden leaned against the car so that the open door provided a small barrier to prying eyes, and unzipped his pants, letting them fall. His excited, dripping cock sprang free since he wore no underwear. "Show me your appreciation for your orgasms this morning, both of you."

Micah crawled to him from his kneeling position while Catherine lowered herself to her knees in front of Jayden. In unison, their hands moved up his thighs while their mouths advanced. While Micah took Jayden's balls into his mouth and began sucking and nipping them, Catherine licked the pre-come from the head before plunging her mouth down over the thick shaft.

Jayden gripped the back of her head and started off slow, inching his way into her mouth and forcing his cock as far into her throat as she could take it. He knew it was probable that his large erection wasn't going to go all the way in, but it felt fucking good to try.

When he released Catherine, she pulled up for a breath and Micah took her place, sucking Jayden's cock right back into warm heaven. The combination of their mouths working him was exquisite. Over the next ten minutes, they went back and forth, taking turns working his shaft and balls until Jayden felt the tightening in his gut. Not wanting to mess up Catherine's make up, Jayden gave Micah the order to open his mouth just as he sprayed his seed over Micah's tongue and down the younger man's chin.

Micah licked up as much as he could before thanking Jayden.

Zipping his spent dick back into his pants, Jayden told Micah to get dressed and get back in the driver's seat. He reached into the car and grabbed Catherine's coat along with the belt and held it open for her while she slipped it back on. With a nod of his head, Jayden indicated she was to get back into the car before he followed her into the backseat.

"You did very well, slut. It's almost time for your day to begin." He cupped her chin and stroked her lower lip with his thumb for a brief moment before announcing over his shoulder, "Micah, I think we may be cutting it a little close for Catherine's appointment, so let's drop her off first, and then you can take me to my office."

"Yes, Sir!" Micah chirped. He put the car into drive and pulled away.

❧❧❦❧

Leaning back into the plush leather of the seat, Catherine's body felt wobbly, like the gelatin salads her *maimeo* had always made. She tried to wrap her mind around the intense scene that had just played out. Master had sometimes played with more than just Catherine during a scene, but he had never had her interact with another submissive like this. The closest had been that long ago night at Bass Hall, where she had been more of an observer than a participant.

Catherine took pleasure in being an exhibitionist for Master. Even greater pleasure came when she was allowed to meet his gaze. She could see the pride and lust looking back at her when he worked her over in front of an audience.

With a content sigh, she felt her nipples perk up again when they rubbed against the stiff fabric of the trench coat. The sting was slight compared to the tight grip Micah had just had on them, and nothing at all in comparison to the feel of Master's clamps biting into them. Just the thought was enough to make Catherine rub her thighs together. They were slick from the juices still leaking out of her from the amazing orgasm Micah had literally sucked out of her at Master's command.

Shocked was the best way to describe Catherine's reaction to the force of that orgasm, considering nothing but finger penetration and tongue action had been used. She hadn't felt Master's cock buried deep inside of her for a week, and it was no surprise she missed it. To top it off, Catherine realized she was also frustrated Master had granted Micah the pleasure of swallowing his come.

Stop it Erin, right now.

Then it clicked: this was Master's way of showing her what was involved with sharing her submissive time, the price she had to pay for the pleasure of serving him and trusting him to meet her needs. She'd asked to have her limits pushed, and Master was granting her request. A smile of satisfaction spread across her face.

"Catherine."

She blinked.

"Catherine, look at me."

Master's rich voice drew her from her inner thoughts, and she looked up at him, feeling herself get lost in his deep, brown eyes.

"You did very well this morning, Catherine," Master continued once he had her attention. "Did you enjoy yourself?"

"Aye, Master. This girl did, thank you."

"As always, it was a pleasure seeing you submit yourself to me with such abandon."

The look that accompanied Master's words could be best described as loving. It was intense, and Catherine lowered her gaze back to her lap.

They spent the next ten minutes in silence while the car hummed along. When the car pulled up to the curb, she felt her nerves kick in. The distraction of playing with Micah had almost made her forget that she was about to spend the day in full submissive mode without Master.

Catherine Eilene O'Chancey, you know that's not true. While you won't be in his physical presence, today is all about being with him in your mind and heart. Every humiliation, every sting of pain, every tingle of pleasure will be received by you while you accept your Master's gracious gift.

On occasion, her inner dialogue could be a pain in the ass and very to-the-point.

Micah opened the car door. Catherine began to scoot forward on the seat, preparing to get out, but Master's hand touched her arm and stilled her.

"Do you remember your rules for today?" he queried in a soft tone.

"Aye, Master. This girl is to check in under 'Jayden's Slut,' and then follow the instructions given her by her attendants. She is to show proper respect and gratitude for all they do to her." She took a deep breath before continuing, "And this girl is to trust that they will not abuse her limits."

"Perfect," he whispered and leaned in to capture her lips with his own.

His tongue licked along Catherine's, demanding entrance. The second her lips parted, it plunged into her mouth, swirling against her tongue. Their kiss was breath-stealing, and then it was over.

Master pulled back; no doubt his smirk was caused by the look on Catherine's face. She was certain that she must've looked similar to an untried virgin. With that, she stepped out of the car, her fingers caressing her lips.

Master's voice made Catherine turn around. The two simple words were said with a hint of desperation that matched the flicker in his eyes, but they were all she needed to find her focus before heading into the building.

"Trust me?"

"Aye, Master. Always."

He pulled the door shut, leaving Catherine to face the building in front of which she'd been deposited. She grinned, even as her gut twisted in on itself.

ഇൻൿ

CHAPTER THREE

ഇൻൿ

Her eyes ran over the facade of the unassuming building, which housed The Silver Spurs Spa. Master was having Catherine walk into a business she frequented with regularity in nothing but a coat and heels and announce herself as a slut. *Let the humiliation begin.* At the thought, there was a tingle between her legs, and she became aware of her naked nipples again. Oh, yes; Master knew what she needed.

The soft tinkle of chimes sounded when Catherine pushed the door open. Stepping inside, her focus darted about to see if she recognized any of the patrons in the waiting room. She didn't, because there was no one else there. *Odd.*

Is that disappointment, Erin?

Stepping up to the front desk, Catherine was met by a waif of a girl who smiled up at her. She wasn't the usual clerk, and Catherine had the first hint that this would be unlike any spa day she'd ever had before.

"Welcome to Silver Spurs. I'm Paige. How can I help you this morning?" Her eyes sparkled, and her voice was lyrical and comforting. She pushed the lengths of blond hair that framed her face back off her shoulders.

Catherine found the pale blue shade of Paige's irises fascinating. They were ethereal. Firming her resolve again, Catherine let her own green eyes meet Paige's amiable gaze. "Hello, Paige, this girl is Jay—Jayden's Slut, and she should have an appointment." Though she would always love the way his name rolled off of her tongue, Catherine stumbled saying Jayden's name out loud. It wasn't something she was accustomed to doing when in the role of his submissive.

The answering grin on Paige's face was contagious, and Catherine found herself smiling while Paige looked over the reservation book.

"Why, yes—yes, you do." She shot Catherine a playful wink. "Are we ready to have some fun today?"

Catherine gave her a tentative nod followed by a quiet, "Sure."

Clapping her hands, Paige moved out from behind the desk and over to the front door, where she flipped the sign to 'CLOSED' while turning the lock.

"If you'll follow me," she invited before heading down the hall that led to the treatment rooms.

Catherine fell into step, expecting to be led to the changing rooms where she'd be able to put her trench coat into a locker and collect one of the spa's luxurious jasmine-scented robes. Instead, they walked past the rooms, not stopping until they were further down the hall in front of a wooden door.

Reaching out to Catherine, Paige began undoing the belt from around Catherine's waist. "Let me take your coat for you."

"Oh. Well, um . . ." Catherine mumbled, at a loss for what to say. She was trying to figure out how to warn Paige that she was bare beneath the coat, but Paige had already pulled it open and was sliding it down Catherine's shoulders. She didn't seem fazed by Catherine's nudity.

"Those shoes are exquisite; the leather looks so supple and yummy! Oh, sorry," Paige said with a touch of bashfulness. "Where are my manners? I can get carried away sometimes, and I've heard so much about you. I'm a little excited that we are getting to meet at last, but we'll talk more later . . ." Pushing open the door, Paige nodded toward the room. "In you go for your . . . ah, massage. Enjoy!" With that, Paige turned and walked back the way they'd come, leaving Catherine to face whatever awaited her beyond the open door.

She's a strange one, but I like her.

Crossing over the threshold, Catherine found herself in what appeared to be a massage room. A comfortable-looking padded table with a cushioned head support sat in the center. The far wall housed a perpetual waterfall. Trickling and bubbling, the sound of the water was almost trance-inducing. To her left, another wall was kitted out with cupboards, and behind her, a linen shelf displayed fluffy, gray towels. A picture window overlooking an expanse of gardens filled the remaining wall.

It seemed she was alone. Unsure what she should be doing, the submissive fell into a standing ready position. Catherine was gambling that anyone she encountered today would be aware of her submissive status, and assuming the position was natural to her. Her chin lowered to the floor while she closed her eyes and let the waterfall sounds pull her into a quiet place.

�& ℭ℥

"Well, look at this pretty little mare standing here," a deep voice spoke from behind Catherine, startling her.

How much time had passed was anyone's guess.

While she did jump, the movement was restricted to her shoulders. Catherine managed to maintain her position, resisting the urge to look around. Her mouth remained closed, since she'd not been given permission to speak.

"Such a fine specimen you are, too."

Rough-tipped fingers trailed down Catherine's spine, slipping between her ass cheeks. Both of his hands were on her, spreading her cheeks apart so that she felt the cool air against her hole. The image of an animal being inspected at market appeared in her head.

"You'll look amazing with a tail."

Catherine clenched on instinct at the words. *Tail?*

The man snickered, and his hands moved up from her ass to her hips, continuing up over her ribcage until he was cupping Catherine's breasts while the 'inspection' continued.

Master said this was okay.

"Hm. Firm. Terrific size: they fill my hands, but don't overflow," murmured the mystery voice. "Lean forward, and place your hands on the edge of the table."

Catherine did as she was told, feeling her ass jut out behind her. She fought against the flare of panic that threatened to rise at having a stranger touch her, reminding herself of Master's final request to trust him.

Her cheeks were spread apart again, and then a lubed finger pushed into her puckered hole with no warning. It felt nice, and she groaned.

He pushed in and out of her a couple of times before adding a second finger, which he commenced scissoring with the first, spreading her—opening her. Before long, a third finger was added to the task of stretching her hole, and her breathing had picked up. Catherine gasped when he reached around with his free hand and started stroking the wet folds he found nestled between her thighs.

"Like that, do you?" he asked, his breath hot against the back of her neck.

Catherine nodded her head and pushed back against his hand to be met with a loud smack. The sharp sting of his hand on her left cheek surprised her.

"Don't be a greedy whore." His fingers disappeared, leaving her feeling empty and open. "However, it's clear you're ready for more."

In the next moment, Catherine felt cool metal being inserted into her backside with a slow, firm pressure. When the plug was all the way in and she was satisfied that she was full again, he told her to sway her hips.

With the first move to the right, Catherine felt something soft and light brushing against the backs of her thighs. When she moved to the left, the sensation swayed with her. Realization set in: the butt plug he'd just put in had a tail attached to it. While she should have felt debased, instead her arousal increased at the sensation.

Oh geez, he wasn't joking about the tail . . . he's turning me into an animal. Well, fuck me.

I think that's the idea, Erin.

The hairs, which tickled her thighs with a light caress, were sending tremors of electricity through her body, forcing her nipples into tight, pebbled nubs.

"Yes. Very fine, indeed. You make a beautiful filly, Catherine. So tell me," he asked – and she could swear there was a childlike giddiness in it – "Have you ever felt the bite of a whip?"

At once, her breath caught in her throat, and Catherine's body froze, while flashes of the last Demon Night she and Master had attended at Dungeons & Dreams went through her mind.

A submissive was suspended by her wrists with chains hanging from the ceiling. Likewise, a spreader bar between her ankles forced her legs wide and they were chained to the floor. Her eyes were closed and her head was thrown back in rapture. Red lines crisscrossed her nude body giving the appearance that she was wearing a fish-net bodysuit.

With a resounding crack, Catherine watched the long tail of braided leather wrap around from behind the sub, the tip landing on the woman's nipple with a snap.

The sub shuddered and whispered, "Thank you, Master."

It was obvious by her demeanor and the perfect diamond pattern over her skin that the man wielding the whip was in complete control and quite good at what he did.

Catherine held her breath when the whipping Master came around the dangling woman, raising his arm and preparing to lash her again. The leather snaked out and made contact with the submissive's naked pussy, and Catherine couldn't hold back the moan that escaped her lips simultaneous with the bound woman.

She couldn't look away from the scene while Master whispered in her ear, "Do you want to be her? Do you want to feel the bite of Sir Jonathan's whip, slut?"

Entranced, Catherine had said the one thing she could say: "Aye, Master."

The deep voice of Sir Jonathan began explaining how the whip could be, ". . . a pleasure tool in addition to punishment for some submissives if they are pain sluts."

Sir Jonathan had approached without Catherine realizing it and now stood in front of her while he finished talking.

Master chuckled against her ear and commented, "Interesting," while she dared a brief glance up into the angular face of Sir Jonathan with his cropped blond hair and piercing blue eyes – then Master was nudging her off his lap so that he could stand.

The grinning face that belonged to the man who'd just stepped in front of her was the same from that night: Sir Jonathan.

Oh. My. God. Master had arranged a session for her with a whip expert: *The* whip expert for their local scene. She shuddered and could feel the wetness increase between her thighs.

"Ah, so you do remember me?" he asked with a quirked eyebrow.

"Aye, Sir. This girl does," she admitted, her tone breathy.

"Good, good. How about we get started then?"

"As you wish, Sir. Thank you."

Inside, she was trembling. A year ago when she'd signed her contract with Master, whipping had been a hard limit. Master had brought it up a few times with her because of her fondness for pain. Until she'd seen Sir Jonathan in action, she'd been unable to view a whipping as something pleasurable. After that night, Catherine had asked Master to change it from a hard to a soft limit, thus letting him know she was ready to explore it in the playroom.

"Since this is your first time under the whip, I'll go easy on you. Don't want to scare you off when you've agreed to try this at long last." He smirked at her with eyes that sparkled with mischievousness. "But first, I want you to prance that fine ass around the room for me, filly. Stretch your legs a bit, since you've been in one place awhile."

Walking around the room as instructed, Catherine could feel his appraising eyes on her. The stilettos lifted her backside; the plug deep in her ass was accentuated by the angle and forced a sashay into her step, which in turn made the tail swing. Simply put, Catherine felt like a human horse.

You're starting to look like one too, whore.

Oh, will you please shut up, and let me focus!

Wondering how she looked, Catherine recalled Master's admission that she would be recorded today, so she tried to peek around in a sly manner to spot the cameras. She couldn't see them and decided it would be best to forget them again. After all, she wasn't there to perform; she was there to experience and enjoy.

"Well done, filly," Sir Jonathan praised when she returned and came to a stop in front of him. "Your Master sent a gift. Open your mouth." His voice was firm but kind when he gave the instruction, retrieving a chocolate brown, leather bridle, complete with reins, from a side drawer.

Catherine opened, and he pushed the leather-covered bit between her teeth. When she closed down on it, it didn't hurt her teeth. Next, he slipped the bridle over Catherine's head. The reins he left dangling between her breasts while he adjusted the fastenings.

Okay, NOW you look like a horse . . .

Oh, just . . . ugh, shut it!

"Damn, you look . . . hot," Sir Jonathan exclaimed while flashing a lopsided grin at her. Another dip into the side drawer, and he pulled out a matching brown riding crop. "How about a little warm-up?" he teased and flicked each of her nipples with the crop.

Catherine hummed at the sensation.

It was all the encouragement Sir Jonathan needed. Letting the crop thwap against her skin – from her shoulders down her body to her calves – he circled around Catherine. The crop landed in what seemed a random pattern over her flesh. The small sting that came when the flat tip of the crop connected soon spread into a warm glow, a slow burn that was spreading from the outside in.

Oh, this is going to be good.

"Let's see how you're doing," he mused several minutes later, while pushing a finger into Catherine's now very wet core, causing her to grunt. Sir Jonathan laid the crop down and picked up the reins with one hand, leaving her to assume he was satisfied with what he'd found. When he gave her breasts a light flick with the reins, her nipples reacted to the leather.

Erin, if your nipples get any harder they're going to pop!

He tugged on the reins again, guiding Catherine while he instructed her: "On the table on all fours, knees shoulder width apart."

Once she was in position, he looped the reins around one of the drawer handles.

"Don't go anywhere." He laughed, and then he patted her rump. "A bit more warm up, and I think we'll be ready." Sir Jonathan's hands were on Catherine's ass, fiddling with the plug. There was a small clicking sound, and then she was overcome with sensation when it started vibrating.

"What's your color, Catherine?" he queried with sincerity after slipping the bit out of her mouth.

The question, and the way he'd asked it, was the final incentive Catherine needed to let go. There would be no more rambling in her head. By checking with her before going any further, Sir Jonathan had freed her to trust him.

"Oh—oh, God . . . green, Sir. This girl is definitely green." She groaned.

"Does that feel good in your ass, filly?"

Catherine didn't answer – couldn't – because at the same time he was asking, he reached between her legs and pinched her clit. Her whole body shook in response.

Going back to the drawer, Sir Jonathan extracted a beautiful whip, while she watched with wide, hungry eyes. Catherine found herself biting her lip and wanting to rub her legs together at the sight of it. It was the same rustic, brown leather as the rest of the set.

He presented the whip handle to her lips for Catherine to kiss in appreciation. Sir Jonathan maneuvered the bit back into her mouth, and then rolled his broad shoulders before taking a step back. "Let's begin. Come when you are ready, filly."

She had time to see his arm rise up in her peripheral vision, and then her world shattered.

The leather landed across her back, caressing from her right shoulder, diagonal across her spine, and reaching for her left side when the end wrapped around the curve of her hip and snapped just on the edge of Catherine's pussy lips.

"Fuck!" she screamed, though it came out muffled, while gushing all over her thighs and the table.

"That's it, Catherine. Good girl, let it go." All playfulness had gone from Sir Jonathan's voice, replaced by focus and care. She knew she was safe.

The next lash crossed her back from the opposite direction.

While Sir Jonathan maneuvered around Catherine, she became lost in the thrill of the experience. The leather bit into her skin just hard enough to make her breath catch, before it was swept away into primal moans, even while the radiating burn dissolved into titillating warmth. She had a vague awareness of his voice coaxing and encouraging her, grounding her to her spot so that she didn't get washed away on a sea of sensation. Her skin was on fire, and if she'd been asked how she felt at that precise instant, the best she could have verbalized would've been 'a big glob of goo.'

At some point, Sir Jonathan had put the whip down, unloosed the reins, and had helped Catherine down from the table. She shuffled along while he guided her around the room with a firm grip, helping her stay upright. Catherine realized he must have slipped the stilettos off,

A Divine Life

for her bare feet dragged along the cool tiles. That was a good thing, because she wouldn't have been able to balance herself in them at that point.

"There, there, filly. You took that like a seasoned pro." His voice was still gentle, like he was talking down a skittish stallion.

They went back to the table, and he was molding her over the edge of it. Catherine felt the harness being removed, and she worked her jaw, stretching it. A half-focused glance at the bit when he pulled it away revealed it was covered in deep gouges—teeth marks. It was going to need a new leather covering, because she'd worked through the material down to the metal bit during her whipping. The vibration in her ass stopped when he switched off the plug.

"Deep breath. Now exhale."

The plug was gone, and Catherine was thankful for the table, given that it was the only thing holding her up. There was a rustle of clothes, and then she felt his large, warm body against her back.

"I'm going to collect my payment now," he whispered in her ear. "Although, the gratification I got from taking your virginity, as it were, with my whip was quite rewarding in itself. That was truly one of the most beautiful acts of submission I've ever seen, Catherine; just beautiful. If you ever need a new Dom, I'd be happy to oblige."

45

He licked up her neck to just below her ear, sucked her earlobe into his mouth, and bit down. She sighed into it, feeling his erection grow against her back.

"I promised your Master that your pussy would stay empty, but that your ass—your delectable, fine example of an ass . . ." his cock slid into her with one thrust, ". . . was mine."

She came hard.

Drizzling warm, scented oil over Catherine's back and ass, Sir Jonathan started off slow. While he fucked her, he massaged the oil into her tender skin. The heated oil and the steady pressure of his fingers worked into the lash marks, quenching the fire that blazed over her back. His hands kneaded across her shoulders, down her arms, and then came from below her breasts.

It was incredible.

While he pushed his cock into Catherine, his hands squeezed from the bottom upward, his gentle fingers closing and pulling on her nipples when he reached the top. Then he would withdraw until just the head of his shaft was still in her tight hole and repeat the process all over again. Sir Jonathan's tempo in her ass picked up, but so did his manipulation of her breasts.

In disbelief, Catherine realized she was getting close to coming yet again.

"Sir, this girl . . . going to . . . come!" she tried to warn him just before her inner walls clamped down on nothing, and her body convulsed. The feeling of his cock swelling inside her was unmistakable. He pulsed deep inside her while she collapsed onto the table.

The room started to fade. Sir Jonathan pulled out, and Catherine hissed through clenched teeth. The sound of the waterfall grew louder. Her backside was wiped with a gentle, warm cloth. As everything went black, she was aware of his large, oiled hands working over her muscles.

The submissive drifted away with Sir's last whispered words: "Thank you, Catherine. It has been a pleasure. Anyone that has the honor of hearing you call him Master is a lucky man indeed."

ഇരുന്ന

CHAPTER FOUR

ഇരുന്ന

They waited at the curb while Jayden followed Catherine's retreating backside with his eyes until she disappeared inside the building. God, he hoped he hadn't made a mistake.

After Paige gave the all clear by displaying the 'CLOSED' sign, Jayden nodded at Micah to go. The twenty-minute drive to Masterson Metalworks passed while he reassured himself that Catherine would be okay today. As her Dom, Jayden knew she was ready to move ahead, but as a red-blooded male who had somehow fallen for that green-eyed goddess, he worried about her being pushed too much.

In that vein, Jayden had taken advantage of his silent partner status at The Silver Spurs Spa to have the business closed for today and his own 'staff' put in place. He'd arranged for the video recordings in part because Jayden knew they were going to be hot as hell to watch, but their primary purpose was so that he could monitor her progress and know she was being taken care of.

At ten o'clock, Jayden strolled into his luxury corner office, grabbed himself a cup of coffee from the machine, and then set about booting up his laptop. If he knew Catherine, and he was pretty sure he did by now, she would crash after her session with Jonathan. She always did when a scene had been intense. That session would be more than she was used to. Jayden had warned his friend to be prepared for Catherine needing to sleep. He'd also insisted that Jonathan provide her with a full body massage, even when she passed out. It was important aftercare that Catherine would need to make it through the day.

Jonathan's video was due to arrive in about an hour and a half, followed by Samantha's arrival there at the office an hour after that. Jayden had some work to get ahead on, because he was taking a few days off next week as a surprise for Catherine.

If today went well, they would need to renegotiate her contract. Some of the changes he was going to suggest would require some personal days as just Jayden and Erin, not Master and Catherine. Inside, Jayden was hoping the changes would be permanent and that this would be the last submissive's contract he'd ever have to pen.

While he'd arranged today for Catherine to test her limits and realize her fantasies, Jayden was also going to be pushing himself. Today was going to be a final hoorah, so to speak, for him. If Catherine was open to what Jayden planned to propose to her, this would be his last day with any submissive except her. The computer finished its final login and security check, so Jayden buckled down and got to work.

ಬಿಂಗ

At eleven-thirty, Jayden was deep into reviewing the latest production numbers out of China when he got a text from Jonathan.

Check your email. She's something else. Anytime I can be of assistance again, I'm game! She's got more stamina than you give her credit for. Later, Jon

Jayden sent a quick text back thanking him, finished up the document he was working on, and then pulled up Jonathan's email. He couldn't deny his nerves were frazzled with anticipation over what he was about to view.

In planning Catherine's session with Jonathan, both men had agreed that she wouldn't be able to handle more than five to ten lashes of the whip before she called Red—her safe word to stop the scene. That was fine with Jayden; it would be a fantastic start. When Jonathan then suggested the horse apparel, Jayden had loved the idea, and it had led him to custom-order an entire set of play toys for today. He'd gone with the rich brown, because he loved the way the color looked against her skin after impact play.

With a few clicks of the mouse, Jayden had opened the video and connected it to his wireless projection screen. He sucked in a breath at the sight of her almost full size before him, nude except for the heels and his collar wrapped around her neck.

He watched while Catherine glanced around for a moment before falling into a submissive stance. Standing there with her head bowed, she succumbed to her natural tendencies. His dick twitched in his pants, and Jayden felt his chest begin to swell with pride and admiration for the once broken girl.

Adjusting himself, Jayden kept his eyes on the screen while Jonathan entered the room and 'checked' her over before fitting her with the harness and tail plug. *Damn, that was just downright erotic.* When Jonathan had her walk around the room, Jayden's dick went from sporadic twitches to a slow, steady swell while he watched that tail swish back and forth. By the time Jon had her on the table on all fours, Jayden's dick was rock hard.

Her eyes widened, and then glazed over when Jonathan asked her about the whip. Jayden felt himself grin, knowing she was remembering Demon Night. It was the same look she'd had that night when she'd watched Jonathan work over his sub.

Then Jonathan took out the whip and had her kiss the handle.

Fuck Me.

Shocked by his reaction, Jayden had to pause the video, needing to catch his breath.

Jonathan's text had indicated she'd done well, and Jayden hadn't received any panicked calls, so he knew that the video wasn't going to reveal his beautiful Catherine having a mental breakdown. Deciding he was ready, he pressed play once again.

On screen, Jonathan began. Jayden watched the first lash make her come without flinching under the cracking leather. Catherine's body absorbed the impact with majestic grace, and Jayden relaxed. Enthralled with the scene before him, he absentmindedly stroked himself through the thin material of his dress pants while he watched Jonathan's arm go up, and then come back down, again and again.

Jayden counted the first ten lashes, and he was astounded that Catherine came twice more. After that, he became mesmerized and quit counting. He could see the insides of her thighs glistening while her juices trickled out of her with repeated orgasms.

Holy shit!

Jonathan hadn't been kidding about her stamina. He moved around her, bringing the whip down across her back, avoiding the tender vital organs to lash over her ass, the bottoms of her feet after he slipped her high heels off, and the backs of her thighs. Then he angled his strike position so just the tip bit at the sides of her tits.

Thirty minutes later, Jonathan backed off and set the whip down. Catherine's magnificent body was flushed pink, red lashes crisscrossing over her skin. She hadn't called "Red." Instead, Catherine had accepted and delighted in what was being done to her by coming innumerable times.

Jayden's cock ached. He couldn't deny that he'd fallen for her a little harder. How had he been lucky enough to have this angel come into his life? *She's perfect in every way,* he thought. Up on the screen, Jonathan leaned over and whispered something in Catherine's ear just before pushing his large, stiff shaft into her ass. She came yet again, while Jayden looked on in disbelief.

A loud groan reverberated around the room when Jayden squeezed his dick in a knee-jerk reaction. He shuddered and moved his hand before chastising himself: *Dammit, a Dom with three subs does not need to jerk off like some hormone-riddled teenager.*

Jonathan proceeded to fuck her for the next fifteen minutes before she announced she was going to come again. While Jayden looked on, Jonathan tensed. It was obvious when he came with Catherine; he threw back his head and released a loud, stretched-out, "Fuck," followed by numerous grunts while he finished off inside her.

Being the responsible Dom Jayden knew he was, Jonathan pulled out, and after discarding his condom, cleaned her up. His friend then set about working oil into Catherine's flesh while she did, in fact, pass out on the table, just as Jayden had predicted she would.

What the Dom hadn't predicted was that the scene would be so all-consuming for his submissive; that she would meld so easily into it. It had been glorious to watch. The lash marks were already beginning to fade. They left behind white welts, into which Jonathan rubbed the special oil.

With ten minutes left until Samantha was due to arrive, Jayden couldn't have been happier at how the day was proceeding. Also, his cock needed some serious attention, so it was a good thing she'd be there soon. He pondered how Samantha was going to react to his news that today would be their last play date, and he was thankful when his dick softened a little.

Samantha had almost been Jayden's collared sub before Catherine came into his life, and until he'd experienced Catherine's skills, Samantha had been the best head he'd ever encountered. To their misfortune, Samantha just didn't like it as rough as Jayden did, and she had been developing a pattern of Yellowing or even calling Red on him when he would try to get her to expand her limits.

Because he hadn't met Catherine yet and didn't want to give up Samantha all together, Jayden had offered her a position as his personal assistant with benefits. They'd renegotiated her basic contract, and he now paid her three times what someone in her position would get in a normal situation. They teased each other over her being his paid whore, but they both knew she was more of a friend. Jayden had insisted on the higher pay because of the specific requirements he had.

She showed up for work whenever Jayden needed her, worked hard, and wore outfits to his specifications—outfits that allowed him to use her body for physical release while at the office. However, what Jayden didn't get was the mental release of working Samantha over with his floggers, crops, and leather straps until her skin threatened to burst from the attention.

That pleasure did not become his again until he'd met Catherine during an open-door night at Dungeons & Dreams—Dallas's premier BDSM club. She'd come unattached, looking for something more, and Jayden had been the one to give it to her. They'd clicked the moment he'd lifted her knuckles to his lips in introduction.

The outer door to the office opened and closed. Jayden's cock began throbbing anew. A few seconds later, there was a knock on his door. "Enter," he called out.

Samantha walked in, wearing a fitted, brown skirt that halted about two inches above her knees and a sleeveless, cream-colored silk blouse. Her shoulder-length, straight, blond hair had been pulled back into a low ponytail against her neck.

"Good day, Sir." She smiled at him.

Rising from his chair, Jayden walked around to the front of his desk and leaned his ass against the edge. "Your punctuality, as always, is appreciated, kitten. I have a matter that needs your attention."

At once she stepped forward and dropped to her knees in front of him. Reaching for his belt buckle, she paused to ask: "May this girl offer you oral service, Sir?"

"You may."

With nimble fingers, Samantha undid his belt, followed by his zipper.

Jayden straightened up and allowed her to pull his pants down to his thighs, hissing when the cool air of the office hit his already seeping cock.

Without another word, Samantha leaned forward and bathed his nuts with her tongue, taking time to suck each one into her warm mouth and swirl them around.

Jayden moaned at the exquisite feeling.

"Enough of the teasing, kitten. Suck my cock."

She licked from his nuts all the way up to the swollen head, sucking the pre-come off the tip, and then ran her tongue through the slit to gather more. Samantha's mouth opened, and he thrust into it. Her lips closed around his shaft, while one hand wrapped around the base of his cock. A steady rhythm was set while she stroked the lower half of his cock and sucked as much of the top half down as she could.

The whole time, Jayden managed to thrust into her throat with a gentleness that shocked him, considering his needy state.

Her other hand moved to his balls, squeezing and pulling on them. He lost the battle when she ran her fingertip along his scrotum, back toward his asshole. Jayden closed his eyes, coming down Samantha's throat to visions of Catherine on the table with the whip lashing against her.

Samantha continued a deliberate sucking motion, making sure to get every drop from his softening dick. Licking Jayden clean, she then pulled his pants back up, tucking his dick into them and refastening and buckling him. Only then did she sit back on her haunches, resting her hands palms up on her thighs.

"Thank you, kitten. I needed that," Jayden praised with a light air. Of course, she didn't see the grin that curled the corners of Jayden's mouth, because her gaze was on the floor like a good little sub. Walking back around his desk and sitting in his chair, Jayden ordered, "Come here."

With a graceful air, she rose and stepped around Jayden's desk, coming to stand in front of him with her hands at her sides.

Jayden let the silence surround them while he regarded her. Had the time come to give up his office escapades? Could he willingly let go of the knowledge that anytime he felt the urge to come or have a quick fuck, all he had to do was press the buzzer and beckon Samantha into his office? Was Catherine worth this sacrifice?

Fuck, yes. She is worth this, and so much more.

At last he was able to speak, "Present yourself, kitten."

She was aware of the drill; he knew no other command was necessary. Grasping the hem of her skirt with both hands, she began sliding it up her long legs. Inch by inch, her toned thighs were revealed, and then the soft, tanned skin above her thigh-highs came into view. While she continued working the skirt up to her waist, Jayden was expecting to see her smooth cunt, but instead he saw satin.

Angered by instinct and habit, he bolted from his seat. Reaching for the lapels of her blouse, Jayden ripped it open, sending buttons skittering across the polished wood floor. He found her small titties were also covered in satin.

That would never do.

৪০০৪

CHAPTER FIVE

৪০০৪

Catherine came to, blinking her eyes in the soft light of the room. Underneath the babbling of the waterfall, she could hear someone moving about, and she had to take a moment to remember where she was. Flashes of her session with Sir Jonathan played through her mind, and she shuddered.

"Oh, you're up! Good. I was about to wake you myself, but it's so much nicer to get up on your own terms, isn't it?"

The woman who'd escorted Catherine this morning was grinning at her. "Aye, Mistress—"

"Oh, no, silly! Just call me Paige. I'm a submissive, like you!"

Rubbing the sleep from her eyes, Catherine noticed Paige was naked with the exception of a platinum link collar that had a silver L hanging from it. When Paige shifted, turning back to the counter near which she stood, Catherine spotted the tail plug drying on a towel next to the sink. The whip was in Paige's hands, and she was rubbing it up and down.

"I'm cleaning up the toys," she explained, as though she'd known Catherine was about to ask. "And oiling the whip, of course. Have to take care of it. An untended whip can hurt like a bitch!" she joked.

Catherine found herself giggling with the pretty blonde.

Their laughter died down, and Paige pointed to a tray next to Catherine. "I brought you some fruit, cheese, and ice water. You'll need to replenish your fluids and keep your energy up for the rest of the day, Catherine."

"Thank you, Paige. And please, call me Erin when it's just us. It's what my friends call me." Catherine reached for a bundle of grapes and a slice of cheddar.

"My pleasure, Erin. After all, what are friends for?"

"Please join me," she offered, nodding her head toward the tray to suggest Paige help herself. "So, how long have you been a sub?" Catherine asked in an attempt to get to know her new friend.

Grabbing a strawberry, Paige's eyes sparkled when she replied, "Five years, but I've belonged to Master Landon for the last three."

They sat in solitude for the next few minutes, nibbling on the food. While Catherine was still, Paige was humming with unused energy. All of a sudden, she jumped up, and her breasts with their rosy pink nipples bounced. Catherine noticed a glint of light when Paige turned, and although she didn't mean to, she found herself staring at Paige's breasts. Realizing her rudeness, she started to look away.

A quiet snigger from Paige made Catherine turn her head back. "It's okay, Erin. Feel free to look at me. I enjoy the attention." Paige shimmied her shoulders so that her breasts jiggled. "Master didn't tell me I *had* to be naked today; he granted my request to be."

"I'm sorry," Catherine mumbled, a tad embarrassed that she was so enraptured with the sight. "It's just that the light caught on your, um, piercings, and I couldn't help myself."

"Oh, for goodness sake. Here." Paige walked right up next to her. "Give me your hands."

Catherine was tentative while she extended her hands out toward Paige.

The moment she could reach them, Paige grabbed Catherine's hands and brought them to her nipples. They were both pierced with little silver rings adorned with more silver L's; a matched set. A warming sensation began to spread through Catherine's belly when she remembered her first time with Miss Katarina.

"Go ahead, pull on them."

Paige moaned when Catherine complied by tugging on the jewelry with a gentle pull.

Fascinated with how pretty the jewelry looked and how Paige was reacting, Catherine had to ask, "The piercings are beautiful. Did it hurt to have it done?" She grabbed another bite of pineapple and popped it into her mouth.

Would Master like it if she were pierced like this? They had touched upon body modification in past discussions as something to consider.

What do you think, Erin? It would be another way he could bind you and taunt you.

"Not at all. In fact, it was quite orgasmic."

Catherine must have allowed the jolt of arousal which hit her show on her face, because Paige laughed.

"Believe me, I like having my nipples played with. Just like you do, I understand." While she commented, she let her own hands ghost over Catherine's now-protruding nubs.

The sensual caress caused a bubble to start building low in Catherine's gut. *Or perhaps it wasn't Paige's touch*, she thought when the quirky sensation became a sharp pain. Catherine had to let out a burp.

"Excuse me," she exclaimed, moving her hand to cover her mouth in surprise. "My stomach must not like the pineapple."

A second burp made Paige jump into action. "Let me see if there's any antacid stuff in the bathroom. You don't want to have to deal with that today. It'll distract from your enjoyment."

Before Catherine could reply, Paige had already scampered into the adjoining bathroom. She heard cupboards being opened and closed, and then Paige reappeared looking victorious—and mischievous.

"Want to play, Erin?" Paige smiled, while shaking a box of antacid in her hand.

"I'm not sure—" Catherine began with skepticism.

"Oh, come on! It'll be fun, I promise." The sub started twisting her upper body in excitement. "Your next session isn't due to start for about an hour, so we've got time."

Catherine nodded, albeit with reluctance, and Paige squealed. While she watched, Paige retrieved a bottle of water from a stocked mini-fridge by the linen shelf and a glass. She soon handed Catherine a bubbling drink, which she gulped down to avoid the bitter taste. With that out of the way, Paige became serious.

"Lay back, Erin. Let me make you feel good."

The words, and the position she was being asked to assume, were so similar to her time with Miss K months before that Catherine's heart began to race with the expectation of what Paige offered. She lay back but kept herself propped up on her elbows to watch what the girl was doing.

"This is allowed, right, and it's safe? I mean, Master told me I was to go with whatever was asked of me, but he didn't mention . . . this." She wasn't sure how to put it into words without sounding snobby. The fact was that Paige was a submissive, and Catherine had only ever been told to obey Sirs or Ma'ams.

Paige was at the shelf, grabbing a couple of fluffy towels, when Catherine asked her question. She looked over her shoulder at Catherine and waved her off. "Sir Jayden made the specific request that I take care of you today. Trust me."

This was news to Catherine, and in the back of her head, small warning bells went off. However, she wasn't given time to dwell on them, because Paige arrived back, telling her to lift her butt while she slid one of the towels underneath Catherine. The other one she set to the side.

"You're going to love this. Then, we'll get you cleaned up for your next scene. And yes, it's safe for occasional fun. You probably shouldn't do it on a regular basis, though." The words were punctuated by Paige pushing one of the tablets into Catherine's pussy.

For several moments, Catherine wasn't sure what was supposed to happen, other than the fact that Paige's fingers felt amazing while they stroked her sex, teased her clit between slippery fingers, and then pinched her lips closed. She let out a garbled sound when Paige, still holding Catherine's labia in a tight squeeze, started moving the flesh up and down so that her clit was taunted further.

Then she felt it. A warm, tingling sensation erupted inside her, and with each second that passed, it became warmer and was soon bordering on hot.

"Paige," she whimpered.

The tingling spread, and Catherine swore she could feel the effervescent effect of the tablet fizzing and popping inside of her. It was incredible and frustrating at the same time, like the ultimate teasing of her inner flesh with no relief, no pressure in sight.

Another wave of sensation swept over Catherine when Paige released her firm hold and spread her lower lips apart, allowing the cool air to dance across her damp folds. The action resulted in a frothy mixture of fluids, which had built up inside Catherine, to ooze out and trickle down toward her awaiting anus.

Catherine cried out with needy desperation, her hands flying to her own breasts to yank and pull on her nipples, while Paige pushed three of her slim fingers into the fizzy mess. "Oh . . . Please . . ." The rocking of her hips was beyond her control, her body acting on instinct. Catherine's orgasm began to build deep within, and she lost track of what Paige was doing to her.

All she knew for certain was that Paige's small hand was stretching her and providing the pressure she wanted, making her feel more full than she could've imagined. When her orgasm hit, it was brutal and fierce, and it took Catherine a few seconds to realize it was her own voice screaming, "Aye" with such enthusiasm.

After the euphoria settled and Catherine could see straight once again, she noticed Paige was standing at the end of the table with her arms crossed over her chest and a smug look on her face.

"So, how was it?" Paige teased.

"How was it? Hmm, let me think . . ." Catherine laughed and threw her arms out to the side. "It was fucking fantastic!"

Giggling, Paige offered her a fresh glass of water. "Here you go, Erin. You need to replace some fluids—again!" She winked.

Thanking her friend, Catherine took the drink and sipped on it. "How in the world did you learn that little trick?"

"Have you had a chance to meet Mistress Katarina Svenson?"

Catherine nodded with a smile. "Oh, yeah. Master set up a session with her for my first candling experience—among other things."

"Miss K is pretty amazing," Paige agreed with a wistful sigh, and at Catherine's quizzical look, she elaborated. "She was my Domme before I met Landon, and well, this little trick was a favorite of hers to torture me with."

A frown marred Catherine's features. "Paige, aren't you supposed to call him Master?"

"Of course, if he's with me, and we're in play mode. Otherwise, it's just Landon and Paige." She shrugged like that was quite common.

Thinking about it, Catherine realized maybe it was. After all, weren't there times she referred to Master by his given name?

"So the two of you are . . ." She hesitated, unsure of how to proceed. "Are you two a couple outside of the playroom?" she blurted, deciding to just throw it out there.

A dreamy look came over Paige's face while she lifted her left hand and showed Catherine what she'd not observed before. "I'd say we're more than just a couple. He proposed to me almost a year ago. We've been planning a Valentine's Day wedding. Four months to go, and I couldn't be more excited!"

Upon Paige's left ring finger sat an elegant engagement ring. The main diamond was a marquis cut, but it was the band that held Catherine's attention. Starting at a narrow point on the left edge of her finger, the white gold band widened as it came across her finger and wrapped around, reappearing on the other side in rose gold when it passed the starting point and swept off to the side. In the gap between the two colored parts of the band, the diamond was wedged, looking like a leaf.

Two delicate solitaires were embedded in the white gold portion of the band.

"Oh, Paige, it's gorgeous, and congratulations!" she exclaimed, choking down the jealous feeling which threatened to rear up. Getting off the table, Catherine set her water down and went to hug Paige, ignoring that their bare breasts were pressing into each other. "I love the two-toned gold."

Paige blushed, and the smile that followed went all the way to her blue eyes while she tossed her long hair back over her shoulder. "He had it custom made to represent the two sides of our lives merging into one." She was glowing with pride.

"That is such a beautiful sentiment." Catherine reached out to finger the L's dangling from Paige's nipple rings. "Seems he is making sure you're branded," she mused, thinking how she wouldn't mind being branded by Master.

"Mm-hm." A shaky laugh escaped. "Funny you should put it that way." Her hands had found their way to Catherine's nipples and were fingering them with a soft touch. "He used to own a ranch outside of town, so he does have a habit of marking what's his."

"So, how does that work? I mean, how does one draw the line between Master and husband?" Was such a complicated relationship possible? Could *Jayden* see her that way? Just thinking his name caused a funny feeling in Catherine's chest. Her thoughts continued, now on overdrive . . .

No. Master didn't do personal relationships. He'd said as much when they'd first signed their contract together. They'd both agreed to the understanding that this was nothing more than a sexual relationship. Hell, he was fucking two other people besides her that she knew of. If there were a chance that he wanted something more with her, he wouldn't have handed her over to complete strangers today. *Would he? Oh, God.* Sir Jonathan's offer to take Catherine on repeated itself in her memory, along with the knowledge that she had more sessions today with an unknown number of Doms. Was that what today was? Had the 'inspection' Sir Jonathan performed not been part of the scene? Was Sir Jonathan looking her over as a potential acquisition? What about Miss K offering to take her on back in February? Catherine's stomach soured again.

"No. No, please, no. I—I can't," Catherine mumbled and began to shake.

"Erin?"

Her world began crumbling around her, and panic took root. Catherine gasped for air, wrapping her arms around her mid-section.

"Erin! What's wrong?"

Paige's shriek snapped Catherine to attention, and she raised her watery eyes to meet her new friend's.

"Paige," Catherine started to cry. "He figured it out. I tried to be so good, so careful. He knows, and he's going to get rid of me!" She thought she'd done so well at hiding her secret over the months, protecting her heart.

Paige had wrapped her arm around Catherine and was rubbing slow circles on her back. With a wince, Catherine became quite aware of every lash mark from Sir Jonathan's whip. They now burned to her core when Paige's soft hands brushed over them. Catherine flinched away from her.

"Shh, Erin," she said in a calming voice. "Who knows what, sweetie? What are you talking about?"

Turning wide eyes on her, Catherine choked out, "Jay . . . Master. He knows I've fallen in—in love with him. I wasn't supposed to. He found out, and now he's interviewing me with strange Doms to get rid of me. I broke the rules and he—" she swallowed a sob, "he doesn't want me anymore!"

Warm arms embraced her. "Oh, Erin, sweetie, you've got it all wrong. He doesn't want to get rid of you. I've never seen a Master so enamored of his submissive as Sir Jayden is with you."

"But—" Catherine started to argue. Her gut was telling her that *she* was right, not Paige. Master had taken her pearl collar this morning and labeled her a slut. She now assumed she was to be auctioned off like cattle.

"No 'buts,' Erin. You have to believe me. I know this is all going to work out for you," Paige said with affirmation.

Oh, how Catherine wanted to believe Paige, but in her mind she scoffed. Of course Paige thought it was all going to be fine. She had her fairytale: a Master and a life partner in one. Arguing with her would be pointless. Sad resolution became Catherine's bedfellow when she came to what she felt was the right decision in her mind. No matter what, Catherine knew she'd always love Master, and because of that, she'd see the day out so that he wouldn't be embarrassed by her behavior in front of his peers. However, when Master made the move to take her collar, she would just beat him to it. She would claim they needed to end their contract for personal reasons, and then try to walk out with her head held high. It would hurt less if Catherine were the one to leave.

Yeah, keep telling yourself that, Erin.

Straightening her back, Catherine looked up at Paige and managed a weak but determined smile. "If you say so. I'll have to trust you for now," she mumbled, while fingering the braided slut collar around her neck.

Paige's mouth curled up at the edges. "That's the spirit, Erin! Have faith in your Master to do right by you."

Sure, faith that he'll pass you to a capable new Master.

Catherine wanted to reach into her head and strangle that inner voice that didn't know when to shut up.

"Come on, sweetie, between the massage oil and the by-product of the antacid you're a mess. Let's get you cleaned up and ready for your next session." The mischievous glint was back in her eye.

"Paige, do you know what I'm doing next?" Catherine was more than ready to be done with the surprises; ready to call this day quits and crawl into the solitude of her room to cry for her broken heart in peace.

Grabbing her hand, Paige helped her off the table. "Yes. I do. And no, I'm not telling. Wouldn't want to ruin the surprise, now would we?"

Oh, no. Why would we want to do something like that?

Together, they walked to the bathroom, Paige leading the way. "Go ahead and use the toilet while I get the water going."

"I can do that, Paige. You don't need to, promise, and the privacy would be nice." She was fighting not to sound frustrated.

"Sorry, Erin, but it's a direct order from my Master. I'm supposed to make sure you empty and then see to your grooming."

Catherine sighed in compliance and went to sit down on the toilet.

"Oh, just a minute. I almost forgot." Paige slapped the side of her head in a 'duh' gesture. "Can you lean over that counter? Go ahead and put your elbows on the edge and rest your forehead on your hands. This isn't the best feeling, but it is required by my Master."

Again Catherine complied, closing her eyes while she listened to Paige open a cupboard and move around.

"Okay, all ready. Widen your stance a little."

Her butt cheeks were pulled apart, and then something thin and hard slid in, making her clench in surprise.

"Doing good, Erin, but I need you to relax and try not to resist the intrusion," Paige instructed, while Catherine felt her bowels filling with something warm and wet.

"Paige! What the hell?" Catherine barked and tried to straighten up.

"Catherine, resume your position. Now," a male voice commanded from the doorway.

ഇൗൽ

CHAPTER SIX

ഇൗൽ

"Samantha," Jayden started in a firm tone, but then paused.

She knew she was required to present herself at Jayden's request when in his office. Samantha was aware that when her skirt was raised, he was to see bare skin at the apex of her legs. When her blouse was open, Jayden should see her dark brown nipples pointing at him off the tips of her little B-cup titties.

Did she want to be punished? The psyche of most submissives not only wanted, but needed—no, *required* punishment in addition to pleasure. The very act of correcting a sub let them know that their Dom cared and was paying attention to their every action, silent or otherwise.

His next thought brought him to the realization that he had been failing Samantha in this regard since his feelings for Catherine had become more than Master and submissive. Disheartened, Jayden saw that he'd been using Samantha as nothing more than a common whore to get his jollies while he'd failed her as a Dom.

After taking a deep breath to steady his voice, Jayden started again. "Samantha, do you want to be punished?"

The look she bestowed on him was direct and pleading, while a tear fell from the corner of her eye. "Yes. Please, Sir."

Well, hell. Sometimes I hate being right.

"Very well, kitten." He used her pet name to let her know that he was no longer angry with her; that he'd acknowledged his transgression. Opening the top drawer of his desk, Jayden punched in the code on the hidden compartment, from which he pulled out a key. Rising from his seat, he directed her, "Follow me."

They traveled the distance of the room to a wooden door at the back of Jayden's office. It was no different from any of the other doors except that it was locked, and no one but Jayden and Samantha had access to the keys. This room was not on the security camera grid for the building.

The door made no noise when Jayden pushed it open and waved her inside. "Standing ready position, Samantha."

Jayden watched her take position in the center of his playroom. The walls were a deep green, and the furniture was mahogany: sturdy, thick pieces with hints of burgundy in the grain. There were no windows. While the décor was similar to Jayden's home playroom, this one was not as elaborate, housing just the basics.

Unbuttoning his shirt and slipping it from his shoulders, Jayden told Samantha to remove her tattered blouse and skirt. After closing the door, Jayden hung his shirt from a hook on the back before slipping his shoes off to set them against the baseboards with neat precision. When he turned back around, Samantha was standing in her bra, panties, garter belt, and thigh-highs.

What he was about to do wasn't something normal, but Jayden knew he needed to forge ahead for both of them. He walked over to the toy cupboard and threw open the doors. Perusing his options, he chose a riding crop with a large paddle tip because it would hurt less than the crops with the small ones. Those always delivered a stinging pop that lasted a while. His goal was not to hurt Samantha, but to correct her indiscretions. For a minute, he considered taking out her temporary collar and placing her in it, but he decided against it in light of what would be happening later. Before returning to her, Jayden also slipped the emergency knife from his first aid kit into his pocket.

His resolve carried him forward to begin. Moving behind Samantha, Jayden administered a few light smacks to the backs of her thighs and outthrust elbows with the crop.

She trembled.

"Tell me, my kitten. Why am I about to darken your skin instead of licking your slit until you are creamy and ready for me to fuck until you come on my cock?" Jayden inquired while working his crop around the front of her body, continuing to apply light smacks against her hips, thighs, and stomach. When her mouth opened to answer, he stepped back to give Samantha his full attention.

In a shaky, quiet voice, she replied, "Your submissive is to present a naked cunt when her skirt is raised, Sir."

Jayden let the crop snap out and thwack against her satin-covered pussy.

A soft whimper escaped her lips.

"Continue," he commanded.

"Your submissive is also to present bare tits with erect nipples at Sir's request." The last word became garbled when his crop snapped against each of her tits in rapid succession.

A return trip to the cupboard had him selecting two more toys. Glancing at his watch, Jayden noted that he had plenty of time to issue a thorough punishment before moving ahead with his original plans for Samantha. He laid the new toys onto the rolling cart he kept on hand, grabbed one more thing from the drawer and slipped it into his other pocket before he returned to Samantha.

"Kitten, I will admit that I've not been attending to your needs. This has been an oversight on my part, and we'll discuss the reason in depth at the end of our time today—though I'd hazard a guess you already know why. In acknowledgement of my error, I will allow you to choose your punishment tool," he offered in concession while nodding at the cart.

Her icy-blue eyes looked over the display: the crop that he'd already used on her, the suede flogger with its knotted ends, and the large wooden paddle with holes drilled into it. The last was his preferred tool for punishment, and Samantha had never felt its bite.

"If it pleases you, Sir, this girl would like the flogger, please." Her voice was steady and sure.

"Admirable choice, kitten, but first, a few wardrobe adjustments are in order," Jayden declared, stepping toward her while pulling the knife out of his pocket. Her audible gasp made him stop and look at her. "Shh . . . I'm not going to hurt you. Much."

Trailing the knife point across the tops of her breasts, Jayden slid the blade under one of her bra straps, and with a flick of his wrist the honed edge sliced through it. The other strap was soon cut as well. Jayden ran the knife through the pretty bow sitting between her tits, and what remained of her bra fell to the floor. He was pleased to see her nipples engorged and solid, pointing out into the room. Next, he dragged the knife down Samantha's stomach, leaving a white line in its wake that became a raised, pink welt when the blood pooled just beneath the surface of her skin. Two swift cuts through the sides of her panties, and he watched them join the ruined bra on the floor.

Taking a step back to assess his handiwork, Jayden could see the dew already gathering on her exposed cunt. His knees folded under him, and he knelt down. Placing the knife next to his foot and out of the way of a potential accident, he then used both hands to pull her pussy lips apart. With a mind of its own, Jayden's tongue snaked out to take a long, slow lick up her slit, swirling around her clit.

The soft sigh of pleasure above him prompted Jayden to remove his mouth and hands and to collect the knife and return it to the cart.

"Are you wearing your plug like you're supposed to be when I call you in for 'special meetings,' or did you forget that rule, too?" Jayden asked her with a cocked eyebrow.

"No. No, Sir, this girl didn't forget. It's in place," she whispered.

"Show me."

Samantha turned around and grabbed her ass cheeks while she bent forward, pulling herself open for his perusal. There, nestled inside her tight hole, was the clear base of the anal plug he'd bought for her early in their relationship.

"Very good; that will stay in during your flogging. Now," Jayden grabbed one of her tits and mounded it up, pushing the nipple out further, "take a deep breath for me." With his free hand, he slipped a nipple clamp out of his pocket and soon had it secured on her. "Exhale, and breathe."

Keening whimpers fell from Samantha's mouth, but Jayden ignored them. He knew she hated the clamps. However, this was punishment, and she'd given him the okay in the past to use them as he saw fit.

"Again; deep breath," Jayden ordered and affixed the other clamp. "You decided your nipples needed to be hidden from me; therefore I will keep them covered."

"Yes, Sir." Her short answer was pitiful and laced with shame.

"To the cross. Face down."

Giving her a minute to carry out his instructions, he followed her over to the St. Andrew's cross in the corner of the room. Observing Samantha while she got into position, Jayden made note of two things: her clamped nubs were going to press into the wood – but that would hurt less than her lying face up so that he had access to them with the flogger – and two, her backside was calling to him in more ways than one. He couldn't wait to lay into it first with his suede, and then with his shaft.

Samantha placed her outstretched arms against the upper rungs of the cross, and Jayden buckled them into place with the attached leather straps. A low whistle sounded through her clenched teeth when her tits pressed into the wood, but he ignored her, choosing not to comment. Instead, he reached down to release the catch at the bottom of the cross that would allow him to spread her legs, and then buckled her ankles in before pushing them apart. When he was finished, she was bound in an X.

"Twenty lashes, Samantha. For your insubordination, and," Jayden laughed, "because you want it. Don't you, kitten?"

"If it pleases you, Sir, this girl would be most appreciative."

"You will count the lashes out, and thank me for each one." Remembering how turned on he got watching Jonathan have Catherine kiss the whip handle, Jayden presented the handle of the flogger to Samantha's lips for her to do the same.

Holding the handle in his right hand, Jayden gathered the tails of the flogger in his left and raised both arms. Bringing them down, he released the tails about a foot away from her body to watch them fan out as they lashed across her right thigh.

"One, Sir. Thank you." She groaned.

Jayden gathered the tails up again and released them across her left thigh with the next swing.

"Ugh—two, Sir. Thank you."

For the third swing, he let the gathered tails land with a solid thud over the center of Samantha's ass, knowing the impact would jar the plug.

"Oh, God. Three, Sir. Th-thank you."

Jayden was calm and controlled while he concentrated on the task before him. Letting her body absorb each impact before he flogged her again was paramount. He was in perfect control while he centered his lashes on her buttocks and upper thighs. The heat would build faster in this manner, but this wasn't for her pleasure. As the Dom worked, every third hit landed over the plug, jarring it. The messier her counting became, the more his cock swelled while she endured the pain he was bestowing upon her.

"Ow! Twelve, S-sir, th-thank you." By now her shaky words were laced with sniffles, betraying the tears that were escaping.

The loud thwack of the flogger connecting with her skin reverberated in the room.

"Shit! Thirteen, Sir. Thank you."

Thwack! He swung again and waited for her count.

"Fuc-fourteen, Sir. Thank you."

The next two swings landed on the soles of Samantha's feet to disrupt her expectations. Two more hit her ass cheeks. Jayden focused the last two lashes over the plug, harder than any one preceding it.

"Oh, my, fuck! Ni-nineteen, Sir. Thank you!" Her breath was coming in pants and gasps. "Twenty, Sir. Thank you." Samantha whimpered her final thanks, and her body slumped against the wood.

Moving with urgency, Jayden returned the flogger to its spot in the cupboard, and then released Samantha from the leather cuffs. After he helped her stand and take a step back, he noticed the leather wrapped wood was wet where her body had leaked fluids during her flogging.

"Well, well," Jayden taunted while reaching down to stroke her dripping cunt. "Did you enjoy yourself?"

In response, Samantha moaned and ground herself against his hand. "This girl did. Thank you very much, Sir."

"Come, kitten. I want you to lie down on the bed so I can soothe your ache."

Once Jayden had made sure Samantha was lying on the soft mattress, he retrieved the special lotion that he'd started having made because of Catherine's fair skin. She bruised with ease. Similar to arnica cream, but with a pleasant floral scent, the handcrafted cream contained herbal oils and extracts that would prevent bruising and soothe any lingering sting. He climbed up next to Samantha and started massaging the cream into her shoulders. Working his way down, Jayden was sure to cover every area where the flogger had made contact.

While his fingers danced over Samantha's rosy flesh, his thoughts wandered to Catherine. Was she still napping off her session with Jonathan? How had she taken to Paige? If she was awake, were she and Paige getting cozy in a newfound friendship? So many questions made him itch with renewed energy, and his cock hardened. Should it have bothered him that the mere thought of his Irish lass got him hard, and not the naked woman he had right in front of him? Finishing Samantha's back, he instructed her to roll over.

She'd had the clamps on more than twenty minutes by that point, so Jayden removed them post haste. Noting the way her purple nipples hardened further when the blood rushed back into them, he scooped up some more of the cream with both hands and worked it into her tits, letting his slick fingers slip and pull over her nipples.

Samantha was writhing and moaning under his touch.

"You did very well, kitten. I think you've earned a special farewell. Lift your knees and spread your thighs for me."

Jayden sat back, giving her room to maneuver. Once Samantha had her arms hooked under her knees, and had pulled herself open, he lay down in front of her and started lapping at the abundance of fluid escaping her.

Stiffening his tongue so that he could push it into her pussy like a little dick, he observed that while she tasted good, her flavor didn't compare to his Catherine. Still, Jayden gave it his all, knowing this would be the final time; he nibbled on her lips, tongued her folds, and sucked her clit into his mouth.

"Please, Sir, may your submissive come in your mouth?" she begged with a formalness he hadn't heard from her in ages.

Instead of acknowledging Samantha's request, Jayden kept licking, and then slid two fingers into her soaking wetness. Her walls gripped his fingers at once, and her hips started rocking against his face.

"Oh, dear lord. Please, Sir. May this girl come?" she screeched out in desperation.

The next few seconds were a blur of activity while Jayden extracted his fingers and sat back. "Come!" was all he had to say before Samantha fell apart.

It was fun watching her writhe while the moans poured from her mouth. Samantha still held her legs up and apart, her sex on full display while it pulsed and her thick come dribbled out of her. He waited for her movements to still before leaning down to give her one final lick, lapping up a mouthful of the essence that had dripped out of her.

"Mmmm . . . Thank you, Sir," Samantha said with a heavy, satisfied sigh.

Good to know one of us is satisfied, he thought ruefully, just as his phone chirped in his pocket with a personal email alert. Confused as to who might be sending him something right then, Jayden unhooked Samantha's legs from her arms and helped straighten them out with hurried but gentle rubbing.

A bad feeling that something had happened to Catherine came over him, and nothing else mattered anymore.

෮෮෬෬

CHAPTER SEVEN

෮෮෬෬

The man's sharp tone made Catherine lower herself back over the counter at once, and for the time being, she forgot her distress over her Master.

"There ya go, darlin'," the voice continued, softer than before. "Paige was just following orders. Now, you wouldn't want to be responsible for my yella rose getting a whippin' for not obeying her Master, would you?"

That must be Sir Landon.

"No, Sir. This girl apologizes," she whispered, dropping back into submissive mode with ease. Her tummy was getting full and tight with the warm liquid. It wasn't the most comfortable feeling in the world, but she didn't dare move from her position.

A rough, callused hand caressed Catherine's bottom, gave it a pinch, and then patted her, again making Catherine feel like an animal being checked over.

"Alright, darlin'. All done. That wasn't so bad, now was it?" he said after several minutes.

"No, Sir." In truth, Catherine was uncomfortable from the bloated feeling, but she was now worried about upsetting him and having him take it out on Paige.

"That's a good girl." He chuckled. "You can go ahead and sit that pert ass of yours on the commode and empty yourself out. Let Paige take care of you with no further impertinence. Understand?" His voice was stern, but somehow comforting in its pleasant calmness. "I'll be seeing you ladies soon."

"Aye, Sir. Thank you."

She raised her gaze to the mirror to try to get a glimpse of Sir Landon, but all she saw was a flash of his back when he walked away. From what Catherine could tell, he was tall and lean. She couldn't help but notice his light, wavy, brown hair before her gaze settled on his nice, tight ass – unless his jeans were lying – and with a start, she recalled the night at D&D where she'd overheard Master talking about Sir Landon's talent with piercing. That was what had led them to talk about the future possibility in the first place; she'd made it clear to him that she wanted it.

So much for that idea now. Why would a Master arrange for his submissive to be pierced when he was getting rid of her?

"Well, come on, Erin. You heard Master," Paige snickered. "Sit that pert ass of yours down, and empty it all out!"

While not pleased with the situation she was in, Catherine was desperate to get the pressure off her belly, so she lowered herself onto the cold seat. She experienced the instant relief of what felt like gallons of water – and other things – pouring out of her. Groaning, she tried to hide her face in her hands while the unladylike sounds continued from below her. "God, Paige, this is so embarrassing!"

Paige's whimsical laugh echoed around the bathroom. "That's kind of the point, sweetie." She put on a mock stern face and deepened her voice, "Humiliation is a Master's best friend."

They both erupted into a giggle fit at Paige's antics. The moment was therapeutic, and Catherine felt her mood lighten a bit.

"Sorry, Erin. I guess you could say it's a fetish of his from his ranch days."

Taken aback, Catherine gasped. "Are you saying he's into bestiality?" She wouldn't judge either of them if he was; it just wasn't something that she could ever fathom participating in.

"No, no! He didn't get off on using enemas on the animals or anything like that! It was just a necessary part of taking care of them at times, and well, the idea stuck with him when he began his journey into this lifestyle." She broke the silence of the moment with a light giggle. Paige directed Catherine after sticking her hand into the shower to check the temperature. "Okay, water's warm, so in you go!"

Catherine wiped up, wincing at the tenderness she felt after Paige's earlier attentions to her nether regions, and stepped into the extra-large marble stall. There were multiple shower heads with different pressures raining down, filling the ample space with steam. The far wall had a bench seat with handles mounted on either side.

Paige's petite hand pressed into her back, pushing Catherine under the water. Its temperature seemed almost too hot at first, but when the hot spray started massaging into her sore muscles, she decided it was magnificent.

A purr rumbled in Catherine's chest while Paige undid her ponytail and scratched at her scalp, encouraging Catherine's red locks to fall down her back. She arched back into the spray to ensure all her hair got wet before Paige spun her around so that her breasts were under the pelting water. Her nipples hardened, and she groaned.

The fruity scent of the shampoo hit Catherine's nose just before Paige's hands found their way into her hair and began massaging it in. Catherine sighed when Paige started at the bottom of her hair, moving up to Catherine's scalp, where she continued to gently scratch with her short nails.

"Ugh, Paige. So good . . ." Catherine trailed off with a small whimper.

With a giggle, Paige turned her around again to rinse the shampoo out before spinning Catherine once more and repeating the process with a thick, creamy conditioner, which she left in. She piled Catherine's red hair atop her head and grabbed some pins to keep it there.

"Now, scrub time!"

Catherine looked over her shoulder to see Paige pick up what looked like a common kitchen brush with stiff bristles and put a big dollop of body wash on it. Beginning at Catherine's shoulders, Paige worked the brush in a circular motion over her backside. Yet again, Catherine was turned around so Paige could carry on with her arms first, then thighs, then belly.

When the brush was placed against the edges of Catherine's breasts, she had to bite her tongue to keep from begging Paige to go faster, be rougher. Much to her dismay, Paige slowed her pace, leaving the submissive quivering and wanting. Paralyzed, all Catherine could do was watch while the brush swirled over her mounds in languid circles. At the feel of the rough bristles going across her nipples at last, Catherine clamped her teeth together, the air whistling through them while she exhaled.

Reveling in the feelings was easy once she'd closed her eyes and let her head drop back. At the surprise of a warm mouth replacing the abrasive bristles Catherine jerked, the nipple popping out of Paige's mouth with a delightful burn when her teeth dragged across the surface.

"Erin, you know I'm following orders, but I also want to do this for you. Master doesn't let me play with girls very often. Trust me, this is a treat." There she went with that damn wink again.

Trust me. Master's words from that morning taunted Catherine, and she became determined. Pure pleasure and enjoyment were at her fingertips if she could ignore the sorrow that threatened to drown her, so ignore it she would. How could she not, considering Paige's ministrations at that moment?

Blissful delight washed over Catherine when Paige closed her mouth over Catherine's nipple and suckled, drawing the peak out away from her body and stretching it with her lips before moving her teeth to the base and nipping. Tiny fingers latched onto the neglected nipple and mimicked the motions of Paige's lips. After several minutes of Paige trading back and forth, Catherine dragged her eyelids open to glance down. Her nipples were elongated further than she'd ever seen them.

Paige chose that moment to lean back and admire her work. "Almost perfect! I'll keep working on them while we finish getting you ready." Her words were cryptic, and she gave both of Catherine's buds a sharp pull.

The desire built, and Catherine felt her labia began to swell with a surge of the natural chemicals in her system. Again, her thoughts tried to wander, but this time, Catherine couldn't stop them.

This is wrong. No one but my Master should be pulling these feelings from me. But if I'm right and he wants to pass me off, then maybe that's why I'm being subjected to all of this today. It's his way of showing me that I can serve and be served by others. Even in his dismissal, he is still taking care of me.

Before Catherine could start crying over her abysmal situation, Paige was yanking the pins from her hair and washing the conditioner out. That done, her nipples were then pinched and used as leads while Paige guided her from the shower. The women were silent while they dried off, and Paige produced a brown leash-type thing out of a basket on the shelf. One clasp was hooked to Catherine's collar before she noticed the two extra lengths hanging from the main chain with clamps on the ends. These were applied to her stretched-out nubs with a quick, deft hand.

"Paige," Catherine sucked in some air to process the sharp bite, "Can I ask why all the nipple torture? Not that it feels bad; I'm just curious." Her words were jarred by her panting.

Giving her a quick grin, Paige chirped the two words that Catherine was beginning to hate: "Trust me!" before she walked out of the bathroom with Catherine in tow at the end of the leash.

It was a surprise when they returned to the massage room, and rather than settle in to await the next scene, Paige took her to her earlier discarded stilettos. She assisted Catherine with stepping into them before leading her out the door into the hallway.

"Paige, what about the customers?" Their nudity could be a shock to some poor, unsuspecting person.

"Don't worry, Erin. Should anyone happen to see us, they won't be surprised by our presence—or lack of clothes."

With a sarcastic roll of her eyes, Catherine quipped, "Let me guess. Trust you?"

To which a beaming Paige nodded.

While they proceeded down the hall, it dawned on Catherine that it was very quiet, except for the soothing music being piped in through hidden speakers. Of course, the spa respected privacy, and all treatments were done in private rooms. What was missing was the soft chatter of customers behind the doors.

The noise level became inconsequential the moment Catherine was led into a new room, this one labeled 'Make Up' with a brass door plate. Upon their entry,

Paige gave the leash a firm tug, yanking the clamps and making Catherine squeak before Paige dropped the handle, easing the pain. With her hands free, she was able to open a bag that had been left just inside the door. Catherine let out a gasp at the gorgeous corset Paige extracted. With fabric the color of milk chocolate, it looked soft like doe skin and was trimmed with emerald green brocade.

"Arms up, sweetie," Paige requested, wrapping the corset around Catherine before doing the hook and eye closures that ran up the front.

It came to just below Catherine's waist, leaving her tummy and hips exposed at the bottom. The top edge was designed to be an under bust, therefore stiff boning was tucked under her breasts, lifting them up and out but leaving her throbbing nipples uncovered.

Paige pointed out the mirror to her right. The sight reflected back at Catherine was beautiful and erotic.

The tawny color of the corset reminded Catherine of Master's eyes and the softness they often held when looking at her. The deep green trim made her think about how he would comment on her eyes and how they were capable of entrancing him, particularly when she was at her most aroused. Catherine shuddered; now was not the time to have such thoughts or to dwell on how much she would miss his eyes.

Seeming to know where Catherine's thoughts were headed, Paige jerked on the leash to get her attention.

Compliant, she allowed herself to be led her over to a reclining cosmetologist chair, climbing in after being instructed to "Hop up" by Paige.

Paige began flittering around, combing out Catherine's hair and blow-drying it with a round brush, setting it in soft waves. Next was the touch up to her make-up. Given that she didn't seem to take any time at all, she assumed Paige was keeping it light. However, when Paige held the mirror up for Catherine to see, she was left speechless. A pair of smoldering, smoky-green eyes peered back at her, and when she gave a half-hearted smile, the deep crimson lips in the mirror smiled, too.

"Wow, Paige! I didn't know I could look like this. Thank you."

"My pleasure, Erin. It's easy when I have such an exquisite subject to work with!" She beamed, the pride in her work apparent. "Go ahead and rest a bit. Master will be in soon to start your next session. I just need to set everything up."

Leaning back, Catherine closed her eyes and soon dozed off to the sounds of Paige moving about, opening and closing drawers while humming to herself.

ഹരുഗ

CHAPTER EIGHT

ഹരുഗ

Jayden's semi-hard cock deflated. His concern regarding the contents of the mystery email was like having a glass of ice water thrown over him. Abruptly, he stood, adjusting himself with blatant motions in front of Samantha. She would think it was because she had aroused him, which was better than the truth. The more time he spent away from Catherine, the more he regretted ever setting this day up. Samantha's naked body just wasn't going to do it for him ever again.

"Take a moment to recover, Samantha. Meet me in the main office in five minutes," he instructed before leaving her alone. His heart was thrumming, and his palms had become sweaty. Jayden raced out of the room, leaving his shirt behind. He needed to get that email pulled up and make sure his Jewel was safe.

"Come on, come on," Jayden mumbled, hating the extra security measures the office computers featured. When the email program loaded at last, he couldn't click on the icon fast enough. However, he was brought up short when he saw that the sender was Jonathan—and there was a file attached.

He hadn't expected anything else from Jon today. Opening the email, he began scanning over the words. His heart rate settled, only to take off racing again when Jon divulged what the attachment was.

Jayden ~
Don't know if you're still at the office, but just in case you are, thought you'd enjoy this. I realized I'd left my camera in the massage room and ducked back in to get it. The girls were in the shower by the sounds of it, and I noticed I'd somehow turned it back to record mode when I was pulling off the video I sent you earlier. Seems Catherine and Paige have hit it off quite well. Enjoy! ~Jon
P.S. If you get tired of her, I want her. You better do right by her, or I'll personally rip your dick off and make you suck it! lol J.

Of course I intend to do right by her, Jayden thought with mild discontent. Also, what was up with his "friends" all trying to steal his submissive? Oh, that's right; like an idiot he'd asked them to offer their domination to her so she could be sure of what she wanted. Two weeks earlier, Jayden had convened with all of today's cohorts and had asked for their assistance with regard to their particular skill sets. However, he hadn't stopped at just making arrangements for Catherine's experiences, but he had also invited Ryan and Shawn to the meeting to discuss new arrangements for Samantha and Micah.

Was this what love did to a person: turn their brain to gooey mush?

If Jayden were honest with himself, he wasn't delusional enough to think that he wouldn't have done the same thing and offered himself when he first met Catherine had she been with someone else at the time. Lucky for him, she'd been in between Doms, and it hadn't had to get ugly. All it had taken was a seductive smile, a kiss feathered across her knuckles, and a whispered command in her ear for her to become putty in his hands.

Jayden shook off the sweet memory. He was just queuing up the video when Samantha walked into the room and came to stand at the end of his desk.

"Ah, there you are, Samantha. It looks like we've got a little bit of entertainment. Come forward and kneel—

inspection position with your back to me." Jayden wanted her like that, knowing it would spread her open and he'd be able to watch her body react to the images on screen, whatever they might be. Leaning back in his chair, Jayden pressed 'Play' the moment Samantha was situated.

They both sat in silence while the video started. For several minutes, nothing but his peacefully napping Jewel showed on the projection screen. Though it pained him to do so – he could've watched her sleep for hours – he ended up fast-forwarding the clip until Paige appeared in the frame. Catherine was adorable when she woke up and took in her surroundings, and her skin flushed at something Paige had said.

His cock was reacting to the image of the two women getting familiar with each other. Watching Catherine, you wouldn't believe she had been with a woman just once before in her life. She was a natural at it, and Jayden gloated, knowing he'd been right about his fire-capped Catherine and the fresh-faced Paige being remarkable together. Paige had a nice body, but for once, he didn't notice it. All he noticed was his Erin's natural softness.

My Erin? Where'd your submissive, Catherine, go? Dude, you're so gone.

Samantha released a soft sigh when, on screen, Catherine laid back on the table and parted her legs for Paige. She let out a slight gasp when Paige's fingers disappeared between Catherine's thighs with the white tablet she'd just held up.

Jayden's eyes scanned the rest of the picture, looking for a clue as to what Paige had just done. When they landed on the box of heartburn tablets, he gave a belly-laugh. He hadn't thought of that particular goodie in years. Oh, this was going to be fun to watch.

Leaning forward and wrapping his arms around her from behind, Jayden used his large hands to cup Samantha's tiny titties. He started kneading and plucking at her tender nubs while Catherine's moans filled the room via the surround sound.

The camera wasn't set up to get a clear shot, but they still had a good enough view that Jayden, and he assumed Samantha, could get the idea. Paige stroked and teased Catherine's pretty, waxed pussy. Catherine loved it, if her cries and squirming were anything to go by.

In sync with the slight movements of Paige's arm, Jayden dragged his nails across Samantha's skin. She quivered and started to lean back into him. His cock had swollen to capacity by that point and was throbbing with need. Though he had Samantha right in front of him, all Jayden wanted was to pound into Catherine hard and fast, then soft and slow.

A push against Samantha's back had her moving forward onto all fours. Her knees were still spread wide, so Jayden had a clear view of her pussy and ass, which was still flushed from the flogging. Grabbing hold of the plug base, Jayden worked it out of her with slow, teasing twists, pushes, and pulls. More prep work would be needed, because his cock was nowhere near as small as the gaping hole that awaited him when the plug came free.

Catherine's whimpered use of Paige's name prompted him to reach into his desk drawer, from which he retrieved the extra tube of herbal cream he kept there. He greased up two fingers, which he pushed into Samantha. She groaned and pushed back against the intrusion. After a few pumps in and out of her, Jayden added a third finger. With each push, he spread his fingers apart, opening her further, until she was as ready as she was going to get.

Pulling his cock out of his pants, Jayden stroked himself a few times before he tore into a condom packet and sheathed his cock. Squeezing some more lube onto his length, he slathered it on. "Stand up, kitten, and sit down on my cock," he ordered.

A garbled groan redirected his attention to the projection on the wall, and his own groan slipped from his lips. The flash of deep pink flesh told him that Paige had Catherine spread open, revealing her inner folds. Her movements told him that Paige was already working three fingers into those folds and adding a fourth.

He knew firsthand how tiny Paige's fingers were; her whole hand, in fact. Jayden became excited at the prospect of what he was pretty sure Paige was about to attempt. Holding his shaft at the base, making it stand up straight, he gripped Samantha's hip to help guide her onto the head of his cock.

Ahead of him, Paige's petite fist began to disappear inside Catherine even as his cock was swallowed by Samantha's well-greased ass, an inch at a time. It seemed like forever before all of him was buried deep, but when it was, he let out a whoosh of air.

"Play with your tits, kitten. Pinch your nipples for me," Jayden commanded while he grabbed her other hip and guided her back up his cock.

Almost like she could hear him, Catherine mauled her own tits.

Samantha dropped her head back.

Getting an even firmer grip on her hips, digging his strong fingers into the supple flesh, Jayden was able to slide her up and down his dick a few times, loosening her further.

"Put your legs over my thighs," directed Jayden while he kept lifting and lowering Samantha on his shaft.

When Paige's fist slipped free of Catherine's cunt with a spray of fluid, Jayden slammed Samantha back down as he thrust up, continuing to do so each time Paige's fist disappeared inside of Catherine once again.

"Play with your clit, kitten, and do not take your eyes off the screen." His words weren't much more than a growl by that time.

Samantha followed his order, dropping one hand to her pussy while the other one kept squeezing and pulling on her nipples. They were both panting.

When Catherine dissolved into keening cries of "Aye," which Jayden was all too familiar with, he started spurting thick strings of come into Samantha's ass, his eyes locked on the screen where his beautiful flushed jewel was covered in oil, come, and sweat. When her weary body began trembling, Paige worked her hand free of Catherine's slick pussy with ease and set about bringing her down from her orgasm with gentle strokes.

While Jayden was aware of his thighs being soaked from Samantha's own orgasm, it didn't matter. All he could register was that another person's hands were on his Catherine.

A growl erupted from Jayden's throat when a surge of possession washed through him.

What. The. Fuck?

A Divine Life

ॐ

CHAPTER NINE

ॐ

"Hello again, darlin'." A pleasant, quiet voice woke Catherine from her nap. "You sure do clean up pretty, but I think I can make you even prettier. How's that sound?"

She opened her eyes to find herself looking into a pair of ice-blue orbs, which were framed by long lashes brushing against the apples of his cheeks. The wavy hair she'd seen earlier fell around his strong, defined, tan face. After a moment she remembered her place and lowered her gaze, while emitting a quiet, "Sir Landon."

Because she was looking down, Catherine noticed he had her leash in his hands right before he gave it a sharp tug, snapping her nipples back to full, aching attention.

"Lovely," he murmured.

"Paige, you may go ahead and remove the clamps now."

"Yes, Master."

Giving Catherine a chance to suck in a deep breath, Paige freed her nipples.

Sir Landon's long fingers grasped her peaks and pinched. Then he tweaked and twisted them while he pulled until even the flesh of her breasts was outstretched. Releasing one nub, his free hand came up and smacked her breast. Catherine felt it in her sex, which was ripening and swelling under the onslaught, and she couldn't hold back a moan.

"Like that, do you, darlin'?" He chuckled. "Well, I think we're gonna have ourselves some fun here today."

Turning to Paige, he gave her an order, "In that box on the counter is a little gift that Catherine's Master sent along for today. I want you to go into the bathroom and put it on, my yella rose."

The room was quiet for a few minutes while Paige disappeared into the bathroom with the box. Sir Landon continued to work Catherine's nipples, stretching them out further and elongating them while they waited.

With the free time, Catherine's thoughts wandered. Why would there be more gifts from Master? Why would he have gone through all this trouble and expense just to turn around and get rid of her?

Perhaps Paige is right, and you've got it all wrong, Erin.

Silly voice, what do you know?

Catherine shook off the nagging feeling that she was wrong in her earlier assessment. She had her pride; it was the one thing that'd she'd fought hard to preserve, and no one, not even Jayden Masterson, could take it away from her. Catherine was going to be respectful of her agreement with him until the collar came off, but then she would end their sexual relationship.

At the sound of Paige's heels clacking on the wooden floor, Catherine glanced up, as did Sir Landon. While his gaze went elsewhere, his fingers didn't quit pulling on her nipples, which had become numb by then from all the tugging and yanking they'd been exposed to. Catherine's lower jaw fell open when she noticed the large cock jutting out from between Paige's thighs. It seemed familiar to her for some reason—if you could call a rubber dick familiar.

Master's gift was a strap-on? Well, Catherine thought with a hint of sarcasm, *guess that's one way of getting around no other cocks in my Master's pussy!*

What was that, Erin? Did you think "your" Master's pussy? Thought you said he didn't want it anymore.

Was there a way to strangle an inner voice?

Sir Landon put an end to the mental argument she was having with herself when he released her nipples and ordered her onto her knees in front of Paige.

"Now be a good girl, darlin', and greet that pole proper."

Ever obedient, Catherine knelt in front of Paige while resting her ass on her heels, and Paige stepped in closer. Not sure what he'd meant by "greet" but remembering the way Sir Jonathan had her kiss the whip handle, she leaned forward and kissed the tip of the dildo before opening her mouth and sucking down the "pole." Once her lips worked their way down the long shaft, she realized that it *felt* familiar, too. Doing her best, she was able to get most of the length into her mouth, but not quite all of it. Then it clicked, and her eyes went wide.

Sir Landon's brash guffawing astounded her. "Oh, gracious! Jayden said you were a smart one and would figure it out. Gotta admit, you did it a lot quicker than I thought possible!" He slapped his knee.

Catherine pulled her mouth off of the dildo and turned to direct a blatant stare at him. "Meaning no disrespect, Sir," she hissed between clenched teeth, "but what ... the fuck ... is so funny?" She was hanging on by a mental thread, being laughed at was not helping.

A loud gasp drew her attention back to Paige, whose lips were opening and closing like a fish out of water.

Startled by her own behavior, Catherine's hand flew to cover her mouth. *Oh no, what did I do? He's going to bend me over a whipping bench and tan my hide for sure!*

"Oh! This girl is so sorry, Sir. Please forgive her," Catherine begged.

To her utter shock, he continued laughing until tears were running down his rosy cheeks. His reaction left her speechless.

Gasping for air, he began to calm. "Oh, Catherine. The look on your face! He does have quite an unforgettable dick, doesn't he? It's recognizable even in synthetic!" It was obvious Sir Landon was fighting not to burst out laughing again.

Poor Paige just looked confused. She was glancing back and forth between them while Catherine struggled to suppress a smile. "Excuse me, Master," she queried, "but what is going on?"

"You go on, darlin', and enlighten her," he said to Catherine while gesturing with a wave of his hand.

"Well, Paige, um . . . oh, geez . . ." Why was saying this so difficult? She decided to be blunt. "I believe that . . . that strap-on is a replica of my Master."

"Huh?" Paige looked down, and Catherine could see her mental wheels turning.

She knew the moment it sank in.

"Oh. Oh! You mean that Sir Jayden is actually this . . . this big?"

That set the three of them off, the small room filling with laughter once again. This was so not the norm, but to Catherine it felt good to laugh; to feel all the tension that had been building over the last hour start to ease from her mind.

"Alright, girls," Sir Landon clapped his hands together. "I think that's enough silliness. Catherine is on a schedule, and we'd best keep her to it." He winked in her direction.

"Catherine, get back in the chair. Paige, go ahead and just grab some lube, seein' as how we lost a bit of time with our antics."

Both women hustled to obey him. Watching Paige's hand glide up and down while she coated the synthetic penis with a generous dollop of lubrication brought a hitch to Catherine's breath.

"That's right, Catherine. Paige is going to fuck you with your Master's dick. I need her to aid in distracting you from a little procedure I'm about to do. Climb on up here, my yella rose, and if Catherine's green, then slide that dick home."

He gave her an inquisitive look, and Catherine whimpered.

"Aye, Sir. This girl is green." *For the most part.* But she wouldn't say that out loud.

It turned out that Paige was rather nimble. After Catherine had lifted and opened her legs, draping them over the arms of the chair to make room for her, Paige hopped up like it was nothing. She scooted in closer until the head of the dildo brushed against Catherine's throbbing outer lips.

The small touch sparked a need in Catherine. She was hungry for this and wanted it. Though her body had been exposed to a lot of pleasure already today, she still hadn't been filled in *this* way. In fact, she hadn't been filled with more than fingers in a week, Paige's earlier probing excluded.

Catherine rocked her hips forward, and that massive piece of rubber pushed past her outer lips and into her core, filling and stretching her. She threw her head back and let out a throaty moan.

"Oh, fuck. Aye, thank you!"

Paige slid the dildo back out just as slow as she'd pushed it in, before thrusting hard. Catherine was vaguely aware of Sir Landon pulling a cart next to them and his warm hands gathering up her left breast. He was squeezing and massaging it from the base, forcing the nipple to thrust out, and it only added to the experience she was having.

Paige was gaining momentum, pulling out before slamming back into her.

Cold metal clamped onto the tip of her nipple, but Catherine just grunted and closed her eyes, giving herself over to the sensations taking hold of her body. Paige withdrew again, and when she forced her way back into Catherine's pussy with a deep nudge, there was a fierce pinch in Catherine's nipple.

"Oh, God! Please give this girl more. Fuck me harder, Paige! So close!" Catherine was screaming by that point.

Rough tugging on her nipple was followed by a cold wetness.

Paige seemed to be fucking Catherine as fast as she could. Her breasts swayed in Catherine's face, mesmerizing her. Sir Landon's hand moved to her other breast. She felt him mounding it up and forcing her nipple up and out, and déjà vu' barreled down on her.

Cold metal clamped down on her nipple with a mean bite; Paige impaled herself in Catherine's pussy like her life depended on it; an angry pinch stole her breath, and then . . .

She was coming. Hard. Squirting out of her, Catherine's orgasm soaked the chair, her inner thighs, and even Paige.

Paige slowed down with a few final strokes before pulling out with a wet sound and a huge grin. "Told ya it was orgasmic, Erin! They're so pretty!" She clapped her hands together in excitement.

A hazy delirium threatened to envelope Catherine. Her heart felt like it was trying to beat its way out of her body through her sex, and while it was true that her nipples were on fire, it was delicious torture, pure and simple.

Looking down to try to figure out what Paige was rambling on about, Catherine's jaw dropped again. Dangling from her angry, red, and raw nipples were two gold hoops adorned with emerald J's. Catherine did the only thing she could in that moment: she burst into tears.

೫೦೮೩

CHAPTER TEN

೫೦೮೩

Jayden knew he'd become possessive of Erin – Catherine – but what Dom didn't feel possessive of their sub? However, the surge of jealousy that washed through him in reaction to what was up on that screen caught him off guard. Jayden Masterson was rarely caught by surprise; at least, he never used to be. However, since his jewel had come into his life, he was finding it happening with more frequency.

"Sir?" Samantha was still perched on Jayden's lap, held in place by his cock.

"I'm sorry, kitten. You did a splendid job. I just got a little lost in my thoughts." He lifted her off of his

114

softening cock, helping her stand up with one hand while the other gripped the base of the condom so it didn't pull off. "Go ahead and shower. Be sure to clean yourself well. Pull on a robe when you get out. We need to have a talk, and then, I have someone who would like to meet you."

Samantha had a questioning look on her face, but she just nodded and supplied a "Yes, Master" before walking backward toward the playroom. The sound of the shower kicking on soon followed.

While Samantha showered, Jayden changed into some dry pants. He went back to his desk and rewound the video to replay the final scene. *I wanted her to explore her limits. It was my responsibility as her Dom to make sure her desires were fulfilled—all of them. What have I done?*

Catherine had responded with beauty and grace to Jonathan and Paige. The look of rapture on her face while she experienced multiple orgasms with them convinced Jayden that she'd enjoyed herself. In addition, she'd done quite well with Micah that morning. With a slight sense of relief, it dawned on Jayden that he hadn't felt the jealousy during their scene together in the car. Perhaps that was the key: being present and knowing he could step in at any time. Having control over the scene allowed him to keep the jealousy at bay and just enjoy.

Even though Jayden was now prepared for them to become a monogamous D/s couple, the fact remained that today he'd opened her world to sharing partners. It would be unfair of him to let her have a taste of that, and then take it away for his own selfish reasons. If being shared was something she wanted to continue, then he would have to deal with it.

A throat cleared behind Jayden, shaking him free of his mental wanderings. "May this girl present herself, Master?"

Sucking in a deep breath, his ire prickled at her chosen nomenclature, since he'd not adorned her with the temporary collar before they'd begun. Jayden turned around to face Samantha. Her medium-length, dirty blonde hair was pulled up into a messy bun on her head, a few wayward tendrils escaping. She was in a short, silk robe that was a mixture of sunset colors that offset her skin tone—and her collar. *Dammit. Who the hell did she think she was, putting the thing on herself?*

"Sit down, Samantha." He gestured to the wingback leather chair in front of his desk, deciding to ignore the collar issue for the moment. They had more serious things to discuss.

Taking her seat, Samantha kept her back was straight, and her hands were folded in her lap. She was attempting to be respectful while waiting for Jayden to begin.

"Samantha, let me start by saying you have been a terrific submissive. I want you to know that I appreciate the sacrifices you've made and the gift you've given me of yourself. However, I feel the time has come for our Master and submissive relationship to come to an end." Jayden stopped, checking her for a reaction.

Her breathing was steady, and she appeared calm. *Good.*

"As we found today, I've drawn away from my duties to you. The reason is that I've grown quite fond of my main submissive, Catherine, and have decided to offer her a monogamous relationship." Jayden paused again, waiting to see if Samantha wanted to interject anything. When she remained quiet, he prompted her, "Do you have anything to say, Samantha?"

She smiled. "Thank you for your honesty, Master. I'm happy for you. She is a beautiful submissive. I wish you both all the best in the world."

"Go on," Jayden urged her when she hesitated. "We are speaking frankly right now, so please don't hold back from me." He offered her a grin to support his statement.

Chuckling, she continued. "I don't mean to sound ungrateful, Ma– Sir, um, I'm just wondering what this will mean for my job."

Jayden laughed. She was such a sweet and innocent thing, incapable of hurting a fly. "Your job, if you still want it, is safe, Samantha. At the same pay. You happen to be the best executive assistant I've ever had, and I would hate to see you go. The main thing that would change would be your freedom to wear what you'd like to work—as long as it is still professional, of course. What you choose to wear underneath your outfits," he grinned again, "would no longer be my business. Oh, and the office door would remain open for any future interaction between us."

Samantha relaxed in her seat. "Thank you, Sir. I love working here, and for the time being, I would like to try to continue on unless it becomes too weird." She scrunched her nose in a cute way as she said this, and a quiet sigh escaped her lips.

"What else is on your mind, Samantha?"

Her eyes snapped up to meet his. "Well, it's just that, would I be able to get a reference or something from you to stay in this lifestyle? I know I have softer tendencies than most, but I can't imagine trying to go pure vanilla again, and um, well, I'm not sure how to go about finding a new Master." Her nerves were evident in the way she played with her fingers.

Rising from his seat, Jayden walked around the desk to kneel in front of her. He allowed himself a chuckle at the look of shock on her face when she saw him on his knees before her. With a gentle touch, he pried her hands apart so that she would stop picking at her nails and fidgeting.

"Samantha, look at me." Once he had her attention, he went on. "As a parting gift to you, will you allow me to help you find a new Master?"

Her eyes began to well with tears. "That . . . that would be lovely, Sir. Thank you."

"Remember I mentioned I had someone I wanted you to meet?" She nodded. "His name is Ryan Bishop, and he's a Dom who is also a member of the club I frequent, Dungeons & Dreams. Like you, he leans to the softer side of BDSM, and I think you two would be a good match. He's been looking for a new sub for about a month. His last sub wanted too much from him." Jayden laughed. "Actually, from what he's told me, she would've wanted too much even from me!"

The joke helped Samantha relax and laugh along with him.

"I invited Ryan to come meet you this afternoon in the privacy of my playroom, if you are agreeable. Until I remove your collar," she blanched at his acknowledgement of it, "our contract, as it is, still stands. We thought it would be best to do a small scene with you under my watch since I know your limits and body language. At the end of the scene, if you both decide you are compatible, I will uncollar you and present you to him. Sound good?"

She was breathless when she whispered, "Yes, Sir."

"That's my good kitten. He should be here any time now. Please go into the playroom and assume your waiting position."

She rose to follow his commands.

"Oh, and Samantha, you will address him as Sir until further instructions are given."

Smiling at Jayden, she nodded and moved backward through the door into the playroom. Her obvious giddiness reminded him of a small child.

Jayden busied himself, printing off a copy of Samantha's limits so that Ryan would be able to have a quick look before he stepped into the playroom with her.

A few minutes later, the intercom buzzed, and the security guard requested authorization to let Ryan into the building. "Send him on up; I'm expecting him. Thanks, Darren."

Picking up the papers, Jayden walked out into the entry office to wait. He figured it would be better to do their initial talk out there, reducing the chance that Samantha would overhear their voices carrying through the open playroom door.

"Jayden, good to see you!" Ryan said, while reaching to take Jayden's outstretched hand in a firm handshake. "After your build-up at the meeting, I'm intrigued to meet Samantha." He smiled. "And the photo you sent me didn't hurt either. She's breathtaking!"

With a satisfied smile, Jayden handed him the sheet. "Here is her checklist from the last time she updated it.

As I've already mentioned, she is currently using the Depo shot as a means of birth control, and she is clean. Do you have a current STD screening? It's just a formality, but I need to be sure. She is still my responsibility until I uncollar her after your scene."

Reaching into his wallet, Ryan pulled out a slip of paper and handed it to Jayden. "No worries, Jayden. I understand and respect you for being so caring of her. You should be the poster child for our lifestyle." He laughed.

While Ryan glanced over the checklist, Jayden continued talking. "So, I did a scene with her this morning. I used her mouth and ass, but her cunt is still fresh. She's just showered and is waiting for you in the playroom. As you can see by her list, she's a lightweight, but like a true sub, she does desire those spankings." Jayden furrowed his brow while he decided whether to share the next bit of information. "In fact, it became obvious to me during our earlier scene that I've neglected her need for spankings for too long. I tried to remedy it with a chastisement spanking, to which she responded rather well."

Looking up from the paper in his hands, Ryan acknowledged him. "Thank you for the information, Jayden. I've got a good feeling that she and I will get along just fine."

Jayden answered, clapping Ryan on the back, "I do, too, my friend—I do, too. Shall we?" He didn't want to rush their meeting, but Jayden was getting anxious to get back to Silver Spurs.

Unbeknownst to Erin, he was going to be present for her last session, and he couldn't wait. Jayden needed to be near her again. He was beginning to feel like he couldn't breathe without her in the same room with him.

ଛେଓଓ

CHAPTER ELEVEN

ଛେଓଓ

"Uh, Erin, sweetie, what's wrong?" Paige's voice was full of concern, and her hands rubbed at Catherine's thighs, offering comfort.

Catherine's shoulders were shaking. Her body gave in, and she was wracked with sobs. The shuddering brought her attention back to her sore breasts and the mocking J's with which she was now branded.

That was it. The decision had been made. She was being given to Master Jonathan.

A burst of anger flared through her. How presumptuous of both of them to assume that she would be okay with this, without even discussing it with her first. *Dammit!* She might be a submissive, but Catherine was not a slave! She'd been in that situation before and refused to relive it ever again.

Are you sure about that, Erin?

At the prodding of her inner voice, Catherine's mind yanked her back to the memory of a dressing room at the local mall, the small room encased in mirrors for viewing the racy outfits offered at Fredrick's. She'd thought that Spencer, her Master at the time, was feeling remorse for his treatment of her earlier that week and wanted to apologize by taking her shopping. He'd never done either before.

She remembered Spencer had come to her about two in the morning and pulled her from the dog bed by her hair . . .

Catherine couldn't get her feet under her; he was walking too fast. He dragged her down the hall with her hair still in his tight grip. Throwing the door to his playroom open, he dumped Catherine in the middle of the room. At his command to look at him, she saw that he was dressed in a pair of disposable painter's coveralls with latex gloves on his hands and a paper mask over his face. She couldn't control the shaking when the fear overtook her. His eyes seemed unfocused and glazed over. He was drunk.

"Get up, Bitch!"

The submissive stood at once, not daring to disobey.

A Divine Life

Spencer attached a set of leather cuffs with O rings to her wrists and ankles. Next, he snapped a spreader bar between her hands and feet. Catherine was being made to stand spread in an X, and she was having trouble keeping her balance. The whole time she fought not to cry; tears would make him angrier.

A rough shove against her back had Catherine falling face forward onto the floor. Without the use of her hands, she had no choice but to absorb the impact with her chest when she crashed onto the cold cement. The whir of a motor echoed in the room while Spencer lowered the suspension hooks from the ceiling. Catherine tried not to flinch while he fumbled around her, connecting the hooks to the cuffs and bars.

"P-please, Master . . . the waist support . . ." she sniveled, but he cut her off with a kick to her side.

"Shut your fucking mouth until I tell you to open it, you filthy whore!" Spencer walked away, and the motor whirred again.

When she was lifted off the floor, the center of Catherine's body dropped, causing her back to arch painfully while her hands and feet were raised. The upward motion stopped when her head was about four feet off the ground. Her hands and feet were about six feet up. Somehow, Catherine brought herself to risk glancing up when she heard his footsteps retreat.

He was retrieving a thick bamboo cane from his toy wall.

At once, Catherine became frantic and started trying to wiggle out of her bonds. Of course, it was useless. She knew from experience that there was no escaping the wrath of his cane. It was his favorite. The pain in her breasts was immediate when he started hitting them with the implement.

"Look at your tits, juss hanging there for my pleassure," he cackled. "Do ya know wass not available for my plessure?" he slurred.

Catherine managed a whimpered, "No, Sir."

"Your filthy bloody twat!" he screeched while he moved the attention of the cane to her spread pussy. When she cried out, he laughed maniacally and brought the cane down across her bent back.

Fear gripped her when she felt him grab the tiny string and pull the tampon from her body.

"Oh, Catherine, I juss wanted a good fuck, but your goddamn bloody hole is disgusting."

Spencer was stroking her face with the hand holding the used item. Catherine could feel the wetness on her cheek mixing with the tears that now poured unbidden from her eyes.

"Yessss, a good pounding of your pus-pussy," he burped, "and all my stresss would've gone away. But I can't put my dick in that messs, so I'm juss gonna have to beat you inst-instead. Open your mouth, slut!"

Terrified of what she thought he was going to do, Catherine clamped her jaw shut on instinct. He pinched her nose, cutting off her breathing until she was forced to open her mouth to gasp for air. When Catherine opened, Spencer shoved in the tampon, pushing it in until the nasty cotton was sitting on the back of her tongue. The gagging and retching was immediate.

"Oh, no you don't, you bitch."

Her face was slapped, and then her jaw was forced closed while Spencer produced a piece of duct tape and sealed her mouth shut. Wide eyes watched him use a pair of scissors to cut a small hole in the center of the tape, through which he pulled the string. At least it pulled the dirty thing forward in her mouth and away from her throat.

She was unable to guess how long Spencer stumbled around her while the cane came down time and again across her weakening body. No part of her was spared. His miserable aim meant that sometimes it would be a solid contact, other times the rough end of the bamboo would scratch Catherine when it slid over her skin. Spencer seemed to enjoy hitting her breasts in particular and watching them swing from the impact. Every time she was on the verge of passing out, he would ram the end of the cane into her pussy, and then get angrier at the blood he found on the end.

Catherine vomited bile into her mouth. Her arms went numb. She reached a point where she couldn't even feel the cane when it connected with her breasts anymore.

Wetness was leaking from her body, and she was positive he'd drawn blood.

The time came when, at long last, the pressure released in Catherine's back, and she was lowered back to the floor. Who would have thought the coldness of hard cement could be a welcome relief to her burning skin? Somehow, she managed to open her eyes at the sound of paper tearing.

Spencer's coveralls had red splatters on them, and he was ripping them away to expose his naked body underneath. He took his shriveled up dick in his hand and aimed it over Catherine's back.

Blissful darkness overtook Catherine as the hot urine set her wounds on fire.

Several hours later Catherine came to, still bound and on the floor. She could feel the dried piss and blood on her. Lifting her pounding head to look around, she found Spencer passed out on his back in front of her. His limp dick was in his hand, and dried come was on his stomach. There were Polaroid photos of Catherine scattered across the floor.

Two days later found Catherine in the Fredrick's dressing room trying on some crotchless, sheer, pink thing that she thought looked hideous. The fresh cuts and bruises didn't do anything to make it look better. Because of the surrounding mirrors she couldn't escape the pathetic sight which peered back at her from the glass.

Spencer barged in with a glare in his soulless black eyes and locked the door. "So pretty in pink, Catherine." Stomping toward her, he snatched her ponytail and used it to hold her while he clamped his mouth over hers and forced his tongue between her lips. "Bend over and spread your ass cheeks for me. I need to come."

Catherine didn't want to obey, but she feared how much worse it could be if she ignored him. While she got into position, Spencer unzipped his pants and pulled his hard dick out. With no warning, he shoved it into her backside with no lube or preparation. She squeezed her eyes shut to try to block the tears, while biting the inside of her cheek to squelch the scream that wanted to be freed.

"Open your eyes and watch me fuck you, whore. See what I'm doing to you, and get it in your head that you are nothing but a warm fuck hole."

Her backside was a burning inferno while he thrust to the rhythm of his words. Opening her eyes, the pitiful tears escaped down her cheeks, mimicking the way she wanted to run and hide from the relentless mirrors.

"Know that your body is mine. I can and will do what I want with it. I'll bury my big cock in your ass, your mouth, and your gaping twat whenever I want!" His thrusts gained speed while he worked himself up with his words. Suddenly, he pulled out and told Catherine to turn around. Grabbing her ponytail again, he shoved his dick into her mouth, knowing she'd never dare to bite. With a firm grip on her fiery hair, Spencer resumed his frantic *thrusting, just the tip of his short dick hitting the back of her throat when he was all the way in.*

"That's my girl, open wide and suck my big cock, you worthless whore!"

The familiar swelling and twitching told her to prepare to swallow. Instead he pulled out and grabbed his dick, giving it the final few pumps himself before he shot his load all over her neck and breasts. The come dripped down onto the teddy she was wearing, its tags still attached. Spencer pushed his dick back into her mouth, making Catherine lick him clean. In a final show of power, he scooped some of the come up with his finger and wiped it across her cheek.

"Thanks for the fuck, Catherine. You owed me." He cackled. "Nice to know you're good for something. Now get dressed and pay for that. Meet me at the car," he ordered and walked out of the room after tossing some cash on the floor in front of her.

Catherine sucked in a deep breath, and then another. She needed to calm down. Disappointment and panic gripped her at the reminder that she was a "warm fuck hole" to be used by her Master however he wished.

One thing was certain in her mind: she knew that she needed this lifestyle. Deep down, she would be restless and unfulfilled if she wasn't handing control over to a Dom. Catherine had learned to desire the pain and humiliation, because it allowed her the freedom to let go.

Giving up control released her mind to allow her body to be used by another.

Another certainty occurred to Catherine. She'd gotten careless when she'd developed feelings for Jayden, her Master. If it was his desire to give her to another, then she must accept that. By giving in to the reality and accepting her fate, she was serving her Master, and in turn, herself. At least Master wasn't abandoning her, leaving her to flounder for a way to start over—again.

When Catherine composed herself enough to look up, she found Paige looking over her shoulder. Turning her head to follow Paige's gaze, she was met with Sir Landon's confused stare.

Sniffling and wiping her nose with the back of her hand, Catherine settled. "This girl is sorry, Sir. It's been an emotional day, and she forgot her place. She's now remembered it and is ready to move on."

Sir Landon came forward and lifted her still-trembling hand. "Of course, darlin'. Your mind and body have been through a lot today. Quite understandable."

ഇന്റെ

CHAPTER TWELVE

ഇന്റെ

Jayden allowed Ryan to go ahead of him while they walked through his office and into the playroom. Samantha was kneeling with her thighs spread, palms up on her thighs, and tits pushed forward. Her chin was down, as was her gaze. He noticed her tense when they entered.

"There, there, kitten, no need for alarm. Ryan is with me. I'm going to be in the corner chair, and Ryan will direct your scene. Do you understand?"

"Yes, Master." Her voice was calm and unwavering and did not reveal the nervousness he knew she was feeling.

"You may begin then, Ryan."

"Thank you, Jayden." For a long moment he stood in front of her, looking at her.

While Ryan appraised Samantha, Jayden did the same to him. He was average height, but still a couple of inches taller than Samantha. His sandy hair was cut neat and close to his head on the sides and longer on top. A strong jawline and proud nose gave his features a distinguished look. What Jayden noticed more than Ryan's physical attributes was the aura of kindness that surrounded the man. If he hadn't known better, he never would've pegged Ryan as a Dom; not with his relaxed shoulders and casual choice of wardrobe.

Something shifted in Ryan's stature when he began to take steps around Samantha. While he moved behind her, Ryan let his fingers trail across her shoulders, and she gave a visible shudder, leaning into the caress. She'd broken form. Jayden was intrigued to see if Ryan was 'Dom' enough to correct her.

"Still now, little one," he soothed, and her motion stopped at once. Starting at her shoulders, his hands ran down her sides, out over her hips and under her buttocks, finishing with a firm squeeze of her cheeks as he squatted behind her. "Your skin has a pretty flush to it like you've recently been flogged. Were you a naughty girl, Samantha?" he asked in a tone that Jayden had to admit was sultry.

"Y-yes, Sir." Her breathing became jagged.

Jayden was in awe; Samantha had never responded in such a short amount of time to him. She was coming unglued with just a touch and the sound of Ryan's voice.

"Tell me what infraction necessitated the punishment?" When Samantha didn't answer straight away, he smacked her ass. "Answer me!" demanded Ryan.

"This girl wore lingerie under her clothes today, Sir," she whimpered.

"I see," said Ryan, and his left hand disappeared between her legs.

Judging by Samantha's moan, Jayden assumed Ryan had pushed his fingers into her. This was confirmed when, seconds later, Ryan pulled his hand back to inspect the viscous substance.

"Do you like to be disobedient and naughty, Samantha? Your wet pussy tells me you do."

Samantha remained quiet at the rhetorical question.

Ryan's fingers found their way into her again, pumping in and out while he explained, "If I take you on as my submissive, you will not be allowed panties or bras at any time." His right hand wrapped around her, and he pulled her into his chest. Grasping Samantha's right tit, he squeezed. "These tits are beyond beautiful, but are too small to need the support of a pesky bra." He finished his statement by tugging on her nipple.

Samantha's body reacted and began to grind against his hand. Rather than let her continue, he pushed her forward and removed it.

"On your knees, little one. Place your forehead on the floor with your arms stretched in front of you." Walking over to her, Jayden looked on while Ryan arranged her hands, one over the other. Next, he grabbed her hips and lifted them up, while tapping at her feet until she drew her knees up near her breasts. This left her ass high up in the air and her pink pussy lips pushing out between her thighs. "This will be your waiting position. Remember it." His finger stroked across her pussy.

"We will begin all scenes with six open-handed spanks." His hand came down on her left cheek with a smack. "You are never to consider this punishment." A second smack enforced his words. "Simply warm-up." Another pop echoed around them. "If you have earned a punishment," the fourth spank was disbursed, "that will be doled out following your warm up on a whipping bench."

Samantha groaned when Ryan landed the fifth smack on her rose-tinted flesh. He'd alternated each spank between her cheeks. However, the sixth one Ryan aimed right over her cunt, and she moaned, while thrusting her hips back against him.

Jayden sat there dumbfounded. Ryan was not a big man, nor a loud one. Unless he spoke up, he was easy to overlook in a crowd; quiet, with an air of shyness about him. If not for the fact that he was sitting there witnessing him in action, Jayden would've said Ryan bordered on a Switch personality, meaning he enjoyed being on his knees, too. It was easy to envision Ryan subbing for someone. However, the way Ryan was taking command and demanding Samantha's obedience showed Jayden that he could be a force to be reckoned with.

Straightening up from his squat, Ryan moved to stand in front of Samantha again. "Now, kiss my feet, little one, and then rise before me."

Samantha lifted her head just enough to reach his shoes, onto each of which she placed a dainty kiss. Her movement was fluid when she stretched her long body into a standing position.

When she stood upright, Ryan placed a finger under her chin and lifted her face to meet his gaze. Their stares locked onto each other and became intense; so intense that Jayden felt like he was intruding.

With a smug grin, Jayden gave himself a mental high-five. This was going to work for them, without a doubt.

Ryan placed a soft kiss on her lips before leaning down and sucking each of her nipples into his mouth. His fingers moved back into her slick folds, and Jayden could hear her wetness when Ryan slid his fingers back and forth.

"You are an exquisite piece of art, my little one," he told her. "Come for me. I want to see your body flush and color with the orgasm I allow you to have." He pinched her clit, and her head fell back as she shook, moaned, and then came into his hand.

The petting didn't stop. Instead, Ryan resumed suckling Samantha's nipples while his fingers continued to glide across her noisy sex. Jayden was left taken aback at the roughness Ryan used on her nipples. He knew they had to be sore from having been clamped earlier, in particular because her tolerance for the clamps was low. Yet when he walked closer to observe what Ryan was doing, he found Ryan had a nipple between his teeth and was sawing back and forth on it while he pulled it away from her body. Her skin was flushed, covered in a damp coating of sweat from her orgasm, and Jayden could sense by her rapid breathing that she was approaching another one.

Samantha whined when Ryan released her nipple. Before taking the other one into his mouth, he told her to come again, which she did as soon as his teeth started working and pulling once more. She slumped into his arms, but he caught her with ease, like he'd expected her to collapse.

"Beautifully done, little one. Will you do me the honor of being mine, Samantha?" The words had been uttered so low that Jayden almost didn't hear them.

Her lust-filled azure eyes lifted toward Jayden, asking for permission. He did not hesitate to step forward and undo the latch on the platinum chain she wore around her throat.

"Your servitude has been honorable, Samantha. I release you of your obligations to me," Jayden all but whispered, his voice catching in his throat.

She returned the sentiment with a smile. "Thank you, Sir. This girl feels honored to have served you." Her head swiveled to look back to Ryan. "It would be a great pleasure to be yours, Sir."

"Then so shall you be." His rigid expression gave way to a playful grin. "I'm going to fuck that dripping cunt of yours now." She giggled when Ryan lifted her up and carried her bridal-style to the bed. After he laid her out on the bed with care, he unbuttoned and removed his shirt. Then he began to undo his pants.

That was Jayden's cue to leave. Clearing his throat to get their attention, he announced, "I trust that I am leaving you in good hands, Samantha. I have another appointment that I can't be late for, and I don't want to rush or intrude on your time." He chuckled. "Ryan, feel free to use whatever you wish within the playroom. Samantha knows how to clean it up, and I'll trust you both to lock up when you are done."

"Of course, Sir."

Jayden approached and leaned over the bed to place a soft kiss on Samantha's forehead. "I've never seen you more beautiful, kitten. I'm glad you're happy."

She smiled up at him. "I am, Sir, I really am." A blush crept over her features, and she added a heart-felt, "Thank you, Jayden."

"Anytime, kiddo. I've really got to be going." When Jayden pulled the playroom door shut, the last thing he saw was Ryan sheathing himself between Samantha's wide-open thighs while their moans echoed off the walls.

ഇര‌ങ

CHAPTER THIRTEEN

ഇര‌ങ

A switch had been thrown.

Catherine needed to serve, and if Master no longer wanted her, then she would find her satisfaction in the hands of another. Sir Jonathan had been fair. He'd used her body well, given her the pain she needed, and allowed her to achieve release multiple times before he sought his own. He would be a good Master.

Looking at Paige, who still knelt between Catherine's thighs, the dildo bobbing with each breath Paige took, and then at her new jewelry, Catherine knew what she had to do. Directing her attention back to Sir

Landon, she spoke. "Sir, if it pleases you, this slut would like more."

His pale eyebrows scrunched up. "What are you askin' for, darlin'? Look at me when you answer."

"This slut would like to thank you and your submissive for the beautiful jewels, and for the reminder of what I am," she answered without hesitation. "Please allow this slut to pleasure you."

Sir glanced at Paige before turning back to Catherine with a thoughtful look. "Is that really your wish, Catherine?" His voice was kind and gentle, and she knew that if she dwelled on it, she would have another breakdown.

"Aye, Sir. It would be a great relief to this girl's mind to be allowed to see to your needs." Her eyes were fixed on the bulge in his jeans while she made her confession. Watching the bulge grow and hearing Sir's breath hitch brought a small smile to Catherine's face.

He perused her face; she gathered he was searching for any sign of uncertainty. Catherine knew he would find none. Her mind was made up, and her heritage shone true when she stood firm in her decision. Catherine O'Chancey could be as stubborn as the best of them.

"Alright then, darlin', so be it. Paige, step down and kneel to the side."

A wave of pure calm washed over Catherine once Sir Landon took control of the scene.

"Understand, Catherine. My yella rose here is currently being denied orgasms as punishment for an infraction. I will allow her to assist as long as she does not come. Is this clear?"

"Aye, Sir." Her mind soared, while her breathing became easier.

"Hop on down then, darlin', and stand to the side for a moment with Paige."

The submissive slipped out of the chair and assumed her standing ready position.

Sir stepped up to Catherine and cupped her breasts, letting his thumbs flick against the rings. She seethed at the pleasurable pain that radiated up into her chest, making her skin spark and sizzle. His hands closed, squeezing ever so slowly and making a show out of forcing her nipples to push out further.

Fuck—that hurts!

Mm-hmmm . . .

"Your tits sure are gorgeous, darlin'. I knew I could make ya prettier with my needle." His words seemed to drip and ooze over her, changing the sharp sizzle to a vibrating heat that covered her. Then he grinned, dimples breaking up the sharp planes of his face when he leaned in and let his warm tongue lap against Catherine's protruding nipples.

"Mmmm, thank you, Sir." The moan she emitted was porn-worthy.

All male, the Dom stepped back and leaned against the edge of the chair Catherine had just vacated. "Paige, get over here and use your teeth to free my cock. Keep your knees spread while you crawl."

It was mesmerizing to watch Paige crawl over to him. Catherine could see the dildo between Paige's legs, swinging back and forth, and she couldn't help comparing it to the way Master's cock would swing when he moved around the playroom naked. Her pussy pulsed.

Once Paige reached Sir, she raised herself up onto her knees while keeping her hands behind her back. As instructed, she used her mouth to undo the button and lower the zipper on his jeans. Paige sat back on her haunches while he gave his hips a little shimmy and the denim fell down to pool at his ankles. He lifted his foot, and Paige leaned forward to grasp the bottom of his pant leg with her teeth; when she backed up, she pulled it free.

Catherine didn't watch her do the other leg because her eyes had drifted up to take in the bobbing shaft that had been revealed.

It wasn't as long as Master's, maybe two inches shorter, but it was wider. Oh yeah, it was much wider. Thick ridges of veins covered his cock, and she clenched her thighs, thinking of how the texture would feel inside her.

He chuckled, and it was deep and throaty. "See something you like, darlin'?"

"Oh, aye, Sir." Catherine saw the throaty, and raised it a husky.

Sir's hand wrapped around his thick shaft, and he started stroking. "Why don't you come on over here and have a taste then? On your knees, crawl to me, darlin'," he ordered.

Eager to obey, Catherine crawled to him as fast as she could. Arriving in front of him, she rose up onto her knees and waited for his okay to proceed.

"Kiss my cock in greeting, Catherine," he commanded, and her pussy flooded when she placed an open-mouthed kiss on the tip, tasting the salty pre-come that had gathered there. "Mmm, good girl," he moaned. "Now open those pretty little lips for me."

Being cheeky, she let her lips part slightly, then licked them.

"Wider, Catherine. Now." The gentleness was gone from his voice, having been replaced with a lusty growl.

The next switch was thrown, turning off all the ramblings in her head. Catherine had one objective: to serve the Dom she was kneeling before. Her mouth opened wide, and he placed the head of his cock between her lips. Instead of pushing into her, Sir placed his hands on either side of her head and pulled her down onto him. He was able to guide Catherine about half way down before she couldn't go any further because his skin was dry. She was grateful when he pulled her back off.

"Stand up, darlin', I think we need some lube."

The submissive stood up, and Sir reached between her thighs, running two fingers over the outside of her pussy lips before pressing against her hidden clit. On the second pass, he pushed one finger between her folds and slipped inside her.

"My goodness, you're drippin' like honey." He pulled his hand back and licked his finger. "Mmm, taste like honey, too."

"Oh, please, Sir," Catherine whimpered.

"Please what, Catherine?" he cocked his eyebrow at her.

"Please use this slut's juices to lube your beautiful cock," she begged without shame.

"I like the way you think, darlin'." Sir shot her a wink while two fingers plunged into her and he wiggled them around.

To allow him better access, she bent her knees. The new position allowed the squelching sounds of her wetness to be heard. Desire coursed through Catherine's body, making her nipples erect and tight, which let her feel the pull of the metal in them. Catching her by surprise, the beginnings of an orgasm started to coil in her belly, and her inner walls clamped against his fingers.

Catherine whined at the loss of his fingers when he pulled them back out. They were shiny and slick with her juices. She could feel the hunger building in her while he rubbed the slickness over his cock.

"Now, darlin', where were we? Ah, yes, back on your knees, Catherine. And open wide this time; don't make me tell you again," he instructed.

When Catherine was back on her knees with her head again gripped in his hands, Sir guided her down his shaft. This time, he was able to pull her all the way down to the base of his cock so that Catherine's nose brushed against his short, trimmed pubic hairs. He held her there while she swallowed.

"Oh! Fuck, girl!" Sir pulled Catherine almost all the way off, and she took advantage, swirling her tongue around the head before he pulled her all the way down again. "Swallow again."

She did—every time he told her to.

"Shit! That feels so fucking good, darlin'! I can't believe you're getting me all the way down." He groaned and moved her up and down again, holding her at the bottom to repeat the swallowing motion. After a few more times, Sir withdrew from her mouth and told Catherine to suck his balls.

To reach them she had to bend over a little. While she took the first one into her mouth, he bent his knees and spread his thighs, giving her more room.

"Yeah, just like that, darlin'. Paige, get your pretty ass over here and put that rubber dick you've got to work." Sir moaned when Catherine released his nut with a pop before moving to the other one.

She could feel the rubber pressing against her pussy lips and arched her back to open herself up more. Paige plunged into her while the Dom grabbed her hair and pushed his cock back into her mouth.

"Ahhh!" It was a feeble attempt at a cry of pleasure.

A few awkward thrusts later, they'd worked out a rhythm. Paige pushed into Catherine when Sir pulled out, and when he pushed back down into her throat, Paige pulled out of her pussy. Neither one of them ever removed their cocks from her. They just pumped in and out of Catherine until Sir Landon spoke again.

"Paige that cock should be good and slick now. Work it into our darlin's pert little ass. Get her stretched for me."

The dildo left Catherine's pussy and pushed into her ass in one slick motion while Sir resumed rocking in and out of her mouth. She felt like she was melting; her nipples tingled, her muscles were tight, and she felt so full. Knowing that Sir Landon was planning on shoving his thick, veiny cock in her ass made her suck with renewed vigor. Catherine couldn't wait.

For the next ten minutes, they worked Catherine with a languid thoroughness. Paige pushed in and out, swirling her hips to spread Catherine open.

"Enough; time for me to tap that ass of yours," Sir claimed, taking his cock from Catherine's mouth. Keeping her hand in his, he climbed up into the chair. Then he scooted to the back edge and dropped his long legs over the sides, under the armrests.

"Come here, Catherine," he ordered while sheathing his cock with protective latex.

She turned around and sat down on the edge of the seat. Before she could make a move to slide back, his chest pressed against her back, while his arms hooked under her legs and lifted her up. Without any instruction, Paige stood and placed her hands on Catherine's ass cheeks, pulling them apart while Sir positioned her over himself. The head of his cock pushed through the tight ring of Catherine's ass, and he let her legs drop over the top of the armrests. Gravity pulled her the rest of the way down until he was fully buried inside her.

"Oh, fuck!" they both yelled at the same time.

The ridges of his cock could be felt against the inner lining of her rectum. Hands on her waist, Sir Landon lifted her about halfway off of his cock so he could slip down into a better angle, and then he dropped her. She swooned with the abrupt intrusion and the new angle, which allowed him to start rocking his hips so that he moved deep inside Catherine.

Through his grunts and the submissive's moans, he gave a last order: "Paige, come lick this slut's pussy. Don't stop till she's comin' on my cock, and then I want you to fuck her."

A glance at Paige revealed her licking her lips and eyeing Catherine with hunger.

Catherine's responding groan was loud and uninhibited while Paige's tongue swiped up between her folds. The Dom filling her backside moaned out his release even as Catherine's body was wracked by her own.

ഇൗൽ

CHAPTER FOURTEEN

ഇൗൽ

After he'd fired off a text on his way out of the office, Jayden made his way downstairs and out of the building, stepping out onto the curb. Micah was waiting with the car and had the back door open for him.

"I'm going to ride up front with you, Micah. I'm anxious to get back over to Silver Spurs, and I need to see any delays we might encounter with my own eyes."

"As you wish, Sir." Micah's grin was loaded with suggestion.

A labored sigh tumbled from Jayden's lips while he slipped into the passenger seat and watched Micah walk around to the driver's side. A lot was riding on Shawn Carpenter and Micah hitting it off. If they didn't, then Jayden needed to figure out what to do with Micah. The young man had dabbled in the lifestyle with Jayden under no official contract or rules, but Jayden's newfound commitment to Catherine was going to require that Micah look elsewhere to satisfy his needs. Just like with Samantha, Jayden felt obligated to steer Micah into the right hands.

He felt really good about his resolution with Samantha. Without question, there had been more than just a physical connection in that room. In their first scene, Ryan had already pushed Samantha farther than Jayden had ever been able to. The reason for that, Jayden surmised, was that whatever she'd seen in Ryan's eyes had brought forth her complete submission and trust.

Strumming his strong fingers on his thigh, his leg bounced with restlessness while they pulled out into traffic. Jayden couldn't wait to get back to his Erin. Having discussed Landon's piercing session in complete detail, Jayden had felt it wouldn't be necessary for the scene to be filmed like the other sessions had been. He knew he'd be inbound while it was taking place and arriving about the time it finished, thereby eliminating the necessity to email the recording over to his office. More important, Paige would be the one bringing Catherine to orgasm, not Landon. As one part of an engaged couple and as his best friend, Jayden trusted

Landon enough to not have to monitor the scene. There was also the consideration that Paige, as a sub, had no interest in taking on Erin. Her loyalty was to Landon, first and foremost.

After the piercing, Erin had one remaining session for today—until Jayden got her back in his playroom at the villa, anyway. There were two sessions if he wanted to be technical, but as both would be handled by Shawn, Jayden was counting it as one. He smiled at the thought of her final scene, and what it would mean to both him and Catherine.

Catherine didn't know it, but Jayden would be the one pushing her to explore her final limit, drawing the day's final orgasms from her luscious body while at Silver Spurs. Shawn wouldn't be interested in engaging in a sexual act with her, and frankly, Jayden didn't want anyone else touching her. Shawn's hands would be the last pair of male hands besides his own to touch her for quite some time, if Jayden had any say about it. A childhood friend, it hadn't surprised him that Shawn grew up to be an artist. A very flamboyant artist.

Shawn was a Dominant looking for a male submissive. His tastes were particular, however, and so he had been looking for quite some time. He wanted a good-looking, younger sub, and he had been quite intrigued when Jayden had suggested the possible match. A potential sub had to be available, as in uncollared, and Shawn preferred someone fresh and moldable. Micah's willingness to please at any moment, paired with Shawn's jovial nature, made Jayden feel confident that the two would hit it off. The day was looking better the closer he got to his final destination: Erin.

"Micah, can I ask you a question?"

He smirked at Jayden, side-eyeing him while keeping his focus on the road. "You just did, Sir."

Jayden had to laugh. "You little shit; I should take you over my knee for that!"

At once the playful smile on Micah's face dissolved into a look of hunger and want. "If it would please you, Sir."

"About that, Micah. I think you're ready for more formal training and entrance into my lifestyle," Jayden began.

Micah's face lit up.

Yeah, definitely need to fix this, now. "However, I won't be in the position after today to be your mentor any longer." Jayden could almost feel the atmosphere shift in the car at his declaration. Micah's shoulders slumped. "But I do have someone in mind that I think you should meet."

Eyes fixed on the road, Micah's hands tightened on the wheel, but he didn't say anything, so Jayden went on.

"His name is Shawn Carpenter, and he is looking for a new sub—a sub with specifications that *you* happen to match. When we get to Silver Spurs, why don't you come on in with me, I'll introduce you?"

"Yes, Sir," he whispered, his lips trembling so the words were a bit garbled.

"Micah, trust me. I will never be able to fulfill your needs because . . . well, because I just don't swing that way. You know that. Even if I weren't about to enter a new phase in my relationship with Catherine, I'd still suggest you meet Shawn." Jayden kept his voice low and calm in an attempt to ease Micah's fears.

A couple of quiet minutes later, they pulled into the parking lot. Micah turned off the car before responding. "Thank you, Sir. I would appreciate your help, and I would love to meet Mr. Carpenter." His pouty lips turned up in a shy smile.

Jayden clapped him on the back. "That's the spirit! Come on; I need to see my girl!" Ecstatic and vibrating with energy, Jayden hopped out of the car, not waiting for Micah to come around and open the door.

Catching up to him, Micah laughed. "Where's the fire, Sir?"

A responding chortle bubbled out of Jayden's mouth. "In my dick, Micah, and Catherine is the only thing that can put it out!"

With a jangle, Jayden extracted his key ring and unlocked the door to the spa, relocking it once they'd gone inside. Glancing at his watch, he noted that Paige should be almost finished prepping Catherine to transfer her to Shawn's room. *Perfect timing.* Jayden led Micah down the hallway toward the room where her next scene would begin. The plan was for Jayden to wait outside the door until Paige had Catherine situated and Shawn had begun with her before Jayden would enter the room.

Deciding he was in too much of a hurry, he made the call to change up the plans by going ahead and waiting inside the room. Catherine would be blindfolded anyway, so she wouldn't be able to see him when Paige brought her in.

Determination guided Jayden down the hall, but curiosity made him pause outside the door to the piercing room. Putting his ear against the wood, Jayden tried to see if he could figure out how close they were to finishing. He expected to hear the soft chattering of the two girls, but instead Jayden was met with deep, guttural moaning and panting. *What the hell?*

Restraining his temper for the time being, Jayden turned the handle and pushed the door open a few inches to peek inside. The first thing his mind registered was his beautiful Catherine. Her waist was cinched tight in the doeskin half-corset, while her full breasts bounced up and down with the brands, *his brands,* swinging from her rock-hard nipples. She threw her head back and let out a string of profanities while she got lost in the throes of what looked to be one hell of an orgasm.

Jayden sucked in his breath at the vision before taking in the rest of the scene. Paige was between Catherine's thighs. Meanwhile, large hands gripped Catherine's hips while guiding her up and down a veiny cock that he recognized. Before Catherine's orgasm had finished, Paige was climbing onto the chair and shoving the strap on replica of Jayden's cock into Catherine's pussy. Her body began writhing again as another orgasm overtook her, and the sounds of raw sex bounced off the walls. This was *not* a scene; it was blatant fucking, and his Catherine was in the middle of it.

His vision went red, and he staggered back into the hallway, leaving the door ajar. Jayden's hand grasped at his chest while he tried to get air to move through his lungs.

"Sir? Are you okay?" Micah seemed nervous.

Never one to pull his own hair, Jayden found himself giving in to the desperate action. "Am I okay? No, I'm not fucking okay!" he wheezed out in a whisper. "I'm a goddamn fool!" he lamented while he began pacing back and forth in the hall. He came to a stop at the side of the open door and leaned his forehead against the wall. The panting gasps of pleasure drifting through the door were making him sick to his stomach, and Jayden couldn't breathe.

What the fuck was happening in that room? Who the hell did Landon think he was? And why, *oh God*, why was he fucking Erin? They had agreed Landon would touch nothing but her breasts to do the piercings, so how in the hell had his dick ended up inside of her? Jayden needed answers, and he wanted them right then—before he lost his mind!

Reaching a shaking hand over to the handle, Jayden managed to pull the door closed, thankful that at least the moans had stopped. With a deep breath, he curled his fingers into a fist and rapped his knuckles against the door three times. This was the signal they had agreed on in the event that Jayden needed the Dom to step out during a scene for any reason. In that moment, Jayden, without a doubt, needed to speak to Landon.

He stepped back away from the wall to wait and turned to Micah. "Go down the hall to the third door on the right. Knock and wait for Mr. Carpenter to let you in. Introduce yourself and relay our conversation from the car. I'm sure he can take it from there. I'll be in shortly."

ಜೆ೦ಣ

CHAPTER FIFTEEN
Through a Friend's Eye

ಜಿ೦ಣ

Landon couldn't remember the last time he'd come so hard. It'd taken everything he had not to come down Catherine's throat while she'd worked him over with her talented mouth. While he'd never had complaints about Paige's oral skills, there was no denying that Catherine could suck a dick. Landon was already figuring out how best to approach Jayden about maybe setting up a training session with the two girls. If Catherine could teach Paige her tricks, he would benefit—that was for damn sure.

RAP! RAP! RAP!

Huh? He looked up at the clock on the wall; they were running late getting Catherine to her next session. *Jayden and his damn punctuality,* Landon thought with a chuckle. He was pretty sure the girls hadn't heard the knock. Well, Paige might have, but Catherine was still coming down from her orgasmic high—an orgasm that he'd felt splashing onto his thighs. Too bad they were out of time, in addition to Paige's current punishment for getting snippy and rolling her eyes at him the night before. To watch his beautiful girl's body flush under Catherine's tongue while he had his way with her nipples would've been heaven. His dick started to harden again in Catherine's ass at the vision. *Focus, Landon!*

Lifting Catherine off his dick and setting her on the edge of the seat, Landon gave his instructions. "Off ya go, darlin'; our time's up. Paige, get her cleaned up and ready for her next session."

"Yes, Master."

Catherine was shaky when she slid off the seat and stepped to the side. Her breathing was starting to slow down, and she had a peaceful look on her face.

Landon was next to get off the chair. Moving to grab his jeans, he pulled them on before donning his t-shirt. "How ya doing, darlin'?" He wanted her to verbalize that she was okay. The scene had been intense to begin with, but Landon felt responsible for being extra-sure of her welfare, given the impromptu adjustment they'd made.

She offered him a shy smile, which made him laugh. "Wonderful, Sir, thank you."

"Oh, trust me, Catherine, the pleasure was all mine!"

"This slut is happy to have been of service." Her eyes were cast to the floor.

For Landon, the noticeable difference in her formality between this moment and when they'd first begun raised a red flag. He was going to have Paige make sure Catherine was really okay while they got ready. A silent nod in Paige's direction indicated she should meet him in the corner of the room.

"Paige, I think Jayden's in the hall, and I need to step out to chat with him. You've been a very good girl today. Your Master is pleased," he praised while brushing his lips across hers. The smile he felt on her lips warmed his heart. In a low whisper, he added: "Do me a favor, sugar, and try to talk to her while you're preparing her. I've got an off feeling. Something's not right. But don't take too long; we're a bit behind schedule. I love you, my yella rose." Landon swatted her backside before he headed out the door.

Closing the door behind him when he stepped into the hallway, Landon was not expecting the raging bull he found pacing the hall. He could almost see the steam coming from Jayden's ears. At the sound of the latch, Jayden turned to face him.

"What the fuck, Landon?" he growled.

"Excuse me?" Landon was sure the shock he felt was registering on his face.

"Care to explain why your dick was in *my* submissive, you son of a bitch!"

"Hold up, now," Landon said, raising his hand to keep Jayden off. "Do you care to explain what your fucking problem is, Jayden?"

He took a deep breath. "Landon, we planned her scene down to the last detail. What I saw when I opened that door was *not* in our plan!"

"Okay, buddy, I get that. I need you to step back and relax and listen to me before you say anything else." Landon cocked his eyebrow, waiting to see if Jayden was going to go off again or stay quiet.

Jayden gestured with his hand for Landon to go on, but his lips remained pursed in a tight line.

"Yes, the scene changed. You know, as well as I do that can happen." When Jayden opened his mouth to say something, Landon cut him off. "I told you my concerns when you first asked me to help out today. Most subs couldn't have handled what Catherine has been through. Not only has she endured multiple scenes, but multiple scenes with different Doms—Doms who were complete strangers to her, Jayden. I'm sure her headspace has been like a twister. Not to mention the physical strains on her body; no matter how much release and pleasure she's received from it, it's still a lot."

Landon took a breath. "Jonathan and I love you like a brother, Jayden. That's why you asked us to do this. You assured us she would be fine. We all know her past, me more than the others. It wasn't pretty. She has been handled with the utmost respect today; not just because you asked us to, but because she earned that respect from each of us. Catherine is a beautiful submissive, and I'm not just talkin' about her looks. Her willpower and her soul are something to behold. She gives herself over so completely."

"You don't have to tell me how wonderful she is, Landon. Trust me, I know." Jayden's voice hitched at the end. When he lifted his eyes to look at Landon, there was a mixture of sadness, pride, and love swimming around.

"You love her." It wasn't a question.

"So much, Landon; so very much." Jayden's tone became pleading, "Why? Why did you do it?" he asked with a defeated look.

"She asked for it—" Landon didn't get to finish his sentence. In fact, he just managed to get his face out of the way before Jayden's arm rushed past, connecting with the wall to the side of Landon's head.

"Jesus Christ, Jayden! What the hell?" Landon was trying to stay calm, but a man didn't take a swing at a man without cause. He knew he'd done nothing wrong. Distracted by the sound of doors opening, he wasn't able to dodge the next punch, which caught him right in the jaw.

"Master!" Paige shrieked at the same time Shawn asked, "Everything all right out here?"

Landon shook his head and opened his mouth wide, stretching out his jaw to rub it. "Paige, close the door and see to Catherine," he snapped. "I got it, Shawn, thanks." With his temper flaring, Landon turned to Jayden, who was glaring at him, "You. Come with me. Now!"

Hackles raised and anger evident, Landon stormed past Jayden, letting his shoulder knock into the other man on his way into a vacant room. He seethed, taking harsh, shallow breaths and staring out the window while he waited to hear the click of the latch.

About two minutes later, Landon heard the door close, and with a slow turn, he faced Jayden. The man had a scowl on his face, and his hands with their angry knuckles were clenched into fists at his sides.

"She asked for what, exactly? To be taken advantage of by the likes of you?" Jayden sneered.

"Shut up, Jayden. Just keep your goddamn mouth closed. I should beat your ass for that little stunt, but I'll give you that one because I know what it means to love your submissive. Also, I did allow the scene to change."

The two men stood their ground, staring each other down, and after a few more minutes Jayden's fingers started to relax.

"Now, as I already tried to explain. Catherine asked for it."

Jayden sucked in a hiss, his hands clenching again.

"We had completed the scene. She was so far into her head space while Paige brought her to release that I don't think she was even aware I was piercing her until it was done." Landon took a couple of wary steps toward Jayden and kept talking. "Her tears alarmed me at first, especially when her body started shakin' with the force of them. I'm assuming it was the endorphin rush leaving her body and the pain of the fresh piercing settling in. It only took her a few minutes to start calming down, though. I watched her until she stopped crying. Then she shocked the hell outta me. She apologized, saying it had been an emotional day, and she requested permission to thank me by pleasuring both Paige and me."

Jayden's brow furrowed like something had just occurred to him, and a light bulb went off in Landon's head.

"Jayden, what instructions did you give Catherine with regard to her etiquette for today?"

A loud, resigned sigh echoed in the small room. "I—" Jayden paused to take a deep breath. "Dammit, I told her she was to properly thank each of you for her sessions."

"And what did you have in mind when you told her that?" A grin was curling Landon's lips. He was going to make Jayden work this through his thick skull.

"You're a Dom, Landon, you know what it means," Jayden snapped in retaliation.

"God dammit, Jayden. Get your head out of your ass and say it!" Landon snapped right back.

"Fuck, Landon, I slipped. I forgot that your scene wouldn't put her in a position to ensure you came. But Catherine, my sweet stubborn Erin, followed my orders to the letter."

With a pointed look, Landon softened his voice. "Look, man, when she made the request, I asked if she was sure. I gave her the out, but she insisted, following your orders by the sounds of it." He couldn't help the smug grin on his face. The bastard had sucker punched him, after all.

"Wait a minute. When I opened the door, I saw . . ." Jayden swallowed and started again. "I watched Paige make her come, and then start fucking her, independent of any instruction from you. I wasn't witnessing a scene—just raw sex!" His voice was beginning to rise again.

"Jayden, look at me. I swear Paige was following orders with her actions. I'd just given the order before you opened the door."

His mouth gaped open, and Landon had to laugh.

"Dude, seriously, have you heard of knocking?"

Jayden let out a light laugh, which Landon joined in on, and the tension in the room dissipated. Extending out his hand, Jayden offered his mea culpa. "Landon, I owe you an apology. Will you please accept it?"

With a firm shake, Landon did. "No problem, man. I know you can't help being a dick sometimes," he teased, giving his longtime friend a wink.

This time, Jayden's laugh came from the belly.

"Oh, Landon, speaking of dicks . . ."

"Don't worry, Jayden; your pretty peen is the only dick Catherine's pussy tasted in my room," Landon cut over him to allay Jayden's fears. "Come on, you need to get into Shawn's room. Paige should be walkin' your girl down there any minute."

"So you think my peen is pretty, do you, Landon? Something you want to tell me?" Jayden asked with a smirk.

The cocky shithead. Adopting a fake, high-pitched tone, Landon answered, "Oh, Jay, it's so big and so rubbery and," he sighed and batted his eyelashes, "and so brown!"

Laughing, they walked into the hall, with the air between them clear once again.

"Oh, and Jayden, just a suggestion from one friend to another?"

"What's that, Landon?"

"I don't think you should scene with Catherine after you leave here tonight. Call it a gut feeling, but something is off with her. Keep an eye on her during Shawn's session, and use tonight as an open time. Let her talk through her day with you. She's gonna need to unwind."

After a final clap on Jayden's back, Landon walked away, leaving him with that last thought.

⸎

CHAPTER SIXTEEN

⸎

With their scene finished, the submissive felt a bit like a third wheel while Paige and Sir Landon moved to the corner for a private talk. Catherine gave her fuzzy head a shake and glanced around the room. Noticing a bathroom, she made a quiet exit to relieve herself, splash some water on her face, and get a drink.

Feeling a little refreshed, Catherine came out of the small bathroom to be met with the sight of Sir Landon smacking Paige's butt and walking out the door. Once it was closed, Paige turned to look at her.

"Talk to me, Erin. Please. I want some answers," she implored with a sad smile. "Are you doing okay? We're a little worried with how much you've had to process today."

"To be honest, a lot has come up that I need to think on and sort out, but every time I've started to analyze it, I've had to set it aside so I can focus on my scenes. I'm really sorry I lost it earlier, Paige. Memories from a bad time in my life insisted on popping up," Catherine offered with an apologetic shrug.

"Spencer?" Paige hedged.

"Yeah." Catherine kept her voice low and tried to plan out her words so they would make sense. "I guess it's just been the intensity of today causing it to surface, because I haven't thought of that time in my life in a few months. Maybe this was a good thing; I'd become complacent, so this has helped me remember my place," she stated, nodding her head and trying to close the matter.

Before either woman could say more, a loud thud followed by a cracking sound came from the hallway.

"What was that?" Catherine blanched.

"I don't know. Let me check." Paige rushed to the door and pulled it open. "Master!" she shrieked.

Catherine could hear Sir Landon's voice but not his words before Paige closed the door.

"Well?"

"Uh, it's nothing." Paige's answer was evasive, and then she followed up with, "I hope," under her breath. "Time's short, Erin. Quick, undo the corset and put this on." She handed Catherine a sheer piece of green fabric, which she'd pulled from the bag Catherine had noticed when they came in. "Oh, wait a second. Sorry, I get flustered when rushed." Paige rolled her eyes at her own faults, before grabbing something from the counter. "Lift those boobs for me, sweetie."

Unsure what Paige had in mind, Catherine complied. The antiseptic spray hitting her tips made her flinch, but when the numbing ingredient in the salve soaked in, she exhaled in relief. "Wow, that stuff's great. Thanks."

Paige giggled. "Yeah, it is. You'll want to clean the area and apply this at least twice a day, but if they get really sore or itchy, feel free to use it more often. Breast play will also need to be limited at first and done with extreme care until you've healed."

"How long should that take?" Catherine hoped not more than a few weeks or maybe a couple of months at the most. The idea of missing out on one of her favorite pastimes saddened her; of course, she'd done it before, so she knew that she could do it again. Sir Jonathan had seemed more interested in her ass than her breasts, anyway; she doubted leaving them alone would be a problem.

"It varies from person to person, but the average is about six weeks, although for some women, full recovery can take over a year. Just keep it clean and medicated, and trust your Master to monitor how much he touches them. Now, hurry up and get that corset off!"

With less than nimble fingers, Catherine trembled while undoing the fasteners. She took a deep breath. The binding garment fell away from her ribs, and she laid the corset on a chair, shivering when the cool air hit her sweat-dampened flesh. Salty moisture slid along her skin, pebbling Catherine with goose bumps when it trickled into a couple of the whip welts and brought them to life with a teasing sting.

Holding the item Paige had given her out in front of herself, Catherine soon recognized it was a peasant-style blouse. She pulled it over her head and winced at the feather-light touch of the material against her tender skin. The full sleeves hung loose on Catherine's arms down to her wrists, where they were cinched with green satin ribbons tied into bows. Trimmed with the same green ribbon, the neckline scooped low over her breasts. When the submissive looked down the length of her body, she could see the darkness of her puffy, sore nipples with their dangling emerald jewels through the gauzy fabric.

Paige retrieved the corset from where it had been discarded and came forward to wrap tiny arms around Catherine while she bound her back into the garment. With the fasteners closed up, Catherine's breasts once again stood high and proud, pushing out over the top edge. Paige surprised the submissive by placing a quick open mouthed kiss on each of her nipples, causing them to pull into a tight pucker. The material was left damp, and as the air conditioning blew through the room, the fabric chilled against Catherine's nipples, ensuring they would stay pebbled, perky, and aching.

To finish Catherine's makeover, Paige fluffed her hair, following by adding a touch up of gloss to her lips. A final adornment, and they were done; she attached a leash to Catherine's collar and nipples, ignoring the submissive's mewling at the contact. This new leash had hooks instead of clamps now that Catherine had rings in her nipples. The ends of the hooks snapped together, pinching the fabric of her blouse between them with ease.

"All finished," Paige announced while stepping back to look over her handiwork. "You look beautiful, Erin."

Somehow, the submissive felt more naked and vulnerable in this state of undress. Catherine's breasts were covered but visible through the flimsy material; meanwhile, her bottom and quivering sex were left unconcealed and available. She became quite aware of the collar around her neck when Paige began to lead her toward the door. Remembering the pretty silver paddle that labeled her as Jayden's Slut made her brain kick into overdrive.

You know, Erin, those emeralds hanging from your pretty tits are awfully close to the color of your eyes. The ones that your Master is so fond of.

Her mind began racing. Catherine recalled in hazy bits the tenderness with which Master's voice and words had explained that today was for *her* pleasure. "An anniversary to be celebrated," had been his exact words.

Realization dawned, and her breath hitched. Had she made the wrong assumption about the J's branding her? Instead of being a mark of Sir Jonathan, was it possible that they were Jayden's? Had Catherine been marked as *His?* The cobwebs continued to burn off while she acknowledged that the memory of Spencer was just that: a bad memory. Spencer's demise had freed her from forced slavery, giving her the chance to begin afresh and to find a Master who wanted her willing submission. She'd found Jayden. He was the man who had become that Master for her. Her heart raced with the acceptance of one small fact: by his own admission, he'd wanted Catherine from the first moment he had seen her—and she had wanted him. *How could she have forgotten that?*

She thought back to that morning. *Was it really just this morning? So much had happened since then!* The gentleness of the kiss Master had given her before sending her inside; the way he'd seemed to linger, not wanting to pull away. Ideas and possibilities swarmed around Catherine's mind. Again, she marveled at the thought that he'd marked her as His. *Was it possible?*

Could it be? Had Master developed deeper feelings for her?

A shocked gasp slipped from Catherine's lips when she let the idea sink in and a wave of hope coursed through her.

"Everything all right, Erin?" Paige's eyes twinkled.

The huge smile that broke out on Catherine's face couldn't be withheld. "Yes, Paige. I think everything just might be perfect."

"Of course it is, sweetie!" Paige responded with an enthusiastic hug. "Okay, time for the blindfold, and away we go!" she squealed.

"Paige," Catherine whined, "is the blindfold necessary?"

"Silly Erin. It's Master's orders!" She winked at Catherine before her baby blues disappeared from sight when the blindfold slid into place and plunged Catherine into darkness.

ഈരുഈ

If anyone besides Landon had said such words to Jayden, he would've blown them off. Nobody knew his jewel better than he did. However, considering Landon's day job, it was rare that he was ever wrong when it came to reading people. It wasn't smart to blow off advice from a man who made his living as a therapist. Besides, Jayden could admit that his friend was right. Catherine would need tonight to work through all she'd experienced today. Hell, he was going to need it, as well.

In a wayward thought, Jayden wondered if what he was experiencing was anything close to what hormonal women went through every month.

Jayden hurried the short distance down the hall to Shawn's designated space for the day. He was looking forward to seeing his jewel captured by that man's talents. While walking, he reflected on the conversation he'd just had with Landon, knowing he'd been a complete asshole toward his friend. He'd thrown a tantrum like a three-year-old. Jayden knew he was lucky that Landon was such a nice guy; he should have dragged Jayden's sorry ass to a whipping bench for his antics. Instead, Landon had taken the punch like a gentleman, and then had fucking forgiven Jayden.

The price for Landon's forgiveness was a wakeup call about what he stood to lose: Erin. Landon had seen right through Jayden and had forced him to acknowledge his true feelings out loud for the first time.

I love Catherine Eilene O'Chancey.

The thought didn't terrify Jayden or leave him confused. In fact, it was like a piece of a puzzle fitting neatly into its spot, completing the picture. His stomach fluttered, and his heart raced when he anticipated telling Catherine.

Confident that the rest of the day would go well, Jayden reached up and gave three light taps on the door when he reached it. He didn't think Paige had brought Catherine down yet, but just in case, he didn't want to walk in. Fulfilling Catherine's final fantasy required her to be ignorant of his presence.

"It's open!" Shawn's deep voice answered.

Momentary stupefaction awaited Jayden when he stepped into the room and what he saw left him speechless. In the corner of the room, Shawn squatted in front of Micah, doing something with his hands. When his friend stood up, Jayden could see that Micah was naked and in a submissive kneel. There was a ball gag in Micah's mouth, and his hardened cock was enclosed in a metal cage, along with weighted clamps that were attached to his scrotum. *Wow, Shawn's wasting no time.*

"Hiya, Jayden," Shawn greeted while he flashed an enthusiastic grin. "Micah here told me what you guys talked about, and I think he may be perfect."

They both looked over to Micah, who had his eyes closed and a look of serenity on his face.

"Hope ya don't mind if he stays for the session? I figure he's already seen Catherine in an intimate setting, and I can use the time as sort of an interview for him."

"No problem; that'll be fine, Shawn. So, can I see your final draft before the girls get here?" Jayden inquired without masking his excitement.

"You betcha, Jay. I've got it on the tray here," he said while he adjusted himself. The telltale sign of Shawn's fondness for Micah would have been hard to miss; Jayden had to look away.

A Divine Life

Stepping in closer, Jayden found his breath swept away when he saw the prepared stencil. "Wow, Shawn! That's going to be perfect. I can't wait to see it on her skin." Jayden grinned at him. "So, the words will be black, the orchids white, and the rope a mixture of traditional red and green, right?"

"You got it, stud! I figure it'll take about an hour to get the outline down, and then I'll let her take a break. After that, a couple of hours to get the color filled in."

"Sounds good, my friend. We'll still have some daylight left, so we can stay on track with the second part of her session. Damn, this is going to be beautiful!"

A knock on the door ended their discussion. Jayden moved to an overstuffed recliner in the corner of the room that allowed him a clear view of the table where Shawn would be working on Catherine. Settling in, he nodded to Shawn to go ahead.

Shawn cracked open the door, and Jayden watched while Paige handed off a leash to him. She planted a tiny kiss on Catherine's cheek, and he could hear Paige's pleasant voice telling his girl that she would be fine.

Shawn introduced himself to Catherine while he led her to the center of the room where his work table sat. However, Jayden couldn't hear any of the words Shawn spoke because he wasn't able to focus on anything but the gorgeous creature before him. Her skin was flushed and vibrant; her lips were full and glossy. When

177

Catherine's tongue snaked out to moisten her lips, his cock sprang to life in his pants.

Taking a shuddering breath, Jayden let his gaze continue down his submissive's body. Catherine's sheer, green blouse was ethereal against her skin, allowing him to just make out her delectable nipples. He would have to wait to see them up close. The corset cinched her already small waist into a luscious hourglass shape. The stance she'd assumed, with her feet about a foot apart, gave Jayden a clear view of her slick, swollen, lower lips.

In that moment, it took everything Jayden had not to lunge for her and bury his tongue into her honeyed folds. His cock became harder. *Fuck!*

This was going to be the longest afternoon of his life!

ಬಿಂಜ

CHAPTER SEVENTEEN

ಬಿಂಜ

Paige gave her new friend a quick peck, telling her that she'd be fine. Catherine smiled because she knew Paige was right, she *would* be fine, and then giggled when Paige gave her ass a light swat before the echo of her retreating footsteps sounded in Catherine's ears.

"Hello, Catherine," said a deep-timbered voice. "I'm Shawn Carpenter." She felt his large hand grasp hers in a firm handshake.

"Hello, Sir." The submissive's response was cordial, while out of habit she dropped her gaze downward behind the blindfold.

He let out a laugh that wrapped her in warmth and set her at ease in an instant. "We're going to be a little informal with this session, okay, doll? Think of me as a friend, not a Dom. You can just call me Shawn."

She could hear the smile in his voice and took a liking to this new man. "Well, in that case, Shawn, please call me Erin. Um, if it pleases you," she added the last bit with a hint of awkwardness. After all, she was all but naked and blind in front of the man, so she couldn't quite drop all pretenses of what she was doing there. Catherine thought she heard a small exhalation from further in the room, but she shook off the impression, unsure.

"Well, Erin, your Master has asked me to do a tattoo for you—" he started to explain.

"Really?" Catherine squealed, grinning wide and unable to hide her excitement.

Shawn chuckled. "Yes, really. By your reaction, I think it's safe to assume you are okay with that?"

"Oh, aye, Sir! I mean Shawn." Master was going to have her further marked as His! Catherine wanted to jump up and down, but she didn't dare attempt it in the stilettos she was wearing.

"Perfect! Then let's get started. Let me get this lead off of you first, and then I'll guide you over to the table."

Catherine was patient while Shawn undid the hooks and leash from her nipple rings and collar. She surprised herself at her control; she didn't flinch when he grasped her breasts to unhook the rings. His touch was so gentle. Thinking on it, she realized that she didn't feel *anything*: no stirrings of desire, no reaction at all. In fact, Shawn's touch was almost like that of a brother, so she just went with it.

Taking her hand, Shawn guided Catherine over to what she assumed was the table he'd mentioned, and he helped her sit up on the edge. "Comfy?"

She nodded.

"This is going to be cold, but it will clean the skin and allow the stencil to transfer. Ready to begin, doll?"

Catherine nodded again, but she still hissed when the cold, wet cloth made contact with her skin just above her mons. She paid attention to the cloth's path while he wiped it over her hips and around her lower back, across the top of her ass cheeks, and back to her front. The tattoo was going to wrap all the way around her, which explained why she had been left bare from the waist down. There was a soft crinkle of paper before she felt the gentle pressure of Shawn's fingers when he began pressing the stencil against her skin. Sure enough, the paper followed the path the cloth had taken. After a minute, he began to peel the paper away, leaving behind whatever pattern Master wanted on her.

"Wish I could invite you to lay back and relax, doll, but until I get the outline done, I'm afraid you're going to have to stay sitting up so the stencil doesn't smear on your back."

"No problem." Catherine was no stranger to holding her position.

He went on, "The plan is to get the outline knocked out; after that you'll get to take a breather, stretch your legs, and so on. However, Erin, if you need me to stop sooner, you just have to let me know, okay?"

"Aye, Sir." His throat cleared, and she corrected herself, "Aye, Shawn. I'm sure I'll be fine," Catherine proclaimed while she wiggled on the table, centering herself on her tailbone a little better.

"Good girl. Let me grab my stool, and we'll begin."

Wheels squeaked, and then she felt his hand on her thigh, alerting Catherine to his position in front of her. The tattoo gun came on with a click and a humming buzz, and the sound went straight to the submissive's groin. She could sense the first tingles of excitement building inside.

"Do me a favor, Erin. Can you try leaning back on your hands? That's it," Shawn coaxed while she angled her body back. "Just while I get this lower part." His finger brushed right above her pubic mound before he pressed into her flesh to hold it taut, and then the needle bit into her skin.

Again, his touch didn't seem sexual to Catherine, just courteous, like he was letting her know where he was. The needle pelted into her flesh, stinging for the first couple of minutes. Soon enough, she found that place in her head where she could just let go and feel sensation; pain-induced euphoria. Her head lolled back, and Catherine relished the prickling of the needle that angled from her pussy up toward her hip. Shawn's hot breath blew over her core in and out in a steady rhythm as he worked. Every few minutes, the buzzing would stop—so he could reload the ink, she guessed. Each time it resumed, she felt herself become a little wetter in anticipation of the sting.

Shawn was quick and quiet while he embedded the ink. Silence surrounded them, with the exception of the gun's buzzing and their breathing. Every once in a while, Catherine thought she heard additional breaths from the corner of the room, but again she dismissed it, allowing herself to melt away with the tiny pricking of the needle, followed by rough rubbing each time Shawn wiped away the excess ink.

Before long, Shawn had her turn around on the table so that her back was facing the edge. He then directed her to lean forward so that her elbows rested on her knees. The buzzing resumed, and the needle laid the ink, angling down to her ass. When the insistent sting tickled the space right above her ass crack, Catherine giggled.

Shawn let out that soft, warm laugh again. "Enjoying yourself, Erin?"

"Mm-hmm . . ." she moaned.

On he worked, rising back up out of the dip in her lower back to travel to her opposite hip. There was a pause so Shawn could help her turn and lean back on her hands again, opening her front back up before he maneuvered back in between her legs. The trail of ink continued over Catherine's hip and dipped below her belly and across her mons until, at last, she felt him back where he'd begun.

Catherine couldn't deny that she was dripping wet. The tattoo thing could become a dangerous addiction. Her pulse thrummed beneath the surface of her hot skin, and she welcomed the feel of the cool cloth when Shawn wiped her down.

"Excellent, Erin. You took that like a trooper. Outline's all done now, so let's take five. I want you to stretch and move around a bit. My assistant is going to help you."

Assistant? So she hadn't been imagining another person in the room. Knowing she'd been on display all this time made her pulse spike. There was also a growing curiosity as to why Shawn wasn't doing anything sexual to her. Catherine would've expected to have a vibrator inserted into one of her orifices or something, but Shawn was being nothing but professional. *Odd.*

More eager to stretch than she realized, Catherine started to slide forward off the edge of the table when long fingers grasped her hips. A tingling warmed her flesh where they connected. The hands' owner helped her to get steady on her feet before his fingers ghosted up the front of her body, timid digits brushing her erect, sore nipples. She trembled under a sudden surge of need.

Jayden?

Sensing a mouth hovering above her, Catherine inhaled with surprise and caught a whiff of a musky scent. Before she could lean forward to capture the teasing mouth, it was gone, and she indulged in a huffing pout. Catherine was already so wound up from the pleasurable sensation of the tattoo gun that she was craving any kind of actual sexual contact; in other words, she was no longer thinking with any clarity. Lust and desire were ramping up, claiming control of her fractured emotions.

Mystery fingers having found purchase on her elbow, Catherine allowed herself to be guided forward around the room. The movement felt good in her back and thighs, but what delighted her even more was the way the fingers continued to caress her—light and fleeting, moving across her hips and ass, but never applying enough pressure to give Catherine satisfaction. With each almost-imperceptible touch, she felt an electric current jolt her body, taking it on a slow ride to ecstasy.

Uncertain if it was being handled by someone she couldn't see, the weird connection she felt that reminded her of Master, or the intoxicating scent of that musk, Catherine was reaching the point at which she would explode with one good touch.

All too soon, the couple stopped moving, and the man helped Catherine back onto the table. Cuffs were snapped onto her wrists, and she was assisted down onto her back. She offered no resistance when her arms were pulled above her head so the cuffs could be connected to something at the top of the table. Closing her eyes behind the blindfold, she focused her hearing; his tread was light while he walked back to the bottom of the table. Smooth fabric brushed her inner thighs when the man wedged himself in between them, and then those long fingers pushed into the fleshy part of her thighs, a silent instruction to spread.

Catherine hesitated, knowing the moment she complied her secret would be revealed: thighs wet and slick with the moisture that had oozed out of her while she walked. There was a sharp pull on her nipple rings, and her legs fell open at once when hot, searing pain tore through her chest.

Shit, I want to come.

Lips brushed the wanton woman's thighs, laying gentle kisses atop her skin. She tried to lift up and push into them, make the contact firmer, but they disappeared.

She groaned as more juice escaped her. *This is pure torture.* "P-please, Sir," Catherine begged in a whimper while praying that Master had given this person orders to make her orgasm, not just tease her into oblivion!

A hot tongue plunged into her core, licking slow and sensual-like up toward her clit. When the tongue reached her hypersensitive bud and sucked, she fell apart.

"Aye, Fuck! Thank you, Sir!" Catherine screamed when a huge orgasm washed over her. One lick from the stranger's tongue was all that was needed to leave her writhing in pleasure.

୫୨୯୫

CHAPTER EIGHTEEN

୫୨୯୫

Her scream of pleasure rocked Jayden back into reality, and he jumped, backing away from her. His woman's body was undulating on the table, and he could see her come flowing out onto the surface. Damn, she was beautiful.

It hadn't been his intention to put his mouth on her. However, walking Catherine around and teasing her with his touches had pushed him to a dangerous edge. When she'd whispered his name in question, Jayden had almost cleared the room so he could make love to her right then. He was pretty sure she wasn't aware that the powerful word had even slipped out, but it reminded him that he was too close; that if he wasn't careful, she would know it was him. That was not information Jayden was ready for her to have just yet.

Ten minutes after Shawn started the break, Jayden decided to get his woman back on the table. Knowing she would need something to focus on for the next part of the tattoo, the Dom elected to bind his jewel to the table. Shawn had explained that the outline was always easiest to endure. The pain would become more intense when it was filled in, because he had to go a little deeper and spend more time in one area to ensure full coverage. For Jayden, it was imperative that Catherine be still to avoid any slip-ups, considering a mistake couldn't be erased.

Thinking he would give her one last small tease to keep her on edge, Jayden had wedged himself between her thighs, pushing against them to get her to open wide. Her resistance had surprised him, so he yanked on her nipple rings and was rewarded with her parting legs, revealing a visual feast.

Oh, yes. We're going to have fun with those little beauties in the playroom, Jayden thought, already envisioning the ways he could attach ropes to stretch her breasts for flogging. Imagining what it would feel like to wrap his lips around her nipples and work the rings with his tongue and teeth made him groan under his breath. Landon had said a minimum of six weeks before heavy play resumed—if she was healed. It might kill them both, but he would do his best to behave and let her recover.

Jesus, he needed to pull back. His dick was uncomfortably hard from the scenes playing out in his mind. With reluctance, Jayden moved away, leaning down to place light kisses across her thighs. Catherine tried in vain to push up against him, and he smiled while maintaining a safe distance—until she begged.

She fucking begged, and that was it.

Who was he to say no to that angel in the flesh? Well, besides her Dom, but Jayden didn't want to deny her anything at that moment. He dove in, burying his tongue all the way into her core before he dragged up through her folds, seeking out her engorged clit to suckle into his mouth. His jewel's orgasm was instantaneous and magical to behold.

Somehow, Jayden was able to pull his gaze away from her – maybe it was the quiet snicker he heard behind him – to glance over at Shawn. His friend stood next to Micah, stroking the young man's hair and pinching his nipples. Shawn had a grin on his face, and he shook his head at Jayden, acknowledging without words that Jayden was a lost cause.

Jayden shrugged his shoulders as if to say "sue me" and sighed, before going back to the corner recliner after a last, longing peek at the oasis taunting him from the table. His cock was screaming at him to do something. A lick of his lips rewarded him with his jewel's sweet flavor, and one thought surged: *Fuck it.*

Being extra quiet, he undid his zipper and pulled out his swollen dick, gripping it tight. He ignored the brief flash of pain in his equally swollen knuckles. Punching the wall – and Landon – had been stupid. Jayden's eyes closed, and he heard Micah whimper when he started to stroke.

Of all the things the submissive had endured in the past few hours, as many times as she'd found release, none of it compared to what her body had just experienced. Rocking her hips with wanton suggestiveness, looking for friction that wasn't there, Catherine embraced the hot fire that seared her from within.

How was it possible for just one stroke of a tongue to cause her to come so undone?

Shawn's soft laugh reached Catherine's ears, along with a muted whimper. "Well, doll, *that* was something to see!" He chuckled again. "Almost makes me wish I liked pussy."

What? Oh. Oh! "Are you, um, I mean . . ." The blindfolded woman didn't know how to ask without being rude.

"It's okay, Erin. Yes, I'm gay. But I also know something beautiful when I see it. You, my dear, are one of the most beautiful things I've had the pleasure of laying eyes on in a long time."

Heat raced over Catherine's skin when she succumbed to a blush from the heartfelt compliment. She heard water running; then a warm cloth was being wiped across her thighs.

"Lift your bottom for me, Erin. You've made a bit of a mess on my table."

The heat flared to life again. "I'm sorry, Si–Shawn," she whispered, choking on her embarrassment.

"Oh, don't worry about it, doll. Like I said, that was something to see."

The warm cloth wiped her underside and came up through her still-pulsing folds. Catherine whimpered at the contact, and then brazenly pushed into it.

"Greedy little thing, aren't ya, Erin?" Shawn asked, and she could hear the humor in his tone. "You're gonna have to wait on that, doll. We've still got work to do. Now, how are you feeling? Any soreness or tender spots?"

His voice was laced with a level of concern that comforted Catherine. "Nah, I'm good. Ready to get back to it!" If she wasn't going to get some kind of penetration any time soon, then she wanted to feel the needle. It would distract her from the longing ache between her thighs. She heard the stool roll up, and his large hand took hold of her thigh.

"Sure thing, doll. I'm going to start filling in your outline now. I'll warn you that this next phase is a bit more intense. I have to push the needle in deeper to set the color, in addition to just moving slower to get it all filled in. You let me know if you need another break." There was a pat to her thigh, and the machine came to life with a buzz.

The next hour was peaceful. In her center, the fire had simmered down to a low throb while the needle danced over her skin. Catherine centered herself by controlling her breathing. When the pain became sharp, she tugged against her wrist restraints, thus redirecting her focus. It was worst when he worked over her hip bones because the sting became the sharpest, and as a result, her desire flared between her thighs.

Shawn had completed about half of the tattoo when he turned the machine off. "How we doing?" he asked, rubbing Catherine's outer thigh with a light stroke.

Having succumbed to an in-and-out doze, her voice was sleepy when she replied with a yawn, "I'm fine, Shawn. You're really good at this. I've been napping," she admitted.

He snickered. "Good to hear, doll. Listen, I need to take a break myself. My hand's starting to cramp a bit. Why don't you go ahead and take that nap, and I'll be back in about twenty minutes?"

"M'kay." A soft blanket came down over the drowsy woman, and she drifted off.

ಸಿಂಖ

CHAPTER NINETEEN

ಸಿಂಖ

Jayden's frustration was mounting; he just wanted to beat off and relieve the pressure in his balls. However, he knew he had more control than that, and he opted to stretch it out and build up his craving. His teasing stroke slowed and his eyes popped open when he overheard Shawn telling *his* jewel about his sexual preferences.

Really? He's telling her he'd consider going straight for her? In front of me, no less!

The Dom's mind was put at ease while he witnessed the platonic kindness Shawn displayed when cleaning Catherine and calming her. Jayden's hand gripped tighter around his cock again and slid upward. Shawn, Jayden realized, wasn't making a pass at her; he was just treating her like a little sister or a good friend. His large palm passed over the swollen head, gathering the leaking dampness, and then moved back down.

At hearing Micah whimper again, Jayden swiveled his head to look at him. The young submissive's gaze was locked on Jayden's hand, watching its steady movement. A lowered glance revealed to Jayden that Micah's dick was swelling inside its metal confinement.

Shit, that's gotta hurt! Jayden thought, and eased up on the tension of his own cock in sympathy.

For the next half hour, the Dom teased both himself and Micah, whose eyes were filled with yearning while they darted between Jayden's show and Shawn. Other than the occasional flicker toward Micah, Jayden kept his eyes trained on his jewel, monitoring her body language.

Her breathing would pick up, and she'd pull against her cuffs. The slightest of squirms ripened the air in the room with the scent of her arousal whenever her legs shifted apart. Jayden would find his hand moving faster and his balls tightening when that happened. Several times, he had to let go of his cock to get himself back under control, but the moment his turgid length began to soften, he would take it in hand again.

In the back of his mind, Jayden knew Shawn was keeping an eye on everything going on around him. With each pause to reload the ink in the gun, he was assessing the situation with all three of them – Micah, Catherine, and Jayden – and loving it.

When Jayden had met with Shawn one-on-one to sort out the details of his role for the day, they had come to an agreement about payment for Shawn's services. Shawn had all but begged to suck Jayden off to experience the Dom's legendary cock himself. Jayden had compromised with him by agreeing to jerk off in the room so Shawn could see, but not touch. Knowing Jayden wasn't going to back down, Shawn had accepted. The fact that Micah had offered himself to Shawn at Jayden's suggestion was a huge bonus for them all.

Despite Jayden's valiant effort to hold his orgasm at bay, he reached a point at which he knew he was going to have to come soon. It then dawned on him that he had no convenient receptacle for his seed when it spilled. So he pulled up his shirt, revealing chiseled abs, and Micah let out a longing whimper, which caused Shawn to pause and look over at both of them.

Taking control of the situation, Shawn gave Catherine a brief explanation about needing a break. Her soft breaths and mumbled answer let Jayden know she was not too far from a nap.

Shawn motioned for Micah to follow him, but as Micah started to stand, Shawn made a sign for him to stop, and then mouthed, "On your hands and knees. Crawl," before he crooked his finger at Jayden to follow as well.

Letting his shirt tumble back down over his torso, Jayden stood, following the two men while his cock bobbed proudly in front of him. When they reached the door, Jayden was brought to a stop by a shocking admission from his girl: her hushed snore followed by a whispered "Love you, Jayden." Although it was true that he'd already been hard, hearing her subconscious admission tightened his cock further, and his heart swelled. *Oh, to hear her say that while awake.* The knowledge that the sentiment was in her subconscious was inspirational for Jayden; maybe they'd both survive this day after all.

The three men stepped across the hall into another vacant room before Shawn spoke. "Alright, you two; the sexual tension in that room is killing me." He emphasized his words by palming his erection through his pants. "Here's what I propose. Jayden, dude, I can see you are about to blow your wad, and I can't wait any more for a taste of that ass," he declared, nodding toward Micah.

"Go on," Jayden encouraged.

"I want to watch Micah suck your dick while I fuck him," he stated with a simple nod.

Micah moaned at his dick's twitching reaction, and the cage entrapping it bounced.

Shawn was right. Jayden needed to come; he was approaching desperate levels of need. What Shawn was proposing would be an easy way for him to do it without the mess of spilling his spunk, and it wasn't like Micah hadn't sucked him off before.

"Let's do it," Jayden agreed and pulled his shirt off, letting his pants drop to the floor before he could change his mind. He stepped out of the clothes and leaned against the table.

While Jayden undressed, Shawn released Micah from the cage but left the weights attached to his scrotum. The Dom watched with bemused curiosity when Shawn shed his clothes as well. He'd never seen his friend in action as a Dominant, and he was intrigued about the kind of Dom Shawn would be—kind and patient, or demanding and harsh.

"Micah, crawl to me," Shawn ordered while rolling a condom onto his already erect dick.

"Yes, Sir," came Micah's mumbled reply around the ball gag, and then he jumped – well, crawled – into action.

Shawn issued his instructions while untethering Shawn's mouth from the gag. "Open your mouth. You're going to get my dick lubed with your spit so I can fuck that pretty ass of yours." Shawn pushed his thick shaft between Micah's lips before the submissive could say anything. A delighted groan rumbled from Shawn when Micah's tongue and mouth went to work on him like an expert. After he had pumped in and out of Micah's mouth a few times, he told Micah to turn around.

"Now, my pretty little bitch, wrap that hot mouth around Sir Jayden's cock, and push that ass out for me. We don't have much time." Shawn's words were delivered with a smack to Micah's ass the moment his mouth engulfed Jayden's cock.

The familiarity of Micah's mouth allowed Jayden to shut his eyes and give over to the experience. Feeling that knowledgeable orifice work up and down, the tongue swirling over the head a few times, Jayden was ready to thrust forward just when Micah came to a stop near the base. Shawn plunged into the willing man's ass, jolting Micah forward, and the rest of Jayden's cock disappeared. *Fuck*! That was the deepest Micah had ever taken Jayden in, and when Micah groaned because of the intrusion in his ass, Jayden lost it. While Shawn started moving in Micah's backside, Jayden began spurting down Micah's throat.

It felt like he came for five minutes. Micah's mouth stayed on the Dom the whole time, and he swallowed everything given to him. Soon after Jayden's release, Shawn tensed up, alerting Jayden that he was coming, too.

"Ahh, fuck! That ass is tight!" bellowed Shawn, tossing his head back so his black curls were thrown around. "Mm, so fucking good."

With a chortle, Jayden cleared his throat. "Well, on that note I'm going to step out and use the locker room shower to clean up. You two can, yeah, do what you've got to do. What do you think, Shawn? Meet you outside in about forty-five minutes?" he inquired while pulling his trousers back on and gathering his shirt off the floor.

Turning a lazy grin toward Jayden, the sated man nodded. "You betcha. She's done great so far, so I don't foresee hitting any snags at this point."

With a heartfelt laugh and a pat on Shawn's bare shoulder when he walked past, Jayden left to get ready for his scene.

ಐಿಓ

CHAPTER TWENTY

ಐಿಓ

Erin sat on a wide stretch of beach, gazing out over a crystal blue sea; seagulls sang their song in the sky above, while relentless waves pushed and tugged at the shoreline.

"Erin."

In the distance she could make out a man jogging toward her, but she was looking into the sun and therefore couldn't make out his face.

"Erin, come on, doll."

As he got closer, she began to see some of the jogger's features: bronze skin, dark eyes, wavy ochre locks, and a trim, toned body that was quite easy on the eyes. He was haloed by the sun, and his hand was reaching out to her. She began to lift hers in return.

"Catherine, wake up!"

Her eyes snapped open to be met with darkness. *Oh, right, the damn blindfold*. She sighed and tried to swallow down her disgruntled mood. Catherine wanted to go back to sleep and see where the dream was going.

"Hey, sleepyhead." Shawn's voice held amusement. "Have a nice nap?"

"It was about to get better," she grumbled, and he laughed.

"I'm sorry, doll, but I'm back, so let's get this done. Shall we?"

"Aye, Sir," Catherine snarled.

"Down, kitty!" He laughed at her again, his demeanor even lighter than when they'd begun, and he patted the top of her head. "About thirty more minutes should do it. Do you need to pee or anything before we start?"

"No, thank you. I'm good. Let's just get this done. I want to see it!"

The artist chuckled again.

"Something funny?"

"Yeah, sweetheart. You! Let's just say you remind me of someone and leave it at that. Okay, here we go, doll. Homestretch." *Buzzzz . . .*

₧₧₧

Before she knew it, Shawn was turning off the tattoo gun and announcing he'd finished. After unhooking her cuffs from the table, he then removed them from her wrists. "Here, doll, take my hand, and let me help you sit up."

Catherine accepted with grace, and excitement pebbled her nipples, reminding her they would be tender and sore for the foreseeable future.

"It turned out pretty damn good, if I do say so myself," Shawn preened. "Let me wipe you down and get some ointment on it. First, I'm going to take your blindfold off, but I want you to keep your eyes closed while I do the ointment to help them adjust to the light. Then I'll take you over to the mirror so you can see."

The offending item slid over her hair, and Catherine exhaled in relief. "Yeah? I can see it now?" She was bouncing on the table, and he laughed at her exuberance.

"Yes, if you'll hold still for a minute. I've given a set of aftercare instructions to your Master, but the basic rules are to stay out of sunlight for long periods, avoid chlorine, and no extended soaks in the bath until it has healed all the way. You'll also want to use a water-based ointment on it a couple of times a day. Oh, and no rubbing or scratching; just patting it."

His hands were balmy and soothing while they applied the cream to her sensitive flesh. "Okay, open your eyes nice and slow. I've got you."

Catherine's lids fluttered open, and her vision came back into focus a little at a time. Shawn stood in front of her, steadying her while she looked him over for the first time. His wild hair was thick and black, and when her hand snaked up to touch it, she found it silky soft. He flashed a bright smile, which was framed by a tanned face and the kindest brown eyes she'd ever seen—next to her Master's coffee-colored orbs, that was.

"We good?"

"I believe we are! Can I see now?" Catherine's impatience was clear.

"Of course, the mirror is just over there," he explained and thumbed over his shoulder.

She was thankful for Shawn's assistance when he helped her down from the table and held her elbow while she walked over to the mirror. Her legs were a little shaky after being still for so long. They stopped in front of the mirror, and when Catherine took in her reflection, happy tears formed in the corners of her eyes. Twisting right, then left, and then doing a full twirl to let her take in the back, Catherine was left humbled and in awe.

Shawn had created a masterpiece on Catherine's skin; a combination of red and green twisted and entwined to form a silky-looking Celtic braid, which wrapped around her back and over her hips. Each of the knotted rope was frayed and morphed into orchid blooms. Done in white, the orchids burst off of her skin against the rich background. Growing from the bottom petals was black lettering, which was scrawled across her skin just above her pubic mound and connected to the other side, closing the circle.

Catherine spun around and ran to Shawn so she could throw her arms around him in a big hug. "Oh my God, Shawn, it's beautiful! It's absolutely stunning. I love it!" Pulling back, she bounced and twirled back toward the mirror for another look. Her heart soared while she traced her fingers over the words inked into her skin for the rest of forever: *To Serve is Divine.*

Back in front of the mirror and unable to take her eyes off the fresh ink, Catherine stood frozen. Shawn approached her from behind and encased her in his arms. He then rested his chin on her shoulder, making eye contact with the enthralled woman in the mirror.

Taking a deep breath, Catherine noticed he had a light citrusy scent, like tangerines. It was comforting, but nothing like the spicy musk of her mystery lover from earlier. She smiled. There had been something almost familiar about the scent, but she hadn't been able to quite place it. The spice had been strong enough to cover up another underlying odor.

"I'm glad you like it, doll." Shawn beamed, giving her waist a squeeze.

"Oh, Shawn, I do, I swear I do! You have no idea what this means to me."

"I think I've got an idea. He's a lucky man, Erin."

Catherine jerked her head over her shoulder to look at him head on. "I'm sorry, what? I mean, how?" The poor girl was at a loss for words.

He threw his head back and belted out a deep laugh. "Listen, doll, it's written all over your face and shines in those big green eyes of yours."

Catherine gaped at him.

Shawn became serious. He spun her around to face him and cupped her cheek with a tender touch. "Believe me, Erin, I've seen but a handful of people in my lifetime who were what I would consider 'in love.' Even fewer who were in this lifestyle, but I know love when I see it, and trust me, doll, I'm looking at it right now. You love your Master."

Her head started nodding 'yes' of its own accord, and her heart took up a frantic staccato. "I didn't know what true happiness was before I met him, Shawn. Love is such a strong, meaningful idea; I've been trying to figure out all day if Master is willing to entertain it."

His lips brushed against her forehead. "Of course he is, doll. I'm happy for you—both of you."

They shared a contented sigh.

"Okay, enough of the serious talk. This is your day, and I'm not done with you yet." Shawn grinned while clapping his hands together and rubbing them back and forth.

Yeah, this was going to be awkward. "Uh, Shawn, I—I'm not sure," Catherine started, and then paused, taking a deep breath. "Oh, hell! I'm supposed to thank you for your services, and I have no fucking clue what to offer you!" she spat out in frustration and embarrassment.

Confusion marred Shawn's features while he sorted out her words. He stared at Catherine with his eyes wide and his mouth hanging open. When what she was suggesting clicked, he burst out laughing and staggered back, clutching his stomach.

"Oh, doll! Oh, my goodness, you are too precious! You don't need to do a thing for me. Just seeing the delight on your face is all I need." He took a calming breath. "Besides, Jayden took care of my payment," he said still grinning ear to ear.

Paranoia flooded Catherine's veins, and her smile disappeared at Shawn's words. *Had Master taken in yet another lover?* Maybe she was wrong about his feelings for her? "What—what do you mean 'Jayden took care of your payment'?" She fought to keep her breath calm while she choked out the words.

Shawn took in the look on the poor girl's face. "Oh shit, doll! No, whatever you're thinking, stop! I just meant to say that he introduced me to Micah. I've been looking for a sub that meets specific requirements, and I think Micah is going to work out perfectly," he explained in a rush.

Catherine let out the breath she'd been holding. "Dammit, Shawn, give a girl a heart attack, why don't you?"

He laughed, and there was a hint of guilt flushing his dark cheeks. "I'm not saying I wouldn't have liked to tap that ass of your Master's," Shawn wiggled his eyebrows, "but he wouldn't hear of it. He's all yours, Erin. You've got to believe that. I'm sure you know it in your heart; you just need to wrap that pretty little head of yours around the idea!"

With an exhale, Catherine stepped in closer and gave him a hug. "Thanks, Shawn. You've been a really great friend today. So, you said you weren't done with me . . ."

"Nope, I'm not." Now Shawn sported a mischievous look in his eyes. "I work with other mediums besides tattoo ink. Paige will be here any minute to freshen you up, and then I'll see you again out in the gardens." As if on cue, there was a quiet knock on the door, and Shawn called, "Come on in, Paige. She's all yours for the next," he looked at his watch, "ten minutes." A quick peck was placed on Catherine's forehead, and Shawn whispered, "See ya soon, doll."

He patted Paige on the head when he walked past her, leaning in to say something to her under his breath.

"Hi, Paige."

"Hey, sweetie! Let me see!" She was bouncing on the balls of her feet.

Taking her time, Catherine turned around in a circle so Paige could view the entire tattoo. Surprising herself, she warmed with pride over her new ink and wondered when she would get an opportunity to show it off.

Paige squealed. "Oh my God, Erin! It's so pretty. Do you love it? Did it hurt?" she threw the questions at Catherine one after the other while her fingers came close, and then hovered right above Catherine's skin like she wanted to touch it.

"Geez, Paige, take a breath. Yes, I love it, and no it didn't hurt. It was relaxing, truth be told. I ended up napping."

Giving in and allowing her finger to stroke one of the orchids, Paige asked, "Do you know why he picked the orchids? They seem so fragile but strong."

Catherine smiled. "Well, Master has told me I remind him of an orchid for the reasons you just gave, and there's a happy florist down the street from my house who gets a weekly order from him."

Paige's eyes filled with teary emotion. "That is one of the sweetest things I've ever heard. Wow, he's good."

They both laughed when Catherine nodded her head.

"Okay, then; tell me about the rope."

"I have to make a guess on this one until I get a chance to talk to him and confirm it. My last name is O'Chancey, which is Irish. By using something from my culture – my history – I think he wanted to have a symbol that I am my own person, a willing participant in this lifestyle." Catherine wasn't sure if that's what Master had in mind, but it felt right to her when she expressed her ideas.

Her friend let out a dreamy sigh before she startled them both back into the moment with a sharp clap of her hands. "Well, I love it, Erin! Okay, time to get busy. You go pee, and then I'll work my magic, and we'll be on our way!" Paige chirped.

Done with the bathroom, Paige touched up Catherine's make up again and pulled the front and top sections of her red hair into a clip at the back of her head. Next, Paige assisted the submissive into a gauzy skirt, which matched the peasant blouse and reached mid-calf, being careful not to let the waistband drag over the new ink.

"You do realize that I feel more naked in this see-through stuff than when I was just walking around with nothing on?"

"It's sexy, Erin." Paige was giggling while she responded, and Catherine didn't miss the blindfold she held in her hand.

"Aw, Paige, do I hafta?" Catherine whined at her. "Shawn already said I was going out to the gardens, so why can't I see where I walk?" she implored.

"Damn that man's big mouth," she complained with a huff. "That's neither here nor there, Erin. You have to be blindfolded so you don't see what's happening out there. It's supposed to add to the experience."

Paige made a valiant attempt at convincing her, but Catherine narrowed her eyes and fixed her gaze on her new friend. "Do you know what he has planned for me next?"

Averting her eyes, Paige started looking around the room, everywhere but back at Catherine. "Um, yes," she squeaked.

"Paige, we've become good friends today, right?" Catherine could play sweet and coy if need be, and she started by batting her eyelashes.

"Erin, please, I can't tell you. Our Masters will tan both our hides if I spill!" she pled, having made eye contact with Catherine again.

"Fine," Catherine gave in, "put it on me, and let's get out of here."

"Thank you, Erin. Trust me; it's going to be so worth it." She giggled.

"Paige, I've conceded to not insisting you tell me; you don't need to tease me!" the reluctant girl mock-growled at her friend.

Laughing, Paige slipped the blindfold into place and teased some more, "No, I don't need to, but it sure is fun!"

ༀ

CHAPTER TWENTY-ONE

ༀ

Catherine would have smacked Paige, if she could have seen her. Instead, she growled again, at which Paige just laughed. She then took Catherine's arm and guided the blindfolded woman outside.

This was not Catherine's first time in the gardens; she'd indulged – at Master's insistence – with a gourmet lunch on more than one occasion when spending the day at the spa for treatments. Because of this, she knew the space was surrounded by a high privacy fence.

Stepping out, Catherine could hear muted voices a few feet away that abruptly stopped when Paige cleared her throat, alerting whomever had been talking to their presence.

"Hello again, doll," Shawn's warm voice greeted a now-nervous Catherine. "Thank you, Paige. That will be all."

A moment of panic tried to overtake Catherine when Paige's hand left her arm and she was left standing on her own. When Shawn spoke again, he was much closer, and she jerked in reflex.

"Relax, Erin. We're going to have some fun." Faint clicks could be heard. "Perfect." Even knowing he was right there, Catherine still jumped when he put his hand on her elbow. "Alright, ready for a little photo session?"

So that explained the clicking.

He must have felt her tense. "I told you to relax, Erin. Don't worry; I won't even be processing the film. The memory card will go straight to your Master when he picks you up," Shawn explained with patience. "All you have to do is follow my instructions and enjoy your moment of fame! Ready?"

"Sure, I guess." Catherine wasn't sure, but nothing bad had happened in her time with Shawn thus far today, so she decided to trust him. With her permission granted, he began walking Catherine forward until she felt something brush against her knees.

"That's a hammock in front of you, doll. I'm going to help you sit in it, and then step back to get my camera. Remember, just follow my lead, and we'll get some great shots. Won't be hard with a beauty like you," Shawn complimented, giving her a quick hug before guiding the submissive onto the hammock.

Catherine could feel a light breeze lifting and tossing her hair while the birds chirped in the background. Using her toes, she pushed off the ground, causing the hammock to swing a little. She let the motion affect her and tipped her head back to enjoy the sounds of nature around her and the sun on her face.

Off to the side, the camera clicked and whirred.

In a subconscious gesture, Catherine licked her lips while the concept of what they were doing settled into her head. She could do this; she could even have fun with it.

Faint sounds could be heard while Shawn moved around her, and the wanton female felt the wetness starting to seep between her thighs. She leaned further back into the hammock, locking her fingers in the net to test and make sure she wasn't going to flip herself out of it.

The snapping shutter captured her pose.

In an attempt to achieve some friction, Catherine allowed her thighs a discreet rub against each other. In such a short amount of time, she had become quite turned on, surprising herself.

That's why you're an exhibitionist, Erin.

"You're doing great, doll. Now, take your hands and roam them along your body the way your Master would," Shawn said softly.

A breath caught in her throat at his words. Could she do this? Of course she could—and she would for her Master. Bringing her trembling hands to her knees, she started running them up her body, feeling the skirt gather and lift as she did.

Fast and furious, the camera's sounds broke through the chirping birds.

A hiss escaped her when her fingers came in contact with the fresh ink, and it soon turned into a needy moan. Another click told her Shawn wanted to preserve everything. Her self-perusal continued until she was cupping her breasts through the transparent material. To be naked at that moment would have been heaven.

More pictures were taken while Catherine gave her breasts a gentle squeeze, and then took the rings between her fingers and pulled. Her wet lips fell open in a silent moan.

"That's it, doll; let go. Enjoy that lingering touch. Tease yourself," Shawn coaxed.

One hand kept tugging on a ring while she ran the other up over her chest to her neck, where Catherine fingered the paddle on her collar. A single click hit her ears before a momentary shift of the breeze carried that delicious musk and spice scent from earlier to

Catherine's olfactory lobe. Her heart rate picked up, and she sucked a finger into her mouth.

Shawn continued snapping the pictures and giving her verbal cues, and all too soon, the breeze shifted again, taking the scent with it. Catherine missed it at once without understanding why. Taking her now-wet finger, she slipped it under her blouse and began rubbing her thick nipple.

"Work your skirt up for me further, doll. Does that finger feel good?"

"Mmhmm," the amateur model moaned and kept rubbing her nipple, adding in a light pinch while her free hand found the bottom of the skirt. Slow and steady, she inched the material higher, exposing her pale skin.

Several more images were saved to the memory card.

"Good girl. Part your legs; let your Master see you glisten."

Damn. For a gay man, he sure knows how to talk a girl crazy! Catherine thought, and then she lifted one leg. With care, she found the edge of the hammock and hooked her heel in the netting before letting her knee fall out to the side.

"You're doing wonderful. Now spread those pussy lips for your Master," Shawn commanded; his voice had taken on a deeper tenor—more powerful.

The submissive recognized his Dom persona coming forth and obeyed. With both hands, Catherine reached down and pulled herself open, delighting in the feel of the breeze when it blew across her exposed pussy.

The camera clicked, and she shivered at the naughtiness of it all.

Catherine was slick; so much so that she could feel the juices leaking onto her fingers. Her hips began rocking, and her body ached for something, anything to tame the fire that was building inside.

"Pinch your clit," Shawn ordered, and she obeyed, her moan escaping on the breeze. Another click echoed. "Pull on it while you pinch." More clicks followed.

Harder and faster, her breaths came while she pinched and pulled as commanded. Her nipples were aching, they were so tight. Catherine was quite aware of the metal impaling them. Using her free hand to circle around her opening, she gathered the wetness she found there; all while the camera whirred away.

"Beautiful, doll. Keep going."

Excitement magnified with each beat of her heart. She pushed her finger between her folds and inside while she released her clit to start rubbing slow circles around it. Breaths became gasps when Catherine slipped another finger in to join the first, and she moved her other hand in tighter circles so that she was rubbing right on top of her clit.

The camera caught every move.

Catherine's hips rocked with more force while she worked her fingers in and out of her dripping core. Wanting more but not getting it, she broke the silence with frustrated mewls and could hear her moment being forever saved on digital film.

A calm settled over her the moment Catherine began imagining it was her Master's fingers expertly teasing her and working her into a frenzy. "Mmmm . . . Oh, Master," she whisper-moaned, but her spell was disrupted by a tap on her knee.

"Here ya go, Erin; use this," Shawn directed while he rubbed something through her folds.

Curiosity and shock won out when Catherine extracted her pruning digits to take what he was offering. When her hand wrapped around the familiar-feeling synthetic, she was pretty sure it was the mock cock, and she dripped even more. Throwing caution to the wind, she lifted her other leg and hooked her heel into the hammock, opening herself to the breeze. Catherine groaned with gusto the whole time she eased the dildo into her hungry passage.

"Fuck, that's so hot, doll. Jayden's gonna come when he sees these," Shawn encouraged her while he moved about, firing off shots of her.

A loud smack echoed around her, and she thought she heard a low "Ow" from Shawn. *What the hell?* Uncertainty rising, Catherine started to close her legs when she realized they weren't alone. Once again, she caught a fleeting whiff of that enticing scent when the breeze swirled around her, and she calmed.

"No, doll, keep them open," Shawn barked. "You just keep working that thick cock into your wet pussy." His tone was firm, commanding.

The submissive reacted to the order, and her knees dropped back down. At the same time, she forced the cock all the way inside in one shove. "God!" Catherine could have cried at the feeling of completion and fullness. Savoring the feel of it, Catherine dragged the toy out with almost painful slowness before slamming it back into her body. Her fingers left her clit to begin pulling on her new nipple rings again while she fucked herself with the dildo.

Birdsong carried down from the tree tops as if there was no debauchery happening right below them.

"Oh, God! Shit . . . fuck!" Catherine's profane cries bounced amongst the trees while she came all over her hand and the dildo to the telltale click of her one-eyed witness.

"Perfect, Erin, that was just fucking perfect," praised Shawn.

All Catherine could do was to shudder and shake while she tried to get her breathing under control. With a wet sound, the dildo slipped from her body, and she dropped it next to her on the hammock. Being careful not to rock the precarious netting, she unhooked her heels, and then lowered her feet back to the ground.

She was trembling.

"Give me your hand, doll. We're going to move over by the tree now."

Upright again, her skirt fell back down, and she concentrated on walking without tripping in the heels. Not seeing where she was going was getting old.

"Okay, stop. Now lift your hands. You'll feel a branch above you; I want you to grab it with both hands.

Catherine located the branch with ease and grabbed it. It was low enough that her elbows were still bent.

"You just stay euphoric and relaxed, doll. Don't waste that beautiful orgasm you had. I'm going to tie your hands to the branch, okay?"

Nodding her acknowledgement, the submissive didn't fight the endorphins coursing through her system, instead choosing to revel in them.

She appreciated that Shawn was talking her through his actions. Silk rope wrapped around first one wrist, and then the other, while he secured Catherine to the branch. He stepped away.

"Struggle a little; let me check how secure they are."

Doing as she'd been told, the now-familiar sound of the camera clicking away met her ears while she tugged and pulled against the rope.

"Lovely. Stick your ass out for your Master now, doll."

There were more snaps and clicks while Catherine did as requested. Catherine noticed her senses had sharpened: she could smell Shawn's body wash when he came near, and she could hear him dragging something heavy across the ground.

"Erin, I'm going to lift you up onto a narrow table I've just brought over. It'll be easier if you just stay limp, and let me lift and position you, okay?"

The submissive was still floating from her self-induced orgasm and gave him a single nod. The movement stirred the air just enough that Catherine caught a brief hint of that other scent that had been working its way into her mind all afternoon. All too soon, it was gone. Shawn's warm arms surrounded her, lifting her up. She let him move her around until she was kneeling on the table.

"I'm going to slip your heels off now, Erin."

It was sweet mercy when her feet were freed from the tight leather. She wiggled her toes and giggled when the breeze blew over them.

"Now I'm going to hike up your skirt a little, and I need you to lean back nice and easy. This is a custom-designed fuck table; you'll find that dildo you worked yourself with is now mounted just behind you."

Her breath caught with surprise, and a new surge of need crept along her nerves, exciting every part of her body.

Catherine's skirt slid up the back of her thighs, and Shawn's large hands grasped her ass cheeks. He pried them apart, and she let out an involuntary flinch, given she hadn't been expecting him to touch her that way.

"Shh, it's all right, Erin. I'm just helping you get in place. Your Master wants photos of you bound and mounted. There we go, relax . . . don't worry, it's lubed so it'll go in easy." His voice was soft and gentle while he helped Catherine slide down onto the dildo.

A deep longing for her Master swept through her at the feeling of being filled so full with a replica of his cock. Catherine ground against the intrusion. With her arms anchored above her head, her breasts were lifted and squished together. Desire and want flooded through her, picturing how she must look displayed like this for her Master's pleasure. If only he were there to see her for real, not just through the photographs that Shawn was taking. The camera was clicking away again.

"Do you have any idea how exquisite you look, Erin?"

She shook her head.

"You are beyond stunning, doll! Your Master is going to love these shots."

His words encouraged her to sink further down and rock on the phallus in her ass. She didn't flinch when Shawn grasped her ankle.

"One more adjustment, and then I can finish up. You're doing great, Erin," encouraged Shawn while he pulled her ankle to the edge of the table. He attached some kind of cuff, and then repeated the process with the other ankle.

Catherine was locked into position: hands tied above her head, legs spread wide with knees bent, the mock cock buried deep in her ass. Her sex was stretched slightly open, and she could feel the edge of the table pressing just under the bottom of her ass, bound as she was to the edge of the table. The dildo was the one thing keeping her from slipping off. Catherine felt like a slut; she felt like a seductress, and she felt beautiful in her submission for her Master—even if he wasn't there.

The camera came to life, surrounding her with its audible preservation of every emotion on her face, leaving no part of her hidden but her eyes.

Shawn returned to her side and flipped her skirt up so that, once again, Catherine was on full display. A cool breeze traipsed over her left nipple when he tugged the blouse down, catching it under her breast.

A single camera click chirped before a sharp, repetitive beeping broke into the serenity of the afternoon.

"Well, shit!" huffed Shawn. "Sorry, doll, my battery just died on the camera. I need to run back inside and grab my spare."

"Um, Shawn, please don't leave me out here alone. You've got enough pictures, right?" Catherine could feel her nerves rolling in her stomach, souring it. Her heart pounded in her chest. She didn't want any more surprises; she just wanted to get the damn blindfold off!

"It won't take but a minute. I'll be right back, okay?" He patted her leg, and she whimpered. "Don't go anywhere!" Shawn instructed, laughing at her expense; because really, where the fuck was she going to go?

"Shawn." A door closed, and Catherine had to assume it was the door back into the building. "Shawn!"

Oh, you have got to be kidding me! He did not just leave me out here like this. I know he made sure everything was secure, but so help me; if I slip off this table, I'm going to kick his ass!

"Shawn?" She tried one more time. Nope, the fucker was gone. "Well, fuck me!" she growled to the trees.

A twig snapped behind Catherine.

"I think I just might do that," came a low whisper.

෨෮ඥ

CHAPTER TWENTY-TWO

෨෮ඥ

Catherine froze at the words. *Oh. Shit. Why did Shawn have to leave?* She tried to sniff the air, hoping to detect that erotic scent that would put her at ease, but the breeze had died down and the air was still. Beginning to panic, she resorted to taking shallow breaths to calm herself.

A gloved hand came to rest on her foot and squeezed before sliding up her leg. Her heart raced so that she could feel her pulse in her head and in her traitorous sex, which continued to bubble out wetness. It seemed Catherine had a new limit to discuss exploring with her Master; one she'd never have thought would've appealed to her: edge play. She was enjoying being frightened.

"Well, well. What do we have here?" The whisper was eerie and almost too quiet, too controlled.

His hand had traveled to her thigh and was curving inward. Catherine began struggling in vain. With the way her legs were spread and bound, she couldn't close them, nor could she lift herself off of the mount.

"Wh–what do you want?" Catherine whimpered.

"Oh, I think you know the answer to that," he whispered when he slid a leather-covered finger into her pussy.

Though aroused, Catherine wouldn't let this stranger have his way so easy; she clamped down on his finger with her inner walls and tried to push it out.

"Mm, aren't you tight, you little whore," he growled.

"I am not a whore!" The defense was out of her mouth before she could stop it, yet it didn't feel wrong in the least.

"Oh, but look at you . . ." the man's words trailed off, and her blouse was yanked downward, freeing the other breast. Giving both breasts a hard slap, he chided and belittled her, "With your tits hanging out." He pinched her nipples and tugged the rings. "You're all tied up and spread out like a feast with that cock up your ass and your hungry cunt gripping at my hand." To punctuate his words, he pulled out of her, and then pushed that same finger into her mouth. "Taste how wet you are, slut!"

Catherine's ire was up along with her fear, and she bit down—hard.

The unseen intruder jerked his hand back, his finger grazing the backside of her teeth on its way out. "Motherfuck!" he hissed and proceeded to grumble something under his breath, but she couldn't make out what he was saying.

"Please," Catherine started crying, fat tears rolling down her cheeks, "my friend is going to be back any minute. Please just leave me alone. I haven't seen you, and I promise I won't tell anyone." Her words were delivered with begging desperation. She wasn't so sure he was part of the pre-arranged day; by now, the others had addressed her with her name and had given her some sign that they were a friend and could be trusted. This man, this itinerant person, had done none of that.

With a creepy, low laugh, he spoke again and concerned her even more. "Don't worry about your friend. I've barred the door so he can't get back out here."

The submissive woman's heart sank at the sound of a zipper being undone. She was screwed. *Oh, fuck, please no!* Catherine's thoughts were jumbled, and sweat beaded between her breasts and behind her bent knees. She sucked in a deep breath, preparing to scream.

"Hel—" she was cut off by his leather-covered hand, reeking with her scent, being pressed to her lips. Catherine noted with some satisfaction that he didn't try putting his fingers back in her mouth.

"I think that's enough talk. I'm going to fuck that sloppy cunt of yours now," he said with a muffled snarl.

With renewed vigor, Catherine started struggling, but to her horror she found that her thrashing around was arousing her more. She couldn't escape or ignore the fullness in her backside, and the twisting movements were bouncing her breasts so that she became hyper-aware of her pierced nipples.

You want this, Erin. You know you're secretly enjoying it. You've always fantasized about being raped. You're just getting your wish.

Oh, Shut Up! Now is NOT the time, she argued with herself.

The tip of his cock was pushing against her outer lips, and his hand was still pressed over her mouth.

Now is the perfect time. Think, Erin. You're safe.

Catherine gasped when his thickness slid past her outer lips and dipped deeper into her. It was gentle, not rough like she'd expected, and this confused her.

He didn't go in very deep before he was drawing himself out of her almost all the way, and then inching back in. The stranger groaned. "Hot damn, slut, your cunt is so tight with that dick in your ass. I could fuck you all day," he sneered.

Ashamed of herself, but unable to deny that it felt amazing, Catherine ceased her struggles. She didn't think he was putting his full length in her, and she had to be honest with herself: at this moment, she *wanted* him to.

This is your fantasy, Erin. Enjoy it.

Her ankle was released from its cuff, and then her leg was guided around his waist, resulting in him going even deeper. A shameless groan escaped, and she felt her resolve yielding.

He had the audacity to whimper in response. "Oh, shit—you're so wet. I know you like this. You want this, you little slut, don't you?" The crude words were panted out in a whisper.

In answer, Catherine rocked her hips forward as much as she could, encouraging him to give her more. *Oh, God, I am a whore,* she thought, but in that moment she didn't care.

Don't you remember sitting at that table with Jayden the day you told him how the idea of being taken with force excited you? How, together, the two of you reviewed your limits, shared intense stares and awkward smiles, with whispered promises of things to come—someday.

More slippery fluid worked its way free of her when he undid her other ankle and brought it around his waist to meet the first. In her opinion, he still wasn't deep enough; Catherine wanted him buried as deep inside her pussy as the dildo was in her ass.

"Please. More," she mumbled behind his hand.

By leaning in, he allowed more of his cock to sink in. Dragging his tongue up her neck to her ear, he whispered, "I'm going to remove my hand. Don't you dare fucking scream." He sucked Catherine's earlobe into his mouth and gave it a tender bite before exercising caution in removing his hand from her mouth.

The whore in her moaned and writhed against the invasions.

A small click sounded, and then the woman's arms were dropping. Her wrists were still bound, but Catherine was no longer tied to the branch. Because of his proximity, her arms dropped over his head around his neck; the soft hair on the back of his head tickled her fingertips.

Leather-clad hands cupped her ass, and she was lifted off the mock cock. To her dismay, the movement resulted in the stranger's cock also slipping out of her, and her answering whimper was pathetic. Cool air feathered over her skin while he carried her limp body somewhere else. The whole time, her overripe sex was pressing against the naked flesh of his lower abs, and she squirmed at the feeling of the muscles rippling against her with each of his steps.

Somehow, he managed to lift her skirt out of the way when he laid her back down in the hammock. Catherine could feel the rough fibers of the rope biting into the flesh of her ass, so she lifted her bottom, trying to reconnect with him. He slipped her arms from around his neck, and with a sharp tug, he pulled her legs, shifting her so that she lay across the hammock rather than lengthwise. Her head dropped back over one side while her legs hung off the opposite edge of the hammock.

"Please . . ." The pleading was quiet and unresolved.

A brush of his finger across her lips was followed by a single command: "Open."

Wind swirled around them all of a sudden, and her senses were assaulted. She was surrounded by *that* scent, and underneath was the musk of raw male. Catherine was swimming in it, being pulled into oblivion while she drowned in total submission.

"Aye, Sir," she acquiesced, and she was swept away on a wave of pure desire while her mouth fell open. His thick cock slid past her lips; she lapped at the tangy sweetness of her own juices on his smooth skin, and the stranger – *or was he?* – pulled back out with a hiss. Catherine stretched her neck, reaching with her tongue, wanting to be pacified by that perfect erection. With a grunt, he rocked against her tongue, teasing her. When he slid forward again, she wasted no time closing her lips around him and sucking.

"Ungh. Yes, my slut. So fucking good," he croaked out in a throaty growl.

For hours, it seemed, he taunted Catherine. Never letting more than a few inches work its way into her mouth; never reaching the back of her throat. She wanted to reach up, grab his hips and ass, and pull him deeper, but she couldn't because of her still-bound wrists. Her hips were thrusting at nothing but air to the rhythm of his cock sliding along her tongue. The submissive licked, nibbled, and sucked, sighing in delight whenever she found drops of come leaking from him.

"Oh, hell. I want . . . I can't—" he rambled.

All at once, her mouth was left lapping at air, and she was lifted and being carried bridal-style. She sighed at the softness of the grass when he set her down in it. The skirt was pulled down over her hips and legs, and then was gone altogether. His leather-encased hands ran up her legs, slapping her pussy when she bucked up at him.

The tightness around her waist eased and was soon also gone when the corset fell open. No resistance came when her arms were pushed above her head, but pure delight coursed through her when she felt the heat of his body lay down next to her.

Once again, he pulled a surprised gasp from the licentious female by use of his lips, which enclosed her left nipple and sucked it in until she squeaked in pain. He pulled back and attacked it with rough licks, using his whole tongue, flattening it out, and then dragging it across her aching peak. Catherine arched her back to encourage him to take it deeper even though Paige's aftercare warnings echoed in the back of her head.

The man's hand traveled down her body, over her ribs, and became a light touch when he skimmed over the tattoo, the pressure increasing again when his fingers found and slid between her folds. In short, Catherine felt he was refusing to give her the penetration she so desperately wanted—and now needed.

"So fucking beautiful," he snarled, and his teeth closed on her nipple.

Catherine was in heaven; no, she was in hell. Her need had turned into a fire burning throughout her body, leaving all of her nerves alive and tingling with anticipation. She wanted so badly to come, but at the same time, Catherine never wanted this to end; she was helpless, lost to the whims of the adroit digits manipulating her flesh.

There was a soft *pop* when he released the nipple, and then she felt him crawling down her body; following the lead his hand had taken. The path was burned into her skin with gentle bites chased by quick licks to take away the sting and sealed with tender, open-mouthed kisses. Catherine writhed against the hand stroking her swollen nether lips. It was a beautiful, exquisite torture.

Each controlled movement, executed with care and grace, did not go unnoticed by Catherine. Through the haze of her arousal-induced delirium, one predominant truth was becoming clear.

When his mouth reached her ink, he was mindful of the angry flesh while he feathered over it with tiny kisses. She might have squealed when his tongue replaced his hand. How desperate was the submissive to feel that mouth devour her, but still he just teased with fleeting licks that supplied no friction.

His fingertips brushed against her thighs, and he whispered the same single command from before: "Open."

If only he would speak more, she could be sure of what her gut was telling her, but like his touch, his words were a mere tease that left Catherine to wait for the next clue. Obeying, she spread her legs as wide as she could, pulling her knees toward her chest to open herself even further to him. His long tongue was stiff while he taunted her opening, sliding in and out before sucking her arousal straight from the source.

"Mm, pure heaven. So delicious; so sweet," he mumbled against her pussy, and she rocked upward, craving more of his tongue.

"Oh, God, please." The submissive was panting, harsh rasps of breath escaping her. "Please, please, please." Shaking her head from side-to-side with frustrated moans, Catherine wanted to scream at him to stop bloody whispering. She needed to hear his voice unencumbered. Instead, she just cried out a garbled sound, and he pulled away. His heat was replaced by the coolness of the air.

Catherine held still while he resumed crawling up her body again, treating her right side to the same delicious torture her left side had just experienced. Her quivering sex was left open to the elements once he abandoned it. When he reached her right breast, she sighed in pleasure, happy to have his skilled tongue anywhere on her aching skin at that point.

His hard cock dug into her hip while the man laved her nipple. He shifted himself so that he was kneeling between her thighs, and she could feel the head of his cock brushing against her pussy again. Though blindfolded, Catherine was still able to determine what he was doing: leaning over her, holding his weight up, and running his tongue across her lips, to which she was willing and ready. No more words were needed; the moment their tongues entwined, she knew, but she wouldn't show her hand just yet.

Soft, demanding lips molded against her mouth, and Catherine didn't fight. She let his tongue control hers while he led them in an erotic dance of warmth and wetness, extricating himself to bite and suck on her lips before plunging into her mouth again.

With one hand, he managed to undo the ropes binding her wrists. This was her chance. The moment her hands were free, she reached up and buried them in his hair, pulling his mouth harder against hers. A deep groan rumbled within his chest, and at long last, he reached down to position himself at her entrance.

Catherine was ready to be past the pretenses of a 'fantasy rape;' in her heart she knew the truth that would set her free. Not just Catherine, but Erin, too. She was positive the man about to bury himself within her was none other than Jayden, her Master and lover, and that beyond all reasonable doubt, she loved him. One thing remained uncertain: did he hunger for her love as much as her submission? Would her feelings be reciprocated? There was one way to find out.

It was now or never. Their relationship had changed, and it was time to call him on it. Before he could push into her, she lifted her hand to the blindfold, giving him time to notice and stop her. When he didn't, Catherine slid it off.

After blinking to adjust to the light, Catherine focused on her lover's face. His brown eyes were so dark they were almost black, and his jaw was tight. The sun behind him formed a halo around his silky hair, just like in her dream from that afternoon. He was beautiful and perfect. His eyes softened, and she knew Jayden was hers.

"Make love to me, Jayden," Catherine commanded with an air of bravery.

Time stood still while she held her breath. *Was he going to run? Had she ruined everything?*

And then he smiled his glorious smile.

A caress of his lips against hers made her shiver while he stared into her eyes. Jayden sank into her with one powerful thrust, and as her orgasm claimed her body, threatening to dissolve her into a million pieces that would float away on the wind, he anchored her with one sentence: "I love you, Erin."

ഇൽ

CHAPTER TWENTY-THREE

ഇൽ

Jayden was home. His jewel's tightness pulsated around his engorged cock—pure ecstasy. Once he could feel his balls resting on Erin's slick flesh, he stilled his movements to let her ride out her orgasm. She was fucking gorgeous. Flushed from head to toe, her eyelids were closed but fluttering, and her luscious lips were parted in a sexy 'O'. Her nipples were hardened to tight peaks, and he smiled when the sun glinted off the emeralds dangling from them.

When her breathing steadied, Jayden began to withdraw with an agonizing slowness. She opened her eyes and locked those gorgeous green jewels with his, and a breath of air whooshed out of her. "Say it again."

The Dom in him took notice that this was the second command she'd given him, and it niggled at his need to correct and punish; but the part of him that was nothing but a man in love melted at the pure joy that shined in her eyes with her request. Never would he have thought he'd get so turned on by one of his subs topping from the bottom, but seeing Erin break free from her normal character was sexy as hell—and would need to be explored further at a later date.

Thoughts raced around his head, and he held back his own release by an invisible thread. Jayden continued pulling out until just the tip of his cock rested between her pussy lips. When he looked down, he shuddered at the sight of them together, swollen and glistening, before plunging back into her. Waiting until he was seated within her again, Jayden licked her lips and pressed his to hers. With their mouths touching and their eyes only inches apart, he said what she wanted to hear: "I love you, Catherine Eilene O'Chancey."

He could feel her lips curve into a huge smile right before she gave him a tender kiss and pulled back. *God, her eyes were beautiful in the sunlight. Had there ever been a clearer green?*

Erin then spoke the words that transported Jayden to a fairytale world complete with fucking unicorns and rainbows. "I love you, too, Jayden. So much, *A rúnsearc*!"

Her smile was breathtaking. *Yep, don't know what she just said, but let's throw in some butterflies and talking flowers for good measure, because that accent is amazing.* No doubt clouded his mind that he was in the Land of Happy.

Jayden leaned forward, his heart swelling with joy, and captured her lips. He started making love to her mouth with his lips, teeth, and tongue. Meanwhile, his hips kept up a steady rocking motion, his cock withdrawing a few inches before he was sliding back into her.

The Dom had been so worried whether this last scene was a good idea. They hadn't discussed this particular 'craving' of hers since that long-ago weekend when her mental health was still too unsteady to even consider such a thing. However, the way her eyes had sparkled with excitement when she'd shared her desire for a fantasy rape had finalized his decision: he hadn't known at the time when, but Jayden had known that he *would* make this happen for her.

When planning this day, he decided this would be her final fantasy fulfilled, her last limit pushed for the day. Of course, no one but Jayden would be playing out this scene with her. He couldn't even fathom another person taking what was his, let alone how he would've felt if this had backfired and she'd relapsed with a meltdown in the arms of a stranger.

She moaned underneath him, drawing his mind back to the here and now. *Shit.* Somehow Jayden had gone from taking advantage of a naked woman, bound and helpless before him, to the most vanilla sex he'd had since losing his virginity as a teenager—and it was the most amazing thing ever.

I am making love to my beautiful Erin. The thought brought a choked whine from him when paired with her nails running down his back. It soon turned into animalistic grunting while Erin gripped his ass and pulled him deeper into her.

So. Fucking. Good.

Erin wrapped her legs around him, and it stretched her channel open more so that Jayden could sink further into her. He felt like he was melting into her, like their bodies were trying to dissolve into one another. As they kissed, Jayden could feel her heart beating against his chest. Needing that connection, the two lovers stayed attached as long as their air supply lasted, releasing each other's mouths only at that last second.

To give her a break from his crushing weight, he pushed up onto his arms and let her guide his thrusts with her feet on his ass. The man almost came when the goddess below him glided her hands up her own body and began fondling her tits, sighing out a throaty, "Oh, Jayden . . . just like that, *A rúnsearc.*"

His name from her mouth, neither Sir nor Master, but simply *Jayden*, was the most angelic sound he'd ever heard. If she kept it up, he was going to lose the battle, and he didn't want to come yet because he had a feeling it was going to be the mother of all orgasms. Jayden needed to stall.

Bending his elbows, he dipped down to kiss her parted lips. "I need to taste you again, sweet girl," he whispered and didn't wait for her to reply. Withdrawing his full length from her warmth was not easy, but it had to be done. Jayden scooped Erin into his arms, carrying her back over to the fuck table while she nuzzled into his neck and nipped at his earlobe. *Fuck*. His dick whimpered and shed a viscous tear.

Trying to reclaim his control and re-establish his dominance, Jayden gave her the choice. "Catherine, I am going to mount you again, and then devour your cunt. Which hole do you want filled?" She groaned into his ear and licked his neck. "Tell me now!" he commanded.

"This girl's ass, Master, please fill her ass," she begged.

The Dom was elated that they were on the same page. They were going to be lovers *and* Master/submissive because that's what they both needed now. While the unknown could be daunting, Jayden knew they had quite the adventure ahead of them while they learned the ins and outs of making a dual-sided relationship work. He was excited, looking forward to the days and years ahead.

He lubed two fingers by slipping them into her dripping pussy before he pushed them into her ass, ensuring that she was still loose and slick. Removing his fingers, and chuckling at her pleading mewls for more, he lifted her up by her ass cheeks, and then lowered her down onto the phallus.

She moaned when he dropped to his knees in front of her. "Thank you, Master."

His face hovering just above her pussy, Jayden inhaled a deep whiff and reached up to pet her smooth lips, causing her to squirm. He was pleased with how smooth she was; not a stray hair in sight. Before he blew warm breath over her, he used the inside of his lips to nip at each of the lingering circular scars that made her unique and special. Spencer had given them to her in an attempt to break her, but instead they'd become a symbol of her strength.

"Fuck, Jayden. Lick me!" the woman snapped.

No longer needed as disguise, Jayden took off the leather gloves and began scolding her while he used the gloves to spank her shiny lower lips. "Uh huh, Catherine." The leather made a nice, wet, smacking sound when connecting with her sodden mons. "You will mind your manners and show me respect during a scene." He snapped the glove against her twice more. "I am the Master here, and you are the submissive."

His jewel was so wet that each strike of the gloves was causing splatter, which he licked off her tight tummy. "Now, I intend to lick and suck your delicious cunt, my slut, but it will be on my terms. Is that understood?" Jayden punctuated his words with a final slap of the glove atop her sex.

"Oh, God," Catherine panted. "Aye, Master. This slut is sorry for being impetuous. Please use this *bure* for your pleasure," she acquiesced, accepting her corrections.

She was a sight to behold. Her complete submission to Jayden was the greatest gift she could give to him. Actually, one thing would be better, but he couldn't think about that now. Right now, Jayden had an addiction to feed.

"Spread your pussy wide for me, Catherine." He waited for her slim fingers to grasp her lips and pull them apart, thus putting her hard clit on display for him. One flick of his tongue over it, and she jumped. "Be still. If you move or let go of those pussy lips, I will stop and finish myself off with my hand onto the grass." Jayden knew that 'threatening' her with the denial of his come and her orgasm would help her to focus and accomplish the task he'd set forth for her.

To test her, Jayden pinched her clit, and she didn't move. "Good girl," the Dom praised her.

"*Cailin maith*," panted Catherine.

"I'm sorry?" He'd never pushed her to speak in tongue before.

"It's Irish . . . for good girl, Master. Sorry . . . for speaking . . . out of turn."

"Use your index fingers and take over pinching your clit, but keep those lips spread. I'll be right back, *cailin maith*." His comment was rewarded with glistening gratitude in her eyes.

While his jewel obeyed and he was treated to her little sounds, he walked over to where he'd discarded his pants and pulled the special clamp out of his pocket. When he came back to Catherine, he gave her permission to release her clit.

"I'm going to clamp you now, my pet. Deep breath, now exhale." With her exhaling breath, he placed the clamp so that the teeth bit into the flesh around her clit. Two side chains, which had a hook on each end, extended from the contraption. Jayden affixed the hooks to her nipple rings.

A grin stretched Jayden's lips when she took a breath and he saw awareness dawn on her face: any movement, no matter how slight, was going to cause tugging on her nipples and her clit because they were connected.

"Oh, Master, that feels so good," Catherine whimpered with wide eyes.

Her response delighted him, and he chuckled. "Yes, slut, I'm sure you do like that. Now, Catherine, you have my permission to come when you wish. In fact, I demand you come as many times as possible. For each orgasm you have, you'll get one thrust of my cock. If you run out of thrusts, and I haven't come yet, then you'll have to watch me finish myself." A light tug on the chains emphasized his challenge and made her fall apart. "Well, looksee there, that's one. How about we see how many more I can lick out of you?" he boasted and lowered his mouth to her pussy.

To Jayden's surprise, and much to Catherine's credit, he ate her out for the next twenty minutes. With every lick, suck, and nibble on her swollen cunt she moaned, whimpered, and managed to resist squirming too much. Whenever her movements became too vigorous, he would pull back and smack her pussy. The red-blooded male finally reached a point at which he couldn't take it anymore; he needed to get his cock back inside her.

"You are something else, Catherine." Looking her over, he took in her heavy breathing and drooping eyelids. His jewel was going to need a nap before too long. "I counted eight, you naughty little slut. Let's see if it's enough, shall we?"

The question was rhetorical. Jayden's cock, which was already seeping long strings of clear pre-come, was so hard that he was pretty sure three or four deep thrusts would do the job. It took seconds to position his cock at her slick opening, and then slam home. "Count them, Catherine, and no more coming; it's my turn," he grunted.

"One, Master."

She sighed with pleasure so he pulled out and slammed in again.

"Oooh, two, Master!"

His stomach was tightening, and his balls were burning with heat; he slid out nice and slow, and then inched back into her.

"Ungh. Three, Master." The words were jumbled by her panting as she came around his cock.

"That one doesn't count, slut. In fact, I'll think I'll deduct a thrust for you coming without my permission." In a flash, he pulled out and then rammed his cock back into her hard enough that his balls smacked her ass.

"Oh, God! Four, Master."

That pump, and her resulting breathy response almost did Jayden in. He wanted to try to make it to seven to torment her. Slipping out, he took a breath, and then pounded into her twice.

"Ahhhh! Five and six, M—Master. Oh, God, please, may this girl come?" Catherine had resorted to begging.

This was going to be it for him, Jayden just knew it was. He withdrew, leaving the tip resting in her, and as he thrust a final time into her hot slickness he commanded her: "Come with me now, *cailin maith*!"

Together, they cried out as their dual orgasms rode over them. Jayden collapsed onto her heaving breasts, and she wrapped her loving arms around him. After a moment, he became aware that Catherine was planting soft kisses on his head. He tilted so he could look up at her, and she continued kissing his eyes and nose until he arched further and she could capture his mouth.

Once his heart slowed down to a reasonable pace, Jayden lifted his weight off of her. He unhooked the chains and clamp while she whimpered at his touch on her sensitive nub. "You did a beautiful job, Jewel. Are you okay? Green?"

"The day has been good, Master, but this last hour has been amazing."

How she could look bashful right now was beyond him, but that was the impression he got while she peered at him from under her lashes. Jayden couldn't help but laugh. "Erin, you are a vixen, you know that? How can you sit there and act coy after what we've just done?"

She giggled, and it was the most beautiful sound.

"Here, sweet girl, put your arms around my neck so I can help you down."

Working in tandem, Jayden lifted her off the phallus and set her on the ground. She was a little off kilter, so he kept his arms around her in a loose hug while he stroked her hair and back.

She leaned against his chest and whispered, "I love you, Jayden."

He tightened the hug and kissed the top of her head. "I love you, too, Erin. You've got to be exhausted. How about we head back to my place and order in? I want to give you a bath and get some ointment on your tattoo. We can unwind while we discuss your scenes in front of the fire with some food, and maybe some wine?"

"That sounds wonderful." She yawned, and then took a sheepish look around. "Do I need to get in the car naked or can I put something on?"

A vivid image of her nude and riding next to him in the car blinded him, and he smiled. "As much as I'd like to keep you naked all the time, I do have something for you over here by the door." Hand in hand, they walked over to where he had a lightweight, cotton Capri pant and tank top set waiting. Jayden observed while she pulled the clothes on.

"What?" Erin asked when she noticed his attentive stare.

"Nothing," he smirked. "You are just too beautiful and wonderful not to look at. Are the clothes okay?"

"They're perfect, thank you. The material is super soft and feels good against my, um, tender spots."

"Come on, my beautiful Erin. Micah has the car out front. Let's go home and take care of you."

Jayden grasped her hand, their fingers intertwined, and he took her home.

ೞೞ

CHAPTER TWENTY-FOUR

ೞೞ

The ride back to the villa was quiet. Erin ended up curling against Jayden's side and falling asleep, and he was content to look at her while she emitted adorable snoring noises. How had he gotten so lucky to have this angel love him back?

When they arrived at the house, Jayden attempted to be gentle in waking her, but she was out cold. *Poor thing.* The day had been exhausting for her.

"Micah," Jayden whispered, "can you get the car door, and then run ahead and open the house for me? I'm going to carry her in."

"Sure thing, Sir," he replied before hopping out and running around the car.

Jayden noted that Micah seemed to have an extra spring in his step, and he gathered his time with Shawn had gone well.

"Thanks." The Dom nodded at Micah when he walked through the front door. "Have a good evening, Micah; I'll see you next week. Don't forget, I'm taking off until Thursday morning, which means you're off, too. I'm sure you'll figure out a way to use the days."

"You, too, Sir. Oh, and Sir, thank you. You know, for introducing me to Mr. Carpenter?" Micah grinned, which prompted Jayden to chuckle under his breath.

"My pleasure, Micah. I'm glad it seems to be working out for you. Good night!" Not that he wanted to be rude to Micah, but Jayden had precious cargo in his arms that was beginning to get heavy. He pulled the door closed and turned the lock with his outstretched fingers before carrying Erin up the stairs to his bedroom.

In the process of laying her down so as not to disturb her, Jayden realized that it was the first time he'd had her in his bedroom just because. Any time Catherine had been at the villa, it had been as his submissive, therefore she stayed in the room at the end of the hallway, and scening was done downstairs in the playroom. This felt right. Seeing Erin snuggle into his pillow and murmur, "Love you, Jayden," solidified it for him. She belonged in his bed, in his home, and most definitely, in his heart.

Retrieving the chenille throw from the foot of the bed, Jayden tucked her in, kissing her forehead while answering with a hushed murmur, "Love you, too, Erin." He could swear the corners of her mouth twitched into a smile, which made his heart flutter in his chest.

There was a bounce in Jayden's step while he ducked into the closet to change into a pair of relaxed jeans and then made his way to the kitchen where the take-out menus were stored. Locating his favorite Greek restaurant, he called in an order. After getting his total and delivery time, he hung up and went to his office.

Though he was now on vacation, the workaholic in him decided to use the extra time to boot up his computer and see if there was anything he could address. One thing handled now would be one less thing to be done when he returned. There was just one email message from Samantha, letting Jayden know that she and Ryan had locked up and to: "Get off your email because you're off until Thursday." Samantha had closed the email with assurances that she could hold down the fort until he returned. She also thanked him for the introduction to Ryan, which forced a fresh smile—Jayden didn't deserve the women in his life.

With nothing work-related to distract him further, Jayden was at a loss for what to do. He started pacing his office and soon found himself standing in front of his favorite accessory in the room: a hand-drawn calligraphy copy of *The Submissive's Prayer* mounted in an elaborate frame. The poem was kept in Jayden's office to serve as a reminder that, while he might be the Master, the submissive was always in control and her submission was a precious gift not to be abused. Though he knew the words by heart, Jayden read them aloud:

Allow me the strength to answer questions I can't fathom.
Allow me the spirit to know His needs.
Allow me the kindness to choke back retorts.
Allow me the serenity to serve Him in peace.
Allow me the love to show Him myself.
Allow me the tenderness to comfort Him.
Allow me the light to show us the way.
Allow me the wisdom to be an asset to Him.
Let me be able to show Him each day my love of my service to Him.
Let me open myself up to completely belong to Him.
Let my eyes show Him the same respect, rather I sit at His side, or kneel at His feet.
Let me accept my punishment with the grace.
Let me learn to please Him, beyond myself.
Grant me the power to give myself to Him completely.
Grant me the strength to please us both.
Permit me to love myself in loving Him.
Allow me the peace of serving Him.
For it is my greatest wish, my highest power to make His life complete, as He makes mine.

~author unknown~

After closing his eyes to reflect on the meaning for a few minutes, Jayden then reached out and pressed on the right edge of the frame. A catch released, and he watched the frame swing forward. After typing in the code to the hidden safe, the door slid back. Sitting at the front of the safe was a long, narrow box tucked inside a bag from Dallas' finest jeweler. With care, he picked it up, took out the box, and lifted the lid, reassuring himself of its contents. *Soon. Very soon.*

Hearing the sound of footsteps above, which indicated that Erin was now awake, Jayden stashed the box back in its place, closed up the safe, and returned the frame to its spot against the wall. He rushed out of the office to check on her and caught up with her just as she was coming out of his bathroom, stretching her arms above her head and yawning. Cheeky bastard that Jayden was, he couldn't help but notice her gorgeous tits stretching against the thin cotton. His cock jerked at the sight. *Down, boy. Not tonight. We're going to let Erin recover.*

"Hello, sweet girl. Nice nap?" he asked with a smile, and she jumped. "Sorry, didn't mean to startle you."

"That's okay, and aye, this girl did. Thank you, Master."

"Erin, in here I'm just Jayden. Actually, for the rest of the weekend I'd like us to be just Jayden and Erin, if you don't mind?"

"M'kay," she mumbled, and yawned again.

Jayden was unable to resist closing the distance between them and wrapping his arms around her. She winced when her breasts pressed into his chest. "Tender, are we?" So much had happened, was still happening, that Jayden was finding it hard to remember that she now had some new attributes that would need some TLC for a while.

Catherine nodded her head. "Aye, but in a good way. I don't think there's a part of my body I'm not aware of right now." She giggled, and he loosened his arms around her. When he lowered his mouth to hers, the minty flavor he was met with told him she'd brushed her teeth while in his bathroom.

"Erin, just curious; what did you brush with?"

She lowered her eyes and bit her lower lip. Fuck, the things that sight did to his cock. *Easy, big boy, I already told you no.*

"I hope you don't mind, but I borrowed your toothbrush." She batted her eyelashes at him.

Yeah, can't deny this girl anything. Besides, what was sharing a toothbrush when they'd shared so many other oral treats?

"Erin, sweet girl, you're welcome to anything, and I mean *anything*, I have," Jayden professed and pressed his lips to hers again.

The woman melted into him and her lips parted, allowing his tongue to sweep into her mouth. They shared soft kisses for several minutes while their tongues glided over each other, and then they pulled back to nibble on each other's lips. She sucked his top lip while he gathered her bottom one. Jayden's hands were moving up and down her back, going lower with each pass until he was caressing her firm ass. Realizing this was heading somewhere he'd very much like to go but shouldn't, he gave her ass a squeeze and stepped back from her. Jayden felt cold at once.

"While I'd like to continue, I've ordered dinner, and it should be here in about," he checked his watch, "thirty minutes. Let me draw you a bath so you can wash up before we eat."

Jayden waited for her answer while he absorbed every detail: flushed and breathing heavy; hard, pierced nipples straining at her top; and dampness appearing at her crotch. Shit, he loved the way she responded; she was absolute perfection.

With an adorable pout that thrust out her kiss-swollen bottom lip, she conceded. "Okay, a bath does sound nice, *A rúnsearc.*"

Wanting to take care of every little thing that Erin needed, Jayden took her hand in his and led her back into the bathroom. He closed the plug in the tub and turned on the hot water. As soon as it had warmed, he turned on the cold water to balance it out, and added some vanilla bubble bath. While the tub filled, Jayden returned his attention to Erin. Gripping the bottom of her top, he asked her to lift her arms before sliding the garment over her head, letting his fingertips tease her skin. Her breasts exposed, he bent over and placed a gentle kiss on each of her nipples. "Do you like them?"

"Oh, Jayden, they're beautiful. Sir Landon and Paige did such an amazing job. I didn't even feel it happen!"

Jayden's eyebrow quirked at the reminder of what had happened between those three, but her giggle squelched the jealousy that threatened to rear its ugly head. Moving forward, he helped her out of her pants, and then knelt in front of her to place a kiss on the orchids on her left side while inspecting Shawn's work. It was flawless, as usual, apart from the redness and puffiness of her skin, which was to be expected. "And how about this? Do you like it?" Jayden asked while he stroked his fingertips over the ink.

Erin gasped and grabbed his hand, ignoring his question. "Oh, God—Jayden, your finger!" She was looking at his index finger, which was a bit puffy and starting to turn purple where she'd bitten it. "Oh, *A rúnsearc*, I'm so sorry, I—I swear I didn't know it was you yet, and I was scared."

"Shh, sweet girl. It's okay; no harm done. I guess I played my part a little too well," he chuckled, "what with the new cologne and the gloves. You really had no idea?" It was a real surprise to him that he'd pulled it off.

"No, I guess it was the cologne. Hey, I smelled it during the tattoo; were you in there with us?"

Now it was Jayden's turn to be sheepish. "Yeah, I just couldn't stay away from you any longer, so I had Micah bring me over early. Erin, I do have a small confession about that . . ." He trailed off, afraid of her reaction.

She scrunched her nose in confusion but didn't say anything, so he continued while helping her into the tub.

"I was in there, in the corner, and, well—"

The hot water made her suck in a breath while she lowered her body into it. "Oh, for crying out loud, Jayden; just spit it out!" she laughed.

He blew out a big breath and went on, "I kind of had my dick out and was stroking it while I watched Shawn work on you." She started to say something but he cut her off. "And when he took that break, and you napped, we went across the hall, and, oh bloody hell! Micah was in the room, too. Shawn is taking him on as a sub and had him kneeling naked and caged in the other corner, and we, the three of us, went across the hall—"

Her eyes were widening as he spilled his guts.

"Yeah, Shawn went into Dom mode and commanded Micah to suck me off while he fucked him." Jayden had been looking at his hands while he talked, afraid to look up at her.

She was silent.

Oh, fuck. Why couldn't I have just kept my dick in my pants?

ಶಿುುೊಃ

CHAPTER TWENTY-FIVE

ಶಿುುೊಃ

Jayden held his breath, but began to let it out in slow increments when Erin's tiny hand threaded into his hair. Her nails scratched at his scalp, and it felt so good.

"Jayden?" Her voice was soft. "Look at me, please," she requested.

With caution and uncertainty, he raised his eyes up to her, nervous about what he'd see looking back at him. Her eyes were gentle, and she her lips curved upward in a small smile.

"There you are," she cooed. "Jayden, what are you ashamed of, *A rúnsearc*? I helped Micah suck you off just this morning. I know you play with him. Even if Shawn had touched you as well, isn't that your prerogative? I entered this relationship with you knowing it wasn't just me in your bed, so to speak." Erin kissed his forehead in what he assumed was a gesture of acceptance.

Erin was too good to be real; but she was real. Yet again, she had managed to catch him off guard with her ability to reason and see beyond the bare facts.

"Oh, Erin, thank you!" A dry, relieved sob escaped him. "It's just that—well, I have another confession."

"Go on, then. If we're going to make this work, we can't stop communicating now. Whether you are Jayden or Master shouldn't have an impact on our honesty with one another."

He sucked in a breath and let it out, his lips rippling with the motion. She was right; truth and honesty had to be their cornerstones. "I've been doing a lot of thinking over the last couple of weeks, and I've decided that you are the only one I want in my bed, the one I *need*."

Her bright smile encouraged him.

"I've made other arrangements for Samantha. I mean, she's still going to be my secretary, but that's it now. And as I've just explained, Micah will still be my personal assistant and driver, but his needs are going to be met by Shawn."

"So what's the problem then?" Erin asked, furrowing her forehead.

"I just feel weak for giving in so soon after cutting my ties with them, like I let you down, and can't be good enough for you."

"Jayden Matthew Masterson," she barked at him, "don't you *ever* say you aren't good enough for me! You are the best thing that has ever happened to me."

Nothing more needed to be said; Jayden rushed at his jewel and covered her mouth with his own. There was a vague awareness that his clothes were becoming saturated while he climbed into the tub with her. She was pawing at his shirt, trying to push it up his abs, so Jayden jerked back long enough to rip it over his head and throw it onto the bathroom floor before he was burying his tongue in her mouth once again. Her nipples were like diamonds where they pushed against his chest, and he swallowed her moans with eagerness.

"Please, Jayden, take me! I need to feel you inside me." She bit her lower lip in an enticing move calculated to seduce.

His lips had been running over her neck when her words snapped him to attention. "Erin, love, you've got to be sore. I—I don't want to say no, but I'm afraid of hurting you. You need some recovery time, sweet girl." He tried to kiss away her pout.

Her eyes were fiery, and he could tell her mind was whirling, trying to find a way to get what she wanted. As soon as she smiled, he knew he wasn't going to be able to say no.

"Jayden, you're right." She shrugged.

What? That's all she's got?

"But you do realize that the place where I want to feel you hasn't been touched today? Not much, anyway. Please, Jayden. You can go slow if you want."

The batting eyelashes would get him every time. "Erin," he whined.

There was a glimpse of a smug smile on her beautiful face before she tucked her nose in behind his ear to kiss that soft spot—the one that felt sinful.

Jayden groaned when her hot breath whispered over his ear, "I can feel that you want me, too." Damn capricious cock had its own agenda, no matter what his more sensible head wanted to enforce.

Well, he *had* told Erin she was welcome to *anything* in his home. Jayden bolted upright, the abrupt movement sending water cascading down his body to splash all over her. Erin squealed and tried to cover her face while she bubbled with laughter, but all the man noticed was the way her breasts were pushed together by her arms. The sight spurred him to work faster at releasing the button and zipper on his jeans.

She continued to laugh while Jayden fought to peel the wet denim from his body and avoid falling on top of her—not an easy feat. Trying to balance in a bathtub and wrestle wet denim was not something he would recommend. After what seemed an eternity, during which Jayden almost fell *twice*, he got the last inch of material worked off his foot and couldn't resist a proud "Ta-Da!" while he stood before her with his cock standing firm and upright only inches from her face.

Erin giggled again and clapped. "Bravo! Bravo, *A rúnsearc!*"

All coherent thought left Jayden when she closed the distance and slid her hot, little mouth over his wet dick.

"Fuck, Erin!" he hissed out in surprise.

She ran her hands up the backs of his thighs until she was grasping his ass, which she proceeded to push against, forcing him to go deeper into her mouth. Jayden's hands went to her head, where he let his fingers get wrapped up in her hair. Erin moaned around the organ, while he held her head and started fucking her mouth in a sweet cadence.

"Oh, God, Erin. My sweet, naughty, little Erin, the things you . . . ungh . . . do to me. Shit! *Cailin maith.*" The slow tempo had been abandoned for a needy, fast pump into her mouth. It was amazing how her throat was able to relax and open, and with each thrust, he slipped in deeper. Before Jayden knew it, her nose was brushing against his trimmed pubic hairs, and he could feel her throat muscles contracting as she literally swallowed his cock.

"Holy hell!" He extracted himself from her mouth with a yell lest he shot his load straight into her stomach via her throat. "Erin, you've never gotten all of me in like that. Fuck, I need a minute," he admitted and plopped down on the built-in bench seat. When he was able to open his eyes and look at her, Jayden found Erin smiling like a Cheshire cat. "Pleased with yourself, Erin?"

"Aye!" Erin's enthusiasm was apparent. She crawled through the water, and then knelt in front of him so that her ink was above the water line.

While she leaned in, Jayden was helpless to do anything but watch her tongue snake out in a seductive dance and take long, slow licks up the underside of his erection.

"Yum," she whispered.

Shaking his head, Jayden hooked a finger under her chin and tilted her head up to look at him. "You are insatiable. You know that, right?" he asked with a kiss to her nose.

"Only for you, Jayden," she responded, and then sucked one of his fingers into her mouth.

The sensation went straight to his cock.

"Oh, you've asked for it now, little girl! Stand up and turn around."

Not threatened in the least, Erin snickered while she lifted herself up out of the water, turned around, and, with the slowest pace possible, bent over, pushing her ass toward Jayden. The little minx placed her hands on the edge of the tub, spread her feet apart by a little more than shoulder width, and started swaying in front of him.

From that angle, he could see that her pussy was swollen and wet with more than just bath water. Jayden ran a finger through her folds, and then brought it up to his mouth. "Mm, so delicious."

Erin looked over her shoulder at him and winked, the green of her eyes sparkling.

Naughty girl; but I can be naughtier, Jayden thought, and he grabbed a handful of her ass flesh in each of his hands. He pulled her cheeks apart, and then buried his tongue in her. Jayden had never given a rim job before, never had the desire. Now he wanted to devour every part of Erin he could reach. While he lapped at her puckered hole, she dropped her head and moaned— loud. A shift of his neck let Jayden angle so that he could slide his tongue first into her pussy and then run it back up to her asshole. His hands flexed and released, massaging her ass while he lapped at her from behind.

She was beginning to shake, alerting Jayden that she was getting close to orgasming, but he wanted her on his cock when that happened. Straightening back up, Jayden gripped her hips to guide her back onto his erection, but she stopped him.

"Jayden, please spank me like you did this morning in the car. Smack my pussy and ass. Just a few times, please?" She widened her stance and wiggled said ass at Jayden.

How the hell do you say no to that?

He moved to stand off to the side of her, and then reached down to scoop up some of the hot soapy water and let it dribble across her backside. "Are you sure, Erin?" the Dom asked as his hand came down on her right cheek. *Smack!* Droplets of water splashed off of her and darkened the ends of her red, wavy hair.

"Ugh . . . God, aye, Sir! Again!" She squirmed and gasped.

The water effect had pleased him, so Jayden scooped up another handful, poured it over her, and then brought his hand down on her left cheek with another resounding smack. Her flesh was already turning a glorious shade of pink.

"Mm-hmmm!" She thrust her ass at him, pleading for more. Again he scooped up the warm water and trickled it over her. Just as his hand connected over her pussy, making a loud splat sound, the doorbell rang.

His girl shuddered at the interruption. "No, Jayden, please ignore it. Finish me, *A rúnsearc*!"

Her need wafted off of her in waves, and Jayden felt a little guilty. "Sorry, sweet girl," he said while stepping out of the tub, "that will be our dinner, and I can't ignore it."

Erin stood up; water sluiced over her voluptuous curves. She crossed her arms under her breasts, pushing them up, and huffed.

In retaliation, Jayden gripped his cock and pointed it at her. "You're not the only one being left unsatisfied here! Let me go collect our food. You finish up and meet me downstairs. We'll eat, talk, and maybe get back to this later tonight."

A sigh escaped from her mouth while Erin sat back down into the water and grabbed the loofah.

Jayden couldn't walk out of the room with her disappointed, so he knelt down beside the tub and cupped her cheek with his hand. "I love you, Erin; don't ever forget that."

She rewarded him with a huge smile, turning her face into his hand and kissing his palm.

"Go on, get our food. I'll be down in a couple of minutes. I love you, too, you big tease!"

His playful girl laughed and splashed him with water. Moving fast, he jumped back to avoid most of the spray and grabbed a towel. After a quick rub down, Jayden tugged on a pair of sleep pants, hoping they were loose enough to hide his still-prominent erection. Then he headed down the stairs, grabbing his wallet off the foyer table, and opened the door.

ജ‍ോ‍ങ

CHAPTER TWENTY-SIX

ജ‍ോ‍ങ

As soon as Jayden disappeared from sight, Erin allowed the cheesy grin she'd been holding back to break free. Her cheeks were sore, but she couldn't be bothered; the happiness she felt had to spill over, or she might very well burst.

The waning afternoon had been interesting, to say the least. First and foremost was that he reciprocated her feelings. It was almost comical that they'd found themselves in full-blown love with each other when they'd never even shared a simple kiss before today— the fact that Jayden had an intimate familiarity with her entire body didn't count since it had all been gained as her Master. She looked forward to the days ahead when he would get to know her in depth as her lover.

Giggling over the way they'd fumbled back and forth this afternoon, unsure which role to settle into since Master and submissive had been all they'd known before, Erin lifted her sore body out of the cooling water. While drying off, she noticed a new, unopened tube of ointment on the counter and assumed that it was for her beautiful tattoo.

Looking into the mirror, her eyes misted over while she surveyed her reflection: vibrant green eyes sparkling, red hair a fiery halo about her head, skin pink from the warm water and the whip, and nipples standing proud and decorated. But the ink was what did her in; she couldn't take her eyes off of it.

Before she let herself get carried away on a wave of sappy emotion, Erin shook her head to clear it and hung the towel on the drying rod. Hoping to hold Jayden to his promise of "we'll pick this up later," she wanted to keep her wardrobe on the nonexistent side. A brilliant idea formed, and she snatched the gel off the counter before slipping into Jayden's bedroom—and his closet.

Girlfriends wear their boyfriend's clothes all the time, right?

Are you twelve, Erin? Girlfriend? He hasn't said anything about titles.

She was not going to stand there and argue with herself over semantics. His walk-in closet was huge—and beyond OCD in its organization. Everything was sorted by style and color and hung behind glass doors; Erin guessed this was to keep dust off his clothes. Spinning in a slow circle to take it all in, she stopped when her eyes landed on Jayden's black dress shirts. She smiled. A minute later, she was headed downstairs.

When Erin reached the foyer, she found Jayden leaning against the front door with his eyes closed while he took deep breaths. A more than slight bulge filled out the front of his pants, much to her amusement. It was good to see she wasn't alone in her horniness. She giggled, and his lust-filled brown eyes snapped open.

"Hey there, big boy," she purred at him. "Mind helping me put some ointment on my ink?"

"It would be my pleasure, Erin. Let me just set these down in the kitchen. Come on," he answered in a husky voice, shifting the take-out bags to one hand so he could hold hers with the other.

When they reached the kitchen, he put the bags down on the counter before turning to face Erin. Her heart raced when he strode toward her with a sauntering step that took her breath away. He stopped, leaving about six inches between them.

"You," Jayden kissed her nose, "are quite," he kissed the side of her jaw, "irresistible in my clothes."

Erin was dissolving under his touch. Jayden slid his hands under the open flaps of the black shirt, over the tops of her breasts, and up and over her shoulders. He caught the shirt and pushed it down her shoulders until it was snagged by her elbows. With a sigh, her head lolled to the side, exposing her neck to her lover. He accepted the invitation and bit down with light pressure on the side of her neck, sucking the skin into his mouth.

There was no doubt she would be marked when he was done; not with the fervor behind his suckling. After several minutes, he released her neck, and she shivered when his tongue ran over the skin.

"Did you mark me?" Erin whispered against his face since he hadn't pulled away yet.

Now he moved back, and he looked pleased. "Yes, my jewel, and it won't be the last time I do." Their building moment was interrupted by a growl from Erin's stomach. "I think someone is hungry. For food," Jayden clarified when Erin turned her lust-filled gaze on him.

Abashed, she nodded her head in agreement, covering her protesting, empty stomach with her hands. She stood still while Jayden pulled the shirt back up onto her shoulders and knotted the ends together high on her ribs, under her breasts. Taking the ointment from her, Jayden opened it and applied a liberal amount to his fingertips, which he then smoothed across her ink. When he was done, he feathered a kiss just above her clit before tasking Erin with grabbing some plates and silverware while he rinsed his hands at the sink.

While she pulled the food from the bags and plated it, Jayden grabbed a couple of wineglasses and a nice red wine – an Australian Shiraz – from the wine rack. He then followed her into the dining room, where he poured a small amount of wine into their glasses. They sat down, and he raised his glass to her.

"Happy Anniversary, Catherine, my love."

She clinked her glass with his and whispered, "Thank you, *A rúnsearc.*"

Jayden fixed his eyes on her and set his glass down. "Okay, Erin, you've been saying that all afternoon. Are you going to tell me what it means?"

"Beloved."

Her answer left them both quiet and reflective. They proceeded to sip their wine and eat in silence since they were both starving. No words were necessary between them, however; their eyes were filled with their emotions for each other. When their plates were almost empty, Jayden set his fork down.

"Do you have room for dessert, Erin?"

"I guess I could eat a little bit more; why?"

"I'll be right back." He evaded her question and stood, collected their plates, and then left without giving her any idea of what he was up to. Several minutes later, Jayden returned. In his hand was a tray laden down with a bottle of dessert wine, two small glasses, a jar of what appeared to be golden honey, and a plate of baklava.

"Ooh, this looks so yummy!" she squealed when he set the tray on the table in front of her.

"Yes. It does."

Something in his tone made Erin look up. Jayden was staring at her, and her breath hitched when she realized he wasn't referring to the food. He poured the dessert wine and handed her a glass; she took a small sip and moaned at the sweet flavor.

"Do you like it?" he inquired, and she nodded, taking another small sip. "Here." He dipped his finger into the honey and brought it to her lips. "How does it work with the honey?"

Erin sucked the warm sweetness from his finger and closed her eyes in rapture. "It's divine," she hummed in approval and licked his finger clean.

Jayden's eyes darkened. "Stand up and lose the shirt."

The atmosphere had shifted from the light, playful tone they'd shared through dinner. Out of nowhere, the room was too hot, and the single garment she wore was too tight and restrictive.

"Is that a request or a command?" Erin challenged him. Her heart was racing, and her body was tight with eagerness and need.

"What do you want it to be?" he asked in a breathy whisper.

Elation and confusion took over while she tried to wrap her head around the idea that he was letting her choose. One answer would take her down a familiar path and allow her to indulge in her Master's power, which she had missed since that morning. The other response was the unknown. Erin made her choice: after an emotional day of uncertainty, she needed tangible reaffirmation. She wanted her Master.

"Command this girl, Master." Her pussy pulsed with her request.

"In that case, Catherine, stand up and remove the shirt *now*," he ordered.

Fuck, my girl parts love it when he speaks to me that way.

Obedient, she stood and undid the knot on the shirt to let it fall down her arms to the floor. Catherine stood naked before him. His eyes raked over her body while she awaited his next command.

Jayden pushed the dessert tray to the side. "Sit on the table and lean back on your elbows," he said, lifting the dessert wine to his lips and taking a sip while he waited.

"Now, spread your legs, my little slut."

She made the adjustment while he picked up the pot of honey. Catherine watched him bring the spoon covered with the warm, sticky liquid to her lips. He allowed some to spill over her mouth, and she went to lick it off.

"Don't. Move. Leave it there, *cailin maith*," he ordered.

Hoping her reluctance didn't show, she pulled her tongue back into her mouth, tasting a hint of the honey from her lips.

The Dom sighed and drizzled more honey over her mouth before moving lower to run it over her breasts and nipples in a swirling pattern.

Her hips gave an involuntary lurch when the warmth hit her nipples. Master smirked, and he reached between her legs to pinch her swollen clit. "Uh-huh, I told you not to move. Be very still."

Having set the container down, Master proceeded to lick the honey with an agonizing slowness from her lips before trailing down to her breasts, where he twirled his tongue around her areola without touching her nipples. The action forced her mouth to open, and she began panting.

God, the things this man does to me!

It soon became a battle to keep her eyes open and watch his long tongue follow the swirled honey pattern he'd left on her skin. Catherine wanted to close her lids and just bask in the feel, yet she was fascinated by the sight. When he closed in on her left nipple, sucking it into his mouth, a loud moan escaped the submissive.

Jayden lifted his face from her chest with a grin. "I'm sorry; did you want some honey, too?"

Catherine had to concentrate to manage a nod of her head. She wanted whatever he offered; she couldn't say no to anything. It was pretty simple.

Master's hand went to her right breast, which he squeezed from the base while he pushed it up toward her face. "Suck, Catherine," he commanded.

Wanting to oblige, Catherine stretched her neck, reaching for her own nipple when he pushed it into her mouth. His mouth returned to her other breast, and she almost came under the sensation of them sucking together. She'd never been happier to have been blessed with fuller breasts than she was right then.

When the woman could no longer taste honey on her skin, she refocused her attention on the gold ring impaling her nipple, working her tongue in and around it and cleaning it off as best she could. At least honey was a natural healer, but she still made a mental note that her piercings would need to be cleaned extra well when they were done; an infection was not something she wanted to deal with.

She was trying to slow her breathing when she felt cold liquid splash against her belly and across her pussy. The contrast of the cold against her heated core made her thrust her hips up, which earned her a slap to the side of her breast.

"I told you to be still," he growled, and then ran his tongue through the wine across her belly, letting it dip into her belly button to clean her all up.

Catherine sighed and closed her eyes again, expecting his tongue to move lower and follow the wine and honey trail. However, instead she was surprised when the heat from his body seeped into her own and his mouth closed over hers.

Oh, sweet goddess, he tasted divine. Master's tongue was coated with a mixture of honey and cold wine. He pushed it into her mouth, and she was eager to suck on it. His large cock pressed against her entrance through his sleep pants, and Catherine tried to push her legs further apart to welcome him. The way she was leaning back would not allow her to get any wider, so she lifted her feet to the edge of the table, which did open her up for him. He shifted back, pulled his pants down, and then slid home in one thrust.

Their mouths parted as they both screamed out, "Oh, Fuck!" at the same time.

The submissive braced her palms against the table and hooked her legs over his elbows, while her lover found a steady rhythm: in and out, swirl his hips, in and out, swirl his hips. Catherine felt the pressure build, and she knew she'd be unable to hold back.

"Please, Master, may this girl come?"

Master managed to grunt a "Yes" while never breaking his stride, and she soon exploded around him.

Her orgasm continued, never ending while he kept thrusting and swirling his hips against hers. After another ten minutes, Master slowed his pace and withdrew his length; he was breathing hard, his glorious chest rising and falling with each breath. From the tightness of his jaw, Catherine was sure he'd been fighting his own release.

She tilted her head to the side in confusion. "Master?" Catherine couldn't understand why he wasn't giving in.

His eyes snapped to her face, causing her to gasp at the intensity they held. "On your knees, Catherine," he directed through tight, pursed lips.

Willing and even enthusiastic to service him, Catherine slid off the table and dropped to her knees. Master's cock, glistening with a mixture of the submissive's come and wine, bobbed in front of her face. The sight of it, purple and tight, was enthralling.

How in the hell has he resisted? It's so huge and swollen! Catherine thought, and licked her lips, leaning in to take it in her mouth.

"Wait, Catherine."

She froze with her mouth hanging open.

He stretched above her, reaching toward the table, which allowed his cock to brush against her lips. It took everything Catherine had not to part them more and suck him in. But he had told her to wait, so she waited.

"*Cailin maith*, so beautiful," Master whispered at her when he straightened back up. In one hand was his wineglass, and in the other, the honey. A sexy hiss shot from his lips when he tipped both vessels above his length, dripping their contents onto his cock and turning it into what was going to be the best fucking lollipop Catherine had ever had.

"Now," he ordered after he set the emptied vessels on the table, leaning over Catherine again and pushing his cock toward her waiting mouth.

At once she opened wide, and then moaned when the sweet delight pushed past her lips, over her tongue, and down her throat.

It was Master's turn to brace his hands on the table when Catherine grasped his ass and sucked for all she was worth. Soon his hips found their tempo, and he fucked her mouth.

"Jesus fuck, Erin! So good, sweet girl."

Saliva formed a string from his cock to her lips when she pulled off and moved to his balls, where she bestowed gentle, loving licks and soft sucking. He spread his thighs and lowered his balls to her mouth, making it easier for her to work them with her tongue. Noticing that the tip of his cock was leaking, the covetous woman ran her tongue up the underside to the tip so she could suck his pre-come off of him.

He had called her Erin, so they were back to being just "them," and she decided to push *his* limits. She pushed a finger into her pussy to get it lubricated. Letting her lips close around the head of Jayden's cock as a distraction, Erin eased her coated finger into his ass.

The unsuspecting man tensed while he adjusted to the intrusion, but then her lover growled and shoved his cock down her throat, pulling his body off her finger in the process. She held her hand still to let him make the choice; when he rocked his hips back, he allowed his ass to push against her finger again. Jayden repeated the motion three times before he whispered a pleading: "More, Erin, I need more."

It took her a second to catch on, but she raised another finger to his ass so that when he rocked back, two fingers entered him. He emitted a loud, feral groan.

"Fuck . . . been too long . . . so good," he ranted.

Catherine felt his cock thickening in her mouth—any minute now he would lose the fight. Feeling bold and wanting to send him out with a bang, she had a third finger waiting for him when he rocked back.

Jayden's back arched at the sensation, his ass cheeks clamping and locking her fingers inside him while his cock impaled itself in her throat, and she swallowed. Incoherent grunts and profanities burst forth from his mouth while he started coming down her throat, and she continued the swallowing motion, milking him dry. When he stilled, she removed her fingers from his ass, released his cock from her mouth, and then he crumbled into a heap next to her on the floor.

"Holy fuck, Erin. That was . . . the most amazing, intense, mind-blowing orgasm ever," he panted out. "God, I love you."

Pleased at his reaction, she giggled and kissed his lips. "I love you, Jayden. And I agree; that was pretty hot." She winked at him while licking her lips.

His shoulders shook with amusement while he stood up and offered Erin his hand. "Okay, love, I'm officially spent. Can we just go to bed and have our talk tomorrow?"

"That sounds perfect."

Jayden kept hold of her hand while they went upstairs. When they reached his door, she stood on her tiptoes and gave him a quick kiss. "Goodnight, *A rúnsearc,*" Erin murmured as she turned to go down the hall.

"Erin," he called out, stopping her. "Sweet girl, please stay with me tonight?"

For the first time ever, Jayden looked vulnerable to Erin, like he was afraid she would say no. Raising her hand to his cheek, she cupped it and ran her thumb along his jaw. "I'd love to, Jayden." Erin smiled at him.

His grin was contagious when he scooped her in his arms and carried her to his bed. Jayden set his love down next to it so he could pull the covers back, and then he lifted her again and crawled into bed with her. She snuggled into his arms, and he pulled the covers around them. Their naked, sticky bodies molded to each other while they drifted off into the most peaceful sleep either of them had ever had.

᙮

CHAPTER TWENTY-SEVEN

᙮

Jayden opened his eyes to muted sunlight filtering through the curtains. His body was warm thanks to the angel wrapped around him, her long, red hair splayed across his chest hiding her face. Amazing as it was, his typical morning problem seemed to be mitigated, seeing that he sported a semi as opposed to the usual full-blown wood.

Of course, that lasted until Erin rolled onto her back. With closed eyes, she raised her arms and arched her back, stretching her muscles. The movement freed her breasts from the confines of the sheet. The moment when her hardened, adorned nipples came into view,

Jayden's semi came to full attention, leaving him groaning over the sudden tightness between his thighs.

While Erin yawned and finished her stretch, Jayden watched her eyes take him in, lingering on the obvious bulge under the sheet. "Mm, good morning." She grinned. "Want some help with that?" she whispered.

Staring at the beauty before him, Jayden nodded.

She reached out and tugged the sheet down to reveal his crying manhood. Leaning over him so that her hair tickled his abs and thighs, she took a languid lick from base to tip before sucking the head between her pouty lips, and then popping off. "Hmm, you still taste like honey and wine," she declared before straddling his thighs. Her tiny hand wrapped around his cock, and she soon was guiding herself down. They both let out low groans.

Being mindful of the inked flesh, Jayden gripped above her hips and guided her in a slow, rocking motion. She started to lean forward, but he sat up instead. An errant ray of sunshine had flashed on the paddle on her collar, and it had reminded him that the collar needed to come off so that they could identify their roles easier. He wanted today to be all about being Jayden and Erin. Reaching up to the clasp, he whispered the words, "Your servitude has been surreal, Catherine."

Her breath caught while she responded, "To serve you has been divine, Master."

Jayden's fingers loosened the catch, and the collar slid into his hand. He twisted around to lay it on the nightstand. When he looked at Erin again, she had a confused look on her face. "What is it, Jewel?" he asked while his fingers toyed with the emerald J's marking her as his.

"Well, it's Sunday morning, and it's normal for us to play until six in the evening. I'm just wondering why you took it off early."

"Erin, I want today to be just us, and I want you to be able to speak freely with me," Jayden explained and kissed her nose. "For that to happen, you need the collar off to put you in the right mindset. Okay?"

In answer, her legs wrapped around his waist. He locked his arms around her back, pulling her against his chest. Moments later, their mouths latched onto each other, and their tongues danced. She rocked her hips, and he bucked upward. Between the two of them, it was easy to find a perfect rhythm and maintain it while continuing to tease each other's mouths. Their breathing picked up in minute increments while they made love.

Before long, Jayden felt her clamping around him and milking his cock, while her head fell back and she keened. Unable to withstand any longer, he soon followed, filling her with his seed. As their breathing leveled out, Erin rested her head against Jayden's shoulder. When he was sure he could speak, Jayden nuzzled into her neck and whispered, "Love you, Jewel."

The precious words were rewarded with a beautiful, glowing smile, and she whispered back, "Love you, too, Jayden." She reciprocated when he hugged her tight to his chest.

"How about we grab a quick shower and then some breakfast, Erin?"

"Sounds divine. Coffee would be fabulous right now." She climbed off him but waited while he got off the bed.

Together, they crossed over to the bathroom. Jayden started the water going, and they took turns brushing their teeth, using the toilet, and getting into the steamy shower. They washed each other with caring touches, stopping for lazy kisses while their shower progressed. Jayden paid particular attention to getting Erin's nipples squeaky clean—and her pussy creamy with come in exchange.

After they were done, Jayden stepped out first and hurried to dry off. He had a towel from the warmer waiting for Erin when she stepped out a few minutes later. Once she was dried, Jayden applied ointment to her tattoo and helped her into a fluffy robe before wrapping his own robe around his body.

Hand in hand, they went downstairs to the kitchen. Erin got the coffee going while Jayden pulled items from the fridge for ham, egg, and cheese croissant sandwiches. While he cracked and whisked the eggs, she gathered some fresh fruit and threw together a small salad. It was—normal, just like a regular couple. The love-struck man smiled when the thought drifted through his mind.

Food preparation finished, he plated the croissants and grabbed the salad while she grabbed their coffee mugs, and then they went to the breakfast nook, where they ate in comfortable silence. Sipping on their coffee, both were content to just stare into the other's eyes while they nourished their bodies.

Erin was the first one to break the silence. "So, what are we doing today, Jayden?" she purred while her foot trailed up his calf under the table.

Smirking at her antics, he replied, "Well, I'd like to go over yesterday with you. We also have dinner plans this evening, for which we need to be leaving in a couple of hours. Other than that, we're free."

A moment passed before she stood up and grabbed the plates. "Okay, let me clean these up real quick, and we can get the talk out of the way," she chirped before rushing into the kitchen.

Not wanting to have Erin out of his sight, he followed her and leaned against the counter to watch her move around with ease. She was putting the last dish in the dishwasher when she glanced up and caught him.

Erin smiled and blew him a kiss, which he pretended to catch and place against his lips. It was a goofball thing to do, but Jayden didn't care—he was head over heels for the woman in front of him, and it felt great to be able to proclaim that fact now.

Laughing, she said, "Why don't you take a picture? It'll last longer."

Jayden's mouth broke into a wide smile. "How soon you forget, my jewel. I had several pictures taken of you yesterday!"

Her cheeks bloomed into a luscious pink, and her eyes lowered to the ground while her whole body was wracked with shudders. "Trust me, I haven't forgotten," she whispered, moving toward him.

When she was within reach, Jayden grabbed her and pulled her flush with his body, and his hands moved to her ass. "No?" he queried.

"How could I?" Erin asked and tilted her head up to him. "Shawn was very good at convincing me that I was, um, performing for you."

His smile was back. "You do realize now that you were. Right?" The blush that had faded returned full force, and he couldn't stop himself from kissing her, hard.

They broke the kiss when they were both desperate for air. "Come on, Jewel, let's move this to the living room where we'll be more comfortable."

Jayden took a seat in his favorite overstuffed chair, expecting Erin to sit across from him on the sofa. However, his feisty girl had other ideas; she plopped down on his lap with her legs hanging over the arm of the chair. Erin's robe gaped open at the top, and Jayden was treated to a view of the soft mounds of her breasts peeking out from the material.

"Comfy?" he choked out once she'd stopped wiggling around on his awakening cock and had latched her hands around his neck.

"Mm-hmm," she replied.

"So, let's start with a general question."

His train of thought was derailed when Jayden got lost for a moment in the emerald pools of her eyes. She cleared her throat and grinned at him, and he snapped out of his trance. "Right. Okay, how do you feel overall about yesterday?"

෨෬

How did she feel about yesterday? Erin thought about his question for a minute while she composed her thoughts. "Well, I guess I could summarize it in one word: intense."

"Intense, huh? Please elaborate for me, Erin," he coaxed.

"Besides the obvious physical intensity of the day . . ." She trailed off when his fingers slipped through the opening of her robe and began stroking the valley between her breasts. Swallowing, she forced herself to refocus and continue. "I sort of experienced every emotion I can think of," Erin choked out. The woman was beginning to pant while his fingers traced wide circles around her nipples. In secret, she hoped he would take advantage of the numbing antiseptic spray they were coated in and play with them.

Jayden curved his body inward, placed parted lips on Erin's throat, and then she got her wish when he pinched and rolled a nipple in his long fingers.

Caught off-guard, she gasped and thrust her chest into his hand.

"Desire?" He whispered the question against her neck.

She moaned and nodded her head.

"Excitement?" Jayden inquired with a lick to her neck. His other hand had moved to the tie of her robe, and she felt his hard-on twitch beneath her ass. "Anticipation?" Hot breath whispered over the shell of her ear when he pulled the tie, allowing the robe to fall open and expose her body.

All Erin could do was whimper while the wetness started to flow between her thighs in reaction to his teasing touches. A heavy sigh escaped her when Jayden's lips closed on her nipple and his fingers brushed the outside of her sex. Erin moaned in answer and let her legs fall open; he used the invitation to push a finger inside her at the same time his tongue snuck out to flick her nipple. She whimpered, and he chuckled.

"So beautiful, like a fine-tuned instrument I could play all day," her lover murmured against her heaving breasts.

"Please," she begged while lifting her hips to meet his hand. Instead of giving her more, his finger exited her body, and a kiss was placed right above her nipple.

"Patience, Jewel. Tell me more. You said 'every emotion.' What else did you experience?"

Jayden was making her feel so good now. She didn't want to go into the fear, anxiety, jealousy, and anger that had infiltrated her heart throughout the day, but she also knew that for this new relationship to work, nothing could be kept from him. It was with a heavy sigh that Erin pulled her legs closed, trapping his hand between her thighs, and curled in toward his chest where she laid her head.

"Erin?" His voice was laced with concern. "Jewel, what is it? Please talk to me." He tugged his hand free and wrapped both of his arms around her, pulling her close to him.

She allowed herself a deep inward breath, relaxing when his scent filled her nose. "I—I'm not sure how to describe it. Like I said, the physical parts of yesterday were incredible. Everything that I did, and had done to me, felt amazing—"

"I hear a 'but' in there," he said.

"Aye, but I was also left with a lot of time in between sessions to think. With Sir Jonathan, and even

Sir Landon, I was nervous, even though I recognized their names as friends of yours. By the time Sir Landon completed these," Erin nodded her head at her chest, "I was convinced that Sir Jonathan was taking me on as a submissive; that you were getting rid of me."

The sharpness of Jayden's inhaled breath startled her.

"I tried to ignore the feelings that began to bubble to the surface." Erin took a deep breath; tears were beginning to gather in her eyes, because she knew she had to tell him about the Spencer flashback and where it had led her.

"Shh, Erin. I'm right here, Jewel. You're safe, and no one is taking you from me." He kissed the top of her head, and she snuggled deeper into his chest while he stroked her hair.

"I know, Jayden." She sniffled. "The session with Paige and Sir Landon was incredible. However, when I realized he'd pierced me with the J's, branding me, I—well, I lost it." The tears had started to fall down her cheeks and were leaving a damp spot on his robe.

His voice was soft and gentle. "What do you mean, Erin?" He had begun rubbing slow circles on her back.

"Well, I had begun to question what I was doing there. And I had started to feel like I was being interviewed, so to speak, for new placement. That you had realized I had broken the rules of our contract by allowing my feelings to grow for you—"

Jayden cut her off before she could go further. "Oh my God, Erin! Oh, my jewel, no! I'm such an idiot. I never should have left you alone yesterday," he ranted.

It was Erin's turn to console. "No, Jayden, please calm down. We're okay. Right now we are here, together, and everything is going to be fine. You—you just deserve to know what I went through yesterday because I don't want to keep any secrets from you." They shared a gentle kiss. "Can I keep going?"

After taking a moment to compose himself, he nodded for her to continue.

"So, as I was saying," she smiled at him, "I saw the J's, and the first thing that went through my mind was that you were giving me to Jonathan."

He wheezed again, but didn't say anything.

"I became angry that it hadn't been discussed with me; that I was being passed off like some object."

Jayden was shaking his head back and forth, and his eyes had filled with sadness. Erin kissed him again to remind him these were old feelings, to bring him back to the present with her.

"That was when the old memories washed over me," Erin whispered. "*His* words telling me I was nothing but a worthless fuck hole."

"Spencer?" he choked out, and she nodded. "He was the one who was worthless, Erin. I wish you'd never been exposed to that—that lunatic son of a bitch!"

A single finger stroked his cheek, and it helped to calm them both. "I know, *A rúnsearc.* Me, too. But it happened, and I can't undo it. The memory gave me the strength to accept what was going to happen. I made the decision that I *need* the submissive lifestyle, and that the only thing that mattered was the Master I was kneeling before; which was why I offered my oral services to Sir Landon and Paige. I needed to make them feel as good as they had made me feel."

She lifted her eyes to Jayden's, and her heart broke a little at the tears she saw pooling in them. Erin angled forward and kissed his eyes, licking away the tears when they brimmed over. In return, he squeezed her in a tight hug.

"Oh, Erin, my love. I never meant for you to feel that way. I am so sorry," he whimpered into her chest. "You're so very strong and brave. You are, without a doubt, the most incredible woman I've ever met. I don't deserve you."

"Jayden, please don't say that!" Erin exclaimed. "I love you so much. Remember, these feelings surfaced, and I dealt with them. By the end of the day – no, before then – I realized it was just the hormones and the constant in-and-out of scene head spaces that I had to keep dealing with. You did nothing wrong. All of it, everything you set up for me yesterday, was nothing more than what I had asked for—limits that I'd wanted to explore. You made that possible for me in a safe environment with people you trusted. Once I realized that they had your trust, my trust extended to them as well."

Erin was shocked by the force of his kiss when he latched onto her mouth with his. Between pecks, he murmured "I love you" over and over until she began giggling.

He slanted back and took her face in his hands. "Are you sure you're alright?"

"I'm positive, Jayden. I've never been better. By the end of my session with Sir Landon, I had figured out that the J's were yours—as was I."

"Mine," he growled. "All mine!"

"Aye, *A rúnsearc*." Erin grinned at him. "All yours!"

The couple sat in quiet repose for a short time, soaking up each other's warmth while Jayden's hand traced lazy patterns on her thigh outside of her robe.

"Erin?" he whispered.

"Hmm?"

"You know that I'm yours as well, don't you?"

ഇാൻ

CHAPTER TWENTY-EIGHT

ഇാൻ

Jayden couldn't believe that Erin, his sweet, beautiful Jewel, had been through the mental torture she was describing to him. That she had endured all of that uncertainty and angst, and yet was curled up in his lap still professing her love for him was amazing. There was no doubt in Jayden's mind that he was the luckiest man alive.

Part of him wanted to know what memories had haunted her the day before; he'd thought he knew everything about her time with Spencer. She'd been telling him the horrible tales over the course of the past year—through her journal writing and, on occasion, talking. Full disclosure had been necessary so that he could understand her limits. However, Jayden couldn't bring himself to ask her to relive the memories again; in particular since she'd just done that the day before. That was a task that could be saved for a journal assignment later.

More important than drawing the dead man into their moment, Jayden had to know if Erin understood that he had completely given his heart and soul to her. So he asked, and then waited with bated breath for her answer. When she lifted her watery, jade eyes to his face, the elation and understanding in them made Jayden's heart soar.

Her voice was strong and steady when she answered. "Aye, Jayden, I know. Our hearts beat as one. You've Mastered all of me, but I know you love me not because I'm willing to kneel before you, but because I'm *me*. I know that if I asked, you'd kneel before me in a heartbeat, and I know that we can make this work. From now on, we are lovers and soul mates first; Master and submissive when we need it—if it pleases you?"

The smile on his face stretched from ear to ear. "Erin, have I ever told you that besides strong and beautiful, you are also incredibly smart?"

She giggled. "No, I don't think you have. Smart, am I? Maybe I need to find a schoolgirl outfit to model for you; show you just how 'smart' I can be." She shot him a spirited wink.

Always eager to respond, Jayden's cock hardened at her teasing words, and he groaned.

She ground her ass into his lap, showing him that she was quite aware of what she was doing.

"Ugh, you are also a very naughty girl, Erin," he hissed when she wiggled again.

"Mm, perhaps you need to punish this girl, Master?" she asked with pure innocence.

Damn. This girl, no—this woman was going to be the death of him!

"Do you want to be punished, Catherine?" Jayden moaned when her lips ran across his throat and nibbled on his ear.

He held his tongue and watched while she stood up from his lap, stepped back away from him, and let her robe drop to the floor. Her firm breasts rose up and down with her heavy breathing, and when his eyes traveled to the slit between her thighs, he could see the moisture gathering on her nether lips. With the grace of a dancer, she lowered herself to her knees, which she spread to shoulder width before linking her arms behind her back.

Presenting herself to Jayden in her inspection position, she whispered, "Please, Master, punish this girl. Love me. Give us both what we need."

Fuck. Me.

Sliding forward to the edge of the chair, he paused to confirm. "Are you sure, Erin?"

Without lifting her eyes from the floor, the Irish lass nodded her head in assent and stated, "Aye, Master."

His girl wanted to play, and Jayden wasn't going to deny her. "Very well, then. Catherine, look at me," the Dom ordered while undoing the tie on his robe and pushing it open.

Her head lifted.

"Look at this cock. Do you see how hard you make it, Catherine?" No touching was needed; the cock in question was erect and jutting from between his legs, long and proud, when her eyes shifted to it.

She licked her lips and whispered, "Aye, Master."

Stretching forward, Jayden pinched her nipples at the base, behind the piercing. "These tits are mine." He let his fingers slide forward and hook into the hoops, and he tugged. "I've branded them as such."

An appreciative moan slipped from between her lips.

Continuing his inspection, Jayden ran his hands down Catherine's sides and around her back to grip her ass cheeks with both hands. He squeezed before releasing his grip, bringing his hands down atop her fleshy rump; the sound of flesh on flesh echoed. "This ass is mine; to spank or fuck whenever I want."

She moaned louder and arched her ass out, wringing an amused chortle from Jayden before he moved his hands around to her front. Two fingers slipped through her dripping lower lips; he plunged them deep into her. Out they came, nice and easy, and they were coated. To taunt his submissive, he raised the shiny fingers to her lips and commanded, "Taste my sweet pussy."

When she wrapped her lips around his fingers and sucked, it was all he could do not to throw her on the ground and fuck her senseless. Erin's expert little tongue continued to lick and suck her Master's fingers clean until he pulled them out of her mouth.

Using the hand she'd cleaned, Jayden gripped his aching cock. "However, this cock is *not* mine."

Her eyes shot to his face, filled with confusion, and Jayden smirked.

"This cock, Catherine, is yours. To suck, fuck, and tease however you want. Anytime you want."

Her face was transformed by the beautiful smile that spread across it.

"You've requested to be punished, Jewel, yet I have seen no indiscretions that deserve punishment, so tell me what you want me to do." Erin had caught him off-guard; he kept trying to do the stand-up thing and keep them in a 'vanilla' state of mind while they navigated their new emotions, yet she was too damn seductive.

"Please, Master. Your slut wants to be spanked."

While Jayden was more than willing to play with his jewel, they were not in the playroom, nor was she wearing her collar at the moment, so he was determined to include her in the decision-making process for this impromptu session. He was going to make her call the shots and get a feel for how well she handled having the upper hand. Something she'd said earlier about asking him to kneel had his mind reeling with possibilities.

"Catherine, you will tell me where you want to receive the spanking, and with what I am to inflict the punishment for your . . . cheekiness." He had to fight from smiling when her forehead creased and her nose scrunched up while she thought through his request. Jayden had never let her choose before; he'd always just done what he wanted, and she had let him.

"Um, well, I don't know . . ." she stammered.

"Catherine, did you ask to do this?"

"Aye." The submissive's voice was a whisper.

"Well, you must have had something in mind?" Jayden urged her.

"This girl is sorry, Master, but no, she didn't. This girl just knows she wants to feel her skin sing under her Dom's hand."

It was apparent to Jayden that she was going to need some guidance, so he reached forward and smacked the underside of her left breast. "Do you want your tits spanked, or your ass?" The question was punctuated with a gratifying smack on her right butt cheek.

"Oh, God, aye—please!"

The Dom laughed. "Don't growl at me, little girl. Now, choose one or the other, Catherine."

"Can't this girl have both, Master?" Catherine asked with an adorable, pouty mouth.

He pretended to think about it for a moment. "No, my sweet, you have to choose one, and you still have to tell me *what* I will be delivering the spanking with." Her eyes widened. "Choose something in this room."

Her head turned from side to side while she took in their surroundings.

"You may rise and walk around to make your decision. Once you've made your choice, return to me, and present the part of yourself you want spanked," Jayden ordered. His cock was swollen to capacity and began to leak when she rose to her full height. She swayed her hips when she backed away, taunting him.

He was curious what her choice would be. At first glance, there didn't seem to be a lot of options in the room, so Jayden expected she would come back and ask for his hand, but then he'd also learned to expect the unexpected with Erin. She was a never-ending source of surprises.

Catherine paused at the magazine rack and reached out to touch one with a tentative finger. She looked back at him for a minute, her eyes resting on his hands, but then continued to walk around the room, keeping her front side to him at all times. When she stopped again, it was in front of the kindling basket next to the fireplace.

He was bewildered when she lifted a small stick out and slapped it against her hand a couple of times.

Jayden had to resist the urge to come when his jewel twisted her body and brought the stick down on her own ass. She flinched just a tad and a red line appeared across her cheek. He braced himself to jump to her aid, but she put the stick back in the basket and moved on.

She came back toward Jayden, pausing where he'd laid her trench coat over the back of the couch last night. Keeping her eyes on his, she pulled the belt from the loops and doubled it up in her tiny hand. The Dom held his breath while her arm raised and she brought the belt down over the tops of her breasts. Her eyes closed for a moment, and Catherine shuddered.

Without his permission, his hips thrust upward, and the little minx giggled. It was a moment of clarity for Jayden. Catherine was playing with him—watching his reactions to her choices to help make her decision. *Fine,* he thought, *I can play, too.* Not another second was wasted before Jayden took his cock in a firm grip and started stroking it up and down.

"Catherine, you're wasting time," he all but snarled. Her gaze settled on his hand, following the movement with her eyes, and Jayden could see the lust in them building.

"Mmmm," she moaned. "Does this girl have the choice of just her breasts or ass, Master?" The belt slipped through her fingers.

He opened his mouth to answer, intrigued by what she might be thinking. "I told you the choice was yours, Catherine; anywhere on your body with anything in this room. Just make your decision soon, as my patience is wearing thin." The Dom cocked an eyebrow at his girl.

With a coy mien, she draped the belt around her neck and walked to the edge of the room, where Jayden kept a decorative cane and umbrella basket. She pulled one of the hand-carved canes out and gripped it, running her fist up and down its length and licking her lips.

Jayden's grip tightened on his dick while he watched her movements. Had she lost her mind? Or was Jonathan that good? One time under the whip couldn't have been enough for her to be ready to make the leap to cane play. He couldn't decide if she was being serious with her consideration, or if she was out to vex him.

Still trying to work out her intentions, Jayden returned to observing Catherine, who was now tapping the cane against her calves before returning it to the basket. Next, she pulled out an umbrella. Ever the temptress, she turned her back to Jayden and leaned forward, pushing her ass toward him. Again, she twisted so she could bring the umbrella down over her ass cheeks. The angle was wrong, so solid contact wasn't possible, but they both got a taste of its potential.

Catherine was amazing with her inventiveness. It would be interesting to see what she would do in the playroom if the Dom ever gave her the freedom to play Domme for a session. He had a good feeling he wouldn't be disappointed, and he stored the idea for later. While Jayden didn't kneel for anyone except Landon on the very rare occasion, he had no doubts that submitting to Catherine would be an adventure.

The umbrella slid back into place with a soft whisper, and she turned back around. Her eyes darted around the room before landing on Jayden's. He couldn't wait any longer; he needed to get his hands on her skin and his cock buried in her heat. "Time's up, Catherine. Make your choice and get over here!"

"Aye, Master," she purred and came forward, stopping by the marble coffee table. She sat down on the end and lay back with dainty motions, wincing when her skin came into contact with the cold marble. Her nipples pebbled to hard peaks. She placed a leg on each side of the table and scooted herself back to the middle. "This girl is ready, Master," she announced.

It was Jayden's turn to stand and lose his robe. After tossing the item in the chair behind him, Jayden walked over to Catherine and circled the table, assuming she was offering her breasts since her ass was against the marble. "Explain what I'm to spank your tits with, slut."

The submissive reacted to her Master's words with a shiver that jiggled her gorgeous tits. Jayden's mouth popped open with her next antic: reaching down between her spread legs, she pulled her pussy lips open, putting her engorged clit on display. "If it pleases you, Master, this girl would like you to spank her clit," she ran one finger over the bundle of nerves, "with your long, hard, thick cock." She emphasized each word by tapping her clit.

Well shit, didn't see that one coming!

ෂාⓒ෪

CHAPTER TWENTY-NINE

ෂාⓒ෪

"Your wish is my command—this time." Intent on enjoying himself, he knelt and lowered his mouth to her sex, ran his tongue up her slit, and then sucked her clit between his lips. With a light nibble, he angled back with a grin. "Fucking delicious."

Taking his cock in hand, Jayden crept forward on his knees onto the table until he was positioned above her. In preparation for fulfilling his jewel's request, Jayden gripped the base of his cock and angled it up toward his belly. "Count them, Catherine," the Dom commanded and began to swing his dick down against her clit.

"Ohhh . . . one, Master."

His cock connecting with her skin made a nice, solid sound.

"Ugh . . . two, Master."

On the third smack, some of her juices splattered against her inner thighs. With the fourth, Jayden pushed his length over her clit and thrust his hips forward and back, delighting in the feel of her hard nub rubbing against the thick vein on the underside of his cock.

"Fo–four, Master," she whimpered.

Jayden lifted his erection, and with rapid repetition, brought it down on her again and again. His slut's voice while she counted became more disjointed with each number until she was begging to come after the eighth strike.

"Please, Master, may your slut come?" she panted out.

"No!" he denied her and smacked her clit again with the head of his cock.

"Oh, shit! Nine, Master, please, let me come!" the girl begged, dropping her usual formality in her desperation.

Gripping himself as tight as he could to prevent his own premature ejaculation, he slapped his dick against her and gave the order: "Come, Catherine!"

"Ten! Fuck. Thank you, Master!" she squealed, abandoning her control and letting the orgasm take her.

All his years of practiced composure, and Jayden couldn't wait for Catherine to ride out her release before he was burying his cock deep in her pulsating cunt. Forcing his swollen manhood into her contracting walls was exquisite; she was so fucking tight and wet that it took all of his control to withhold his own orgasm while hers rolled on, squeezing and milking him. Once he was all the way inside her, he held still, waiting for her to come down from her euphoric high. When she did, her eyes opened and looked straight into Jayden's soul with pure love and desire.

The sweet, delirious glaze over her eyes gave way to a mischievous emerald sparkle, and Catherine reached up to slide the coat belt from around her neck. Twisting each end around her hands, she swung the belt over Jayden's head; he felt it land across his ass. Tucking her arms into a curl brought them toward her, the action tightening the belt across his flesh and bringing him closer to her.

On instinct, Jayden tried to resist being drawn in by counter pulling, resulting in his cock slipping free of her body while he pushed back against the flimsy fabric. She curled her arms forward again, pulling him deep into her. That drew a gasp from him due to the all-consuming sensation, and he looked down at her.

"Fuck me, Master. Hard!" she ordered with gusto.

Oh, hell yes! He didn't have to be told twice. Wrenching free, Jayden then slammed back into her, repeating the process many times, her moans of pleasure encouraging him to go as hard and fast as he could. His stomach tightened while his cock swelled, his balls feeling like they would explode any second. That was it, he couldn't hold out any longer.

"Come with me again. Please, Catherine!" Jayden yelled, and hot strings of semen shot from the end of his cock. He pumped and pulsed inside her while her walls again clamped down on him, working everything out of him. Collapsing on top of her, Jayden let his head rest on her ribs just below her breasts. They were both breathing heavily, and her nails dragged through his hair and scraped against his scalp. It was perfect.

Spent and happy, he lifted his head so he could kiss the undersides of his jewel's breasts. When she sighed, Jayden nibbled on the soft flesh, and her hips thrust under him. His flaccid cock began reawakening.

Lifting Erin in his arms, Jayden stood up. The whole way up the stairs and back to his room, he enjoyed the feel of his cock rubbing against her ass. A playful toss onto the bed, and then Jayden lunged at his girl, landing between her spread legs. She was gorgeous when she rose up onto her elbows and watched him. Her still-damp hair draped across her shoulders, the ends coming down and hiding portions of her plump tits.

Lowering his mouth, he returned to her drooling cunt; her head dropped back, but she managed to stay on her elbows while her hands stroked and played with her nipples. A raw hunger had taken over his faculties, and all caution was thrown to the wind while Jayden ate her out like it was his last meal. She came again with a high pitched squeal, and her thighs clamped around her man's head.

Once she relaxed her grip, Jayden sat back on his haunches; his erection protruded out in front of him like a flagpole. Caveman-like, he grabbed her ankles and started to pull her toward him, but she squirmed out of his grasp and flipped over onto her hands and knees. His mouth gaped while she crawled the short distance across the bed toward him.

With no warning, her hot, wet mouth slid down over his cock.

"Oh, Jesus fuck, Erin!"

She moaned while his cock slid deeper into her mouth and throat. The vibrations along with her sucking, sliding movement were going to kill him, no matter how glorious it felt.

"If you keep that up, I'm going to come down your throat." Fair warning to be sure.

Erin shocked Jayden yet again when she pulled off him and sat back with a grin. "Do you have any dildos in here?"

Oh hell, what was the vixen up to now?

"Um, yeah, in the nightstand. I got a few when I got back from China, just in case. Why?"

"Just in case?" Her brow arched, and her emerald eyes twinkled.

"After having you stay in here right before I left, I was undecided as to whether I was going to expand our play areas to include my room on a regular basis. Now I'm glad I didn't. I want this to be our room."

Her earlier excitement dissipated, replaced by a soft halo of adoration. "Oh, Jayden—"

"None of that, Erin. You had something in mind, and now I'm curious . . ."

She clapped, spinning around to pull open the drawer. It took mere seconds for her to glance over the limited selection and retrieve the canary yellow vibrator. It was thicker than Jayden but not as long, and it was covered in ridges. The toy also had a small extension arm with a tiny cup on the end of it. Erin turned on the switch, and her eyes lit up when she felt the power of the piece of rubber and plastic in her hand. She placed her fingertip inside the tiny cup, and Jayden knew she was feeling the tiny metal ball swirling around the inside.

"Oh, my, Jayden, you've been holding out on me. This is going to feel so good crammed in my pussy while this little ball thing circles my clit." Her voice was husky, and he was beginning to think she might come just thinking about what that vibe could do.

The Dom was dumbstruck. Was she really going to lie back on his bed and fuck herself with a toy while he sat there with another hard on that was begging for attention? A hard on, he might add, that she had sucked to its current state!

Teasing and taunting, with seduction in her eyes, she leaned back against his pillows and bent her knees, placing her feet up as close to her ass as she could get them. Jayden had a very clear view of her wet cunt, and he was never more thankful that he'd insisted she learn how to masturbate. His tongue snaked out to lick his lips when she placed the vibe at her opening and started pushing it in. She inserted it about half way, and then slid it out and sucked the mixture of their come off of it.

"You're right, Jayden. Fucking delicious!" Erin winked and slid the toy back in, pushing it deeper that time. Again, she pulled it out and started to raise it to her mouth, but a longing whimper tumbled from Jayden's lips. "Oh, I'm sorry. Did you want to taste, too?" She angled it toward him, offering it to him in the same way he'd teased her with the honey hours before.

It took Jayden about three seconds to scurry over to her and wrap his lips around that dildo. Her come was thick and creamy, and it was so sweet that he enjoyed every second of bobbing his head up and down the toy, cleaning it off. Erin pulled it out of his mouth and set it to the side.

"Put that cock in my pussy and get it lubed, Jayden. I want to feel you in my ass," she whispered.

A Divine Life

Her shyness was endearing, but he didn't buy it—not anymore. That settled it. Jayden knew he needed to get that woman into a leather corset and armed with a riding crop in the not-too-distant future.

Not one to leave his lady waiting, he lined himself up with her sodden opening and nudged inside. She was so fucking wet it made his head spin.

"Now, Jayden, get your cock in me now! Please!"

Neither one was able to contain their feral noises when he rammed home; a few quick thrusts, and she propped her hand against his chest in silent instruction. Jayden slipped out of her and sat back. That time, when he grabbed her ankles, she didn't resist but let him pull her close enough to put them up on his shoulders. Angled as Erin was, he was able to position himself at her backside and work his way into her clenching channel. If he'd thought her pussy was tight, it was nothing compared to getting inside her this way. They took a few minutes to adjust to each other.

Once Jayden was able to glide in and out of her, he picked up the vibe and pushed it into her pussy. Making sure the little cup was positioned over her clit, he flipped the on switch.

Jayden could feel the ridges and vibration of the dildo through the thin membrane that separated his cock from her warm pussy. The moment he began moving both his cock and the toy within her, Erin started coming. Knowing he had to go easy or risk tearing something and hurting her, Jayden took his time, and they both reveled in it. What they were doing was kinky as hell, but the tenderness the position required put it in the category of making love, as far as he was concerned.

Erin's eyes were closed, her lips were parted, and she was panting. Her usual pale, creamy skin was flushed and hot. She was the most beautiful thing he had ever seen. Soaking her up with his darkened eyes, it didn't take long until he was spurting a load in her ass while she shuddered through a final orgasm.

Coasting on a downward endorphin spiral, Jayden pulled out of Erin and collapsed next to her, curling his body around hers. He let out a soft laugh. "I think we need another shower, sweet girl."

"Yeah, that probably wouldn't be a bad idea, except I can't move just yet. I feel like rubber right now." Her giggle was lighthearted and lyrical.

Jayden snuggled into her more. "No problem, beautiful. We have time to recover for a while before we need to get ready." He brushed some red curls off of her shoulder, and then kissed the bare skin; she sighed with contentment, relaxing into his arms.

"So, is there anything else you want to tell me about yesterday? Any other emotions or concerns that came up?" They had gotten a little side-tracked from their discussion, and Jayden didn't want her left with any concerns that could fester and turn into problems later.

"Well," she snickered, "I also had a little bit of a jealousy issue."

"Oh? Do tell," he encouraged.

Erin buried her face in her hand and mumbled something. Jayden was able to make out the words "Shawn" and "payment."

"I'm sorry; you seem to be talking to the pillow and your hand, not to me. Could you repeat that, please?" His fingers found her ribs and tickled.

She huffed but rolled over in his arms to face him. "After the tattoo was done, I tried to offer thanks to Shawn like you had instructed. Of course, by then I'd figured out that I wasn't his particular flavor, so I had no clue what I might be able to do for him."

Boisterous laughter bubbled forth, earning Jayden a glare. "I'm sorry, Erin, but I would have loved to have seen that conversation happen. A beautiful, straight woman coming on to a gay man . . . classic!"

While she acted mad and slapped his chest, she soon started laughing as well. Catching her breath, Erin continued, "Anyway, when he realized what I was getting at – the look on his face was priceless, by the way – he started laughing at me, too. Then he said not to worry about it because you had taken care of his payment." She lifted her eyebrows at Jayden as if to say: figure it out.

"Ah, so you got jealous thinking that I'd been the payment?"

"That about sums it up, but Shawn caught the panic in my face and explained about Micah." Erin shrugged her shoulders.

Jayden kissed her nose. "You are too adorable."

"Well, I might be adorable, but I'm also sticky and sweaty and in desperate need of cleaning up!" she squealed and jumped off the bed, running for the shower with Jayden on her heels.

Profuse giggling met Jayden when he caught up to Erin in the bathroom. She seemed so carefree that he couldn't help but be happy. When she stepped into the shower, Jayden returned her smile and set about relieving himself while he watched her curvaceous figure through the frosted glass. When she submerged herself under the hot water, she let out a throaty moan.

His cock twitched at the sound.

Petite hands came up to push her hair back while the color darkened from scarlet to deep ruby under the water. Like she knew he was watching and wanted to put on a show for him, her hands kept traveling down. Jayden, of course, followed their movement with his eyes.

She slid her hands down over her tits. The pervert in him expected her to keep moving her hands down over her stomach to lower places, but instead, she cupped her tits, lifting and squeezing them from underneath. The minx was trying to ensure he would die a slow, pleasurable death.

Forget twitching, his cock was now swollen and throbbing. Again. Why did it seem Jayden was always sporting wood around this woman? That's right: because she was beautiful, intelligent, feisty, adventurous, and his. He sighed.

"Erin, my jewel?"

"Hmm?" she warbled under the water.

"I'm going to go lay out your clothes for the evening and let you finish up your shower," he stated. Her grunt of displeasure was audible, and Jayden chuckled. "As much as I want to get in there and help you get clean, I know we won't get out until the water turns cold, and then we'll be late. Very late."

She let out a soft sigh. "Okay, Jayden. I understand. I'll try to hurry," Erin agreed while she continued massaging shampoo into her hair. The fresh, clean scent wafted out with the steam, and he became dizzy.

"Take your time. Enjoy your shower." Finishing by blowing her a kiss through the doors, he was stopped by her voice just before he exited the room.

"I love you, Jayden."

Bewitched, his heart fluttered, and he smiled. "I love you, too, Erin."

Perm-a-grin etched onto his face, Jayden hurried into the bedroom and pulled on some lounge pants. Ducking into the closet, he located the bags, which had already been packed, and then he rushed out of the room. First stop at the bottom of the stairs was Jayden's office; he gathered the envelope with the new contract he'd printed out and the jeweler's bag from the safe. Stepping into the foyer, he paused to listen. Good; the shower was still running. He had time. Jayden grabbed his keys from the entry table and took their things out to the car, where he tucked everything into the trunk except the contract—that got tossed into the backseat.

Rushing back inside, Jayden returned to his office and his desk phone. After dialing a number, he tried to be patient while waiting for his call to be answered.

"Hello?" came the familiar, heavy drawl.

"Hi, it's me. Just wanted to make sure everything went okay at the airport."

"Yes, dear. He's a lovely man, and he's excited to meet you," she said.

"As am I to meet him. We'll be leaving within the hour. See you soon." Jayden was having trouble containing his nervous excitement.

"Everything is ready, just like you requested. We can't wait for you to get here. See you soon, dear. Drive carefully." The call ended with a soft click.

The grinning man hurried back up the stairs to lay out Erin's clothes.

CHAPTER THIRTY

Though she didn't want to be, Erin couldn't deny that she was a little disappointed he'd chosen not to join her in the shower. On the other hand, she was a bit grateful, too. When the hot water began to cascade over her skin, she'd become aware of how sore and tender she was everywhere.

While she washed, she wondered where Jayden was planning to take her and considered rushing the shower so they could be on their way. However, the hot water just felt too good on her muscles, so she lingered, letting the powerful spray massage her. After several long, lazy minutes, the fear that the warm water would run out spurred Erin to finish washing her hair, soaping her body, and running a razor over her legs.

Upon stepping out, Erin was met by Jayden, who was standing there holding a fresh, warm towel. "Thank you, *A rúnsearc*," she cooed while he wrapped the towel around her, locking her arms to her body. She melted when he dipped his mouth to hers for a thorough, heart-stopping kiss.

"Your clothes are on your bed in the sub room, Erin. I thought you'd want to get ready in there since all of your things are still down there."

His thoughtfulness touched her.

"I'm going to take a quick shower." He snickered. "That is, if you left me any hot water."

"Hey, you told me to take my time," Erin whined at him.

Laughing, he replied, "Erin, I'm only playing with you. It's no bother. I'll be in and out lickety-split. I'll meet you in the foyer in about thirty minutes."

In a distracted stupor, she nodded; she was trying to get control over the tingles that had erupted across her body when he'd said "playing with you." Without a doubt, the man owned her through and through, and she wallowed in the feeling—like a happy pig in the mud.

Entering the sub's room, Erin gasped. The dress draped across the bed was new, and it was beautiful. Erin stepped closer and ran her fingertips over the material. The extra-soft, cotton knit fabric would feel nice against her piercings and ink; not itchy or constrictive. She teared up a little at the kindness of his gesture.

Holding the garment up to the light, she inspected the dress with care. It was black, with vibrant floral embroidery rising up from around the hem and the cuffs of the wrist-length sleeves. It was a longer style than Jayden usually had her wear. Looking at it, Erin guessed it would fall to her knees, maybe a bit past them. The fabric of the plain, black bodice crisscrossed and would not draw attention to her breasts. It was quite conservative for Jayden's tastes, but it was perfect for her.

Laughter slipped out when Erin took in the lingerie lying next to the dress; there was the Jayden she knew. The pale lavender satin panties were crotchless, and the matching bra was a half cup. Her nipples would rest just above the material instead of being trapped behind it. Again, his actions showed that he'd thought of her comfort.

Looking closer, she realized there were no stockings laid out. Then Erin noticed the dark purple slippers that had been placed on the floor next to the bed. She tittered while slipping her foot into one; it was a perfect fit and felt wonderful, seeing that her feet were still sore from wearing the stilettos the day before.

After patting down to dry off, Erin darted into the bathroom to retrieve the tattoo ointment and apply a fresh coat of antiseptic to her nipples. With her care done, she began working on her make up while standing nude in front of the bathroom vanity. Judging from her outfit, it was obvious Jayden was going for a soft, young look, so she followed through by keeping her colors neutral and light, finishing with a clear gloss on her lips. She scrunched some mousse into her curls and gave them a quick dry with the blow dryer – just enough to take the "wet" out – and then left it down.

Now that the creams had soaked into her skin and wouldn't stain the dress, she pulled on the panties and the bra. She was even more grateful for his choice of lingerie when she worked her boobs into the cups. A full-cup bra would have been uncomfortable. The whisper of a content sigh escaped while she maneuvered the dress over her head and felt it slink down her body. Slipping the tiny shoes on, Erin went to appraise herself in the mirror.

Feeling like a million bucks, the delighted woman twirled around, smiling while the skirt flared out and settled back in against her calves. While the fabric was lightweight and soft, the color and cut hid her lack of lingerie underneath it. Her vibrant hair contrasted against the black for a stunning effect, brightening the green of her eyes. Erin felt very feminine and beautiful.

Erin hurried back to the bathroom to retrieve her perfume. Using a very light touch – her rules forbade lotions and perfumes during scheduled playtimes – she spritzed her neck and wrists, and shot a bit into the room to walk through so the scent would settle on her hair and dress. Erin felt so pretty in the outfit; she wanted the perfume enough to risk a punishment. Glancing around one more time to make sure she hadn't missed anything else Jayden wanted her to wear, she saw nothing. Satisfied with the finished product, Erin headed down to the foyer.

Her lover had not yet come down, so Erin stood there deciding if she should kneel to wait for him or remain standing. It was still the weekend, their official "play" time, but he had indicated more than once that he wanted them to be just Erin and Jayden. She fidgeted, gnawed on the edge of her lip, and looked up the stairs while listening for movement. Jayden had chosen her outfit, which was what he did in Dom mode. *Oh, hell!* Erin started to kneel, but then stood back up each time her mind changed direction. Just as she decided to play it safe and kneel, she heard him chuckling.

"Is this some new dance you're working on, Erin?"

Palm braced against her chest, she spun around, startled. Jayden looked delicious. His damp hair was disheveled and wild. He was in a pair of dark brown Dockers and a simple, plaid shirt of browns and greens;

the top two buttons were undone, and the sleeves were rolled up to his elbows. And he was wearing his glasses.

Erin loved the glasses.

She gave him a sheepish smile. "I—I couldn't decide if you wanted me to kneel or not, Mas–Jayden," she offered in quiet explanation.

"Come here," he whispered.

Open arms awaited her. When she stepped into them, they closed around her. "Erin, my jewel. You make it so easy to love you." He kissed her forehead. "I told you, just us today. You are under your own free will in anything you want to say or do. Just keep it respectful. Okay?"

"M'kay." She exhaled in relief, and then noted she was becoming lightheaded from his proximity and his sweet breath fanning across her face.

Jayden stepped back to look her over. "Twirl," he ordered, and Erin gave him an exasperated look. "Twirl, please. I want to look at you."

This time, Erin did as he'd requested, grinning while she spun.

"Beautiful," he whispered, and then had to clear his throat. "Absolutely beautiful," Jayden said with a stronger voice, and she beamed at his approval. He glanced at his watch. "We need to get going. We've got a bit of a drive to our destination. I hope you'll be comfortable in the outfit I chose."

"It's perfect, Jayden. I love it—the material, the color, the simplicity of it. Thank you."

"Always my pleasure, Jewel. Come. Let's go." Jayden grasped her hand in his and led her out, stopping to lock the house. He guided her to his newest purchase: a dark-colored Rolls Royce Wraith with a camel-colored leather interior that wasn't even on the market yet. Sometimes it was good to know people. Like a true gentleman, Jayden held the door to his 'weekend' car open for her while she slipped in before he hurried around to slide into the driver's seat.

Erin relaxed into the plush leather while he started the car, and they pulled away. Jayden fiddled with the radio for a few minutes before queuing up the CD player. Music laced with a hypnotic bass filled the car.

"So, where are we going?" she asked about twenty minutes into the drive. They'd gotten onto Interstate 20 going west; she was trying to start a conversation so she didn't doze off. A small yawn escaped.

"Uh-huh. It's a surprise, love." His eyes were sparkling, and he grinned at her.

OCBOG

CHAPTER THIRTY-ONE

&OCR

Jayden attempted to keep his focus on the road ahead of him, but his attention continued to be drawn to Erin in his peripheral vision. The poor man was gobsmacked over how she looked; she had a conservative style with a flirtatious, sexy undercurrent. She was stunning in the dress, and he wished he could take credit for picking it out. It had been Paige who'd suggested it, knowing that Erin would be getting the tattoo and the piercing; she would need something soft and comfortable afterward.

When he'd handed his credit card over to Paige to go shopping, it had been relinquished with two requests: the dress needed to have a modest cut, and he wanted the design to show off her hair and eyes. Paige had made the perfect choice. Jayden made a mental note to get in contact with Landon when they got back to thank Paige—to thank them both, actually, for all of their help.

Erin's question hadn't surprised Jayden, but that she'd waited so long to ask did. Noticing the yawn that she tried to cover up left him feeling a tad guilty for wearing her out, but he figured now was a good time to let Erin go over the new contract. With so many changes happening – a budding romance, a new collar, and new experiences to account for – it was best to start fresh. The drive was going to take a few hours, which would be long enough for her to read through it and ask any questions she might have.

"Erin, sweet girl, you look a little sleepy."

She yawned again, and then clapped her hand over her mouth. "Yeah, I guess I am. I'm also very comfortable, and the music is quite relaxing."

"Well, I brought along our new contract if you'd like to read over it," he hedged.

The woman sat up straighter, and her eyes looked more alert at once. "Okay, but do we have enough time for that? I mean, we'll be at the restaurant soon, and we wouldn't want to have to interrupt our contract perusal, right?" Erin asked while batting her eyelashes.

Minx, Jayden thought with a grin. She was trying to be sly and fish for more information about their destination. He could give her a tidbit, and she still wouldn't figure it out: "We'll be in the car for a couple more hours."

He could see the gears turning while she tried to figure it out. When Erin came up with nothing, she let out a cute little "humph" and folded her arms over her chest with a pout. It was adorable, and he sniggered at her frustration.

Her eyes shot to Jayden, and he found the fire in them sexy as hell; so much so that he had to shift in his seat to stop the pinch on his swelling shaft.

"Give it to me," she snapped.

Oh-kay. Not cool. "Catherine," Jayden admonished her. "You will use a respectful tone with me. At. All. Times." The words were firm, with no room for discussion. While it was true that he'd dictated that the day wouldn't be spent under their usual guidelines, Jayden would never accept rudeness from his collared submissive.

Her eyes widened, and the guilt of her action overtook her. Lowering her gaze with respect, she whispered, "Aye, Master. This girl is sorry." She started fidgeting in her seat while their silence filled the car, her right hand moving up to her neck. One slim finger uncurled from her fist and started to move across her throat. She stopped. "Oh, no!"

"What is it, Erin?" Jayden asked, though he was pretty sure he knew the answer.

"You didn't put my pearl collar back on." Her worried eyes met his. "You've had it since yesterday morning."

Now Jayden had to struggle to play it cool, so he chuckled and stared at the road. "I know, sweet girl." He shrugged and felt the heat rise in his cheeks while his chest tightened. "I got you a new one. You know, a new contract, so a new collar." Jayden hoped his explanation was as nonchalant as he was trying to make it sound. His thoughts went to the box tucked away in the trunk.

"Jayden, may I please read over the new contract?"

Much better, he thought, stretching his arm into the back seat to grab the envelope. "Here you go. It's pretty much the same one as before, but I've made a couple of changes." Why was he suddenly nervous about this? She'd been his sub for a year and had already admitted that she returned his feelings of love; he shouldn't be fucking nervous about something as trivial as a contract.

For the next hour, the car was quiet except for the music while she read every word with great care— twice. To be honest, Jayden was becoming more anxious with every minute that passed in silence. He had to talk himself back from the edge numerous times, reminding himself that was just the way she worked. It wasn't the contract itself that she was being so careful with; his girl was just meticulous.

At last, Erin set the papers down in her lap and angled her body toward Jayden. He flashed her a hopeful smile. She took a breath and began. "Well, everything seems in order with it. You've updated my limits as we've discussed, but I do need to ask . . ." she paused, looking at Jayden.

"Anything, Erin. Honesty between us, remember?" Jayden reached across the console and brushed her cheek with his fingers.

"Aye, okay, here goes. So, I know you told me last night that you've ended your sexual relationships with Samantha and Micah. And you've put it in here," Erin pointed at the papers in her lap, "that we will both be monogamous," then she raised her hands to make finger quotes, "except on a case by case basis which the submissive and the Master will discuss prior to any action being taken."

"That's correct," Jayden clarified for her.

"Are you really okay with that?" she mumbled. "Or is the exception written in so that if, for example, you're having a bad day at the office, you can call and tell me that you'll be fucking Samantha or Micah or whomever." Her chin dropped, and she played with a fold in her dress.

"Erin."

Her gaze stayed down.

"Catherine, look at me please."

Erin raised her eyes up, but her posture stayed slumped and curled forward. "Hmm?"

"I did not put the exception in there as a loophole for *me* . . ." Jayden cut his eyes over to watch her reaction. "I put it in there for *you*."

That got her attention, and she straightened up again whilst a look of confusion transformed her face. "Huh? I mean—what do you mean?" she asked.

"Sweet girl, I was serious when I ended those relationships yesterday. I want you—no one but you. If I'm having a bad day, I will just have to deal with it until I can get to you. And I'm okay with that. As for you, I allowed you to explore new possibilities yesterday. You don't think I'd open your eyes to those experiences just to slam the door on ever doing them again if you enjoyed it, do you?"

Her features softened while the confusion melted away. "You are too good to me, Jayden. I don't know how I got so lucky to find you."

"In my opinion, I was the lucky one. To be clear, Jewel, I'm not saying you've got my permission to go playing with other Doms anytime you want—"

"I would never!"

"I know, sweet girl, but I have a feeling that there will be at least a few times we'll need to play with another. However, when that happens, I assure that it will be *we*. I'll never stay away again, I promise. You told me that you enjoyed the intense sessions and the whipping, right? Even the electricity play Katarina did for you a few months back . . ."

Erin's eyes took on a distant, glazed look. "Aye, I did. Very much so."

He watched her breathing get ragged while she savored the memory. Her body language alone told Jayden just how much she'd enjoyed it. And wasn't he all about mastering any techniques that could work his girl into an aroused state that fast?

"I've considered whip training in the past, but I've never been able to bring myself to give it a try, despite Jonathan's frequent prodding. Jon is the best that we know, and he's offered to meet with us anytime to get my skills up to par in one-on-one sessions."

Erin's eyes seemed a little glassy and lust-filled at the direction their conversation had gone.

Jayden went on explaining. "So, you see, the 'exception' clause would apply here because you and I would discuss the logistics of setting up a training scene with Jonathan in attendance before we do it. Details like how much skin you have showing, whether I would use your body while he was still there, whether or not you would want – or I would expect you – to attend to his needs as well; that kind of thing. The same principle applies to what Katarina did for you. I have limited training with electricity, so if you want me to learn her skills, more sessions would be required."

Jayden glanced over at Erin once he'd finished talking, to find that her thighs had parted in the seat and her breathing had become even more ragged. She licked her lips, and Jayden watched her tongue.

"Fuck. You look so sexy right now. Are you wet, Erin?" He almost choked on his words.

She closed her thighs and rubbed them together, closing her eyes. "Aye," she panted.

The man knew he shouldn't do what he was contemplating, but he couldn't help himself. Jayden had told Erin she had free will today, so she could tell him to go to hell if she wanted – so long as she did it with respect – or she could play along.

"Catherine, lift your dress and show me."

℠

CHAPTER THIRTY-TWO

℠

Catherine wanted to squirm.
    She wanted to press her thighs together and try to relieve the pressure building between them. Instead, she let her thighs spread open, hoping maybe that would help. The wanton female couldn't help it; his voice was pure sex. When you added the subject matter, yeah, she was helpless and desperate to get her breathing under control.

He turned his head to glance at Catherine just as her tongue had slipped out to wet her lips, which were becoming dry from her harsh breaths. Frozen, his eyes darkened. It was a look she knew well. In mere seconds, he'd read her body and knew the aroused state she was in. The million dollar question was: what was he going to do about it?

When he asked if Catherine was wet, she had to squeeze her thighs. Scrunching her eyes shut, she gave in and clenched; the movement created much-needed pressure against her pussy. Catherine didn't want to worry about right or wrong or that they were in a car anyone driving by could see into. She wanted to relinquish control. "Aye" was all she could say. In her mind, she begged Jayden to decipher her need for her Master.

Then he went there: Catherine's Master was back, giving her the choice, and she wasted no time making her decision. With daring bravado, she propped her right foot up onto the dashboard and inched the dress up, dragging her nails along her skin as she did. An airy gasp escaped her when the cool air from the vent blew against her skin. The exhibitionist didn't have to look down to know that Master would see her leaking from between her smooth nether lips.

She swallowed down her amusement at his futile attempts to keep his eyes on the road. They got to a red light, and he turned his head to look at her.

"Show me those tits," he commanded.

The garment's neckline was loose enough that Catherine was able to tug the material down and to the sides, tucking it underneath her breasts.

Master sucked in a sharp breath and let out a whistle. "My god, Erin, you are so fucking gorgeous!" The light turned green, and he returned his attention to the road.

For the most part, the road had been free of traffic, with only an occasional passing car. However, there was always the chance that she would be seen with her erotic bits on display. The experience was exciting and thrilling, and it made Catherine's pulse beat faster.

Watching Master's Adam's apple bob when he swallowed, she waited to see if he would take this further or if he was going to just make her spend the rest of the ride like that.

"Do you want to come, Catherine?"

"Always," she giggled, and he rolled his eyes at her.

"You are insatiable, Jewel. Very well, then; come."

The submissive's mouth opened and closed like a fish out of water, and the Dom smirked. "We have about ten minutes. If you really want to come, you better get to it."

What? Oh! Master wanted her to masturbate for him. Of course. He was driving; he couldn't help.

She wasted no time spreading her pussy lips with her left hand, and then using her right index finger to rub circles on her swollen clit; she had plenty of lubrication. Catherine found herself having to resist the temptation to close her eyes, and she watched him watching her instead. His breathing picked up, he gripped the steering wheel tighter, and he parted his lips so that magical tongue slipped out and ran across them.

Catherine had been about to fall over the edge when he growled, "Stop!"

In an amazing show of mind over matter, she was able to hear and obey; she removed her finger from her clit but kept her lips spread.

"Please, Master. This girl is so close it hurts."

He nodded at the road ahead of them. "Sorry, sweetheart, but we're almost there; so we'll have to resume this later. Please fix your clothes, Erin."

They had just passed a sign welcoming them to Sweetwater, Texas. Her large, green eyes looked around at the small town while she tried to figure out what awaited them there. When she had settled both her mind and body, she was able to notice that Jayden looked nervous.

"Are you okay?"

His brown eyes darted her way before snapping back to the road. "Sure."

"Jayden?"

The car pulled onto a dirt driveway with an arching gate. At the top, fancy metalwork displayed: "Flying M Ranch."

Erin reached over to stroke Jayden's arm, and he smiled and said, "Showtime."

The small dirt road they were traveling went on for about a mile. To either side were acres of yellow-green grass waving in the light breeze. And horses. Lots of horses. In the distance, Erin could make out the reflective surface of a watering hole, and the otherwise unbroken view of the horizon was pebbled by the occasional boulder. It was breathtaking. Before too long, tall oaks and cedar trees began to encroach on the road, giving Erin the feeling of passing through a natural tunnel. When they broke free of the tree line, a huge mansion appeared before them. The lawn around the house was neatly landscaped, and she couldn't decide which was more beautiful: the path to the house, the house itself, or the surrounding flower gardens.

"Wow! This isn't a restaurant is it, Jayden?"

He chuckled. "Nope. I never said I was taking you to a restaurant; you just assumed that."

The car circled around a large metal fountain, which depicted a group of running stallions crossing a fjord. He stopped the car in front of the steps to the main entrance and turned off the engine.

"Is that some kind of metal?"

Jayden's eyes followed Erin's line of sight to the fountain. Taking her hand, he locked her in his gaze. "Yes, the bulk of it is iron, but the hooves, manes, and tails are copper."

"How do you know that?"

"Remember, Erin, it's just us. Just Jayden and Erin; okay, sweet girl?"

"Okay, but how?" Erin's heart was palpitating faster with by the minute.

"I've arranged a few days off from work for both of us, and this is where we are staying. After this evening, it will be just you and me. But right now, waiting inside are some very important people who want to meet us. Oh, and I commissioned my craftsmen to make the horses," he added.

While she was elated that he'd planned a getaway, she couldn't for the life of her think of who might be inside the sprawling building. Mind racing, Erin sat in her spot while Jayden went around the car to open her door. The fresh October air was crisp, and she felt like they'd entered another world; their own private world.

He left her standing there gawking at the view and moved to the back of the car. When he set two carry-on suitcases on the gravel, Erin realized that he had thought of everything. Even when he told her they were spending the next few days there, clothes and toiletries hadn't crossed her mind. Couldn't blame a girl for being distracted under the circumstances, though!

The trunk closed with a quiet thud, and Jayden picked up the bags and walked back over to where she stood. Extending his elbow toward Erin, he asked: "Shall we?"

Hooking her arm through his, Erin responded with a delighted, "Let's." A relaxed smile was plastered on her face.

Together, they mounted the steps and walked across the wide porch to the door. Erin made a mental note to spend some time in one of the big oversized rocking chairs that graced the porch before their visit was over. Jayden set one of the bags down long enough to open the door and lead her inside.

The smell of home-cooked food permeated the house, and they laughed when both their stomachs growled at the same time. They'd been so distracted by each other that morning and afternoon that they'd forgotten to eat anything since their quick breakfast much earlier in the day. It appeared they were both starving.

"Jayden, darlin', is that you?" A strong voice that Erin recognized at once came from down the hall.

Erin looked at Jayden in surprise and was taken aback by how young he looked suddenly. The smile on his face was huge, and his eyes were light and bright. She was about to say something when a tall woman with green eyes and shoulder-length, wavy, red hair walked into the foyer. She was dressed in what Erin was sure were designer jeans and a pale green silk blouse. The woman was stunning, as usual.

"Jayden! Erin!" Jillian Masterson squealed, and she rushed up to them, pulling them both into a tight embrace.

Jayden dropped the bags and threw his arms around his mother while Erin slipped back. She found herself grinning just watching them.

Jillian released her son, and then she turned her attention to Erin. "It's so nice to see you again, Erin. Jayden has been keeping you all to himself—come here, darlin'!" She pulled the younger woman into another hug.

When his mother released her, Erin stepped back. "Hi, Jillian. It's good to see you again, too. You've got a gorgeous home."

"Oh, thank you, dear. We're quite happy with it, and we hope that you'll enjoy your time here so that you'll come back often!" Her eyes darted over to Jayden, and Erin wondered at the silent message in them.

Jayden chuckled beside her. "Thanks, Mom. Erin and I have had kind of a long weekend, and we're starving. What's for dinner?"

A throat cleared behind them, and Jayden's beautiful smile returned in full force, as did Erin's.

"Now, son, is that any way to greet your momma? Is your old lady not feeding you enough at home?" he teased Jayden while throwing a wink at Erin. "Howdy, Erin. Welcome to Sweetwater and the Flying M."

"Hello, Malcolm. I'm thrilled to be here. I've no doubts I'm going to enjoy our visit very much," she answered with sincerity while Jayden wrapped an arm around her waist.

Malcolm chuckled, and his eyes twinkled when he cleared his throat. "I'm sure you will. There are plenty of things to do here," he said, looking toward Jayden and winking again.

Jayden's cheeks bloomed deep red, almost like he'd been caught being naughty. She'd have to ask her lover about that; surely his dad didn't know about their lifestyle. *Did he?*

In the last year, she had decided that Jayden was one of a kind. He was beautiful inside and out, and now he wanted *her*, not just her submission. Erin's eyes moved from Jayden to Jillian, and then to Malcolm, while she wondered how she'd gotten so lucky and if life could be any more perfect.

Before she could let the thought sink in all the way, she was jolted back to the here-and-now by a gravelly voice.

"Cat? Is it really you, *iníon*?"

Daughter? Erin spun around in shock. "Da?" she squeaked, and her eyes welled with tears.

ଞ୦ଓଃ

CHAPTER THIRTY-THREE

ଞ୦ଓଃ

It had taken Jayden nine months and one private investigator to locate Smallwood O'Chancey; Woody to his friends, and Da to Erin. He'd been working at a small lake town diner in California as a fry cook when the PI tracked him down. When Jayden learned that Woody had been traveling town to town, picking up odd jobs during his search for Erin, he knew he'd done the right thing in seeking out the man. After the initial contact, it had taken another month of casual communication between the two men to build a rapport so that one, Woody wouldn't hunt Jayden down as the beast that had hidden his daughter away, and two, he could convince Woody to agree to wait for this reunion.

Through her journal and their conversations, Erin had told Jayden she'd left her previous life behind. She'd gone into hiding because of that monster. Even once he was dead, Erin had lived in fear that one of Spencer's friends would remember her and have ideas about how she could be treated. On more than one occasion, she'd endured their laughter and mockery, so she had good cause to worry.

Jayden watched the two of them embrace, and his own heart warmed at the sight. Erin needed her father in her life. It had killed him inside knowing she'd turned her back on her Da for her protection and his. As her Dom and now her lover, Jayden was prepared to take over the role of guardian and would be protecting Erin from now on. No one was ever going to hurt her again.

A small, strong arm wrapped around Jayden's waist, and he looked down into his mother's grass-green eyes. Her tears glittered back at him when she looked up. "I'm so proud of you, Jayden. You did the right thing. I don't know the whole story—"

"Mom, I can't—"

"Shh, dear, I know that, and I don't want you to tell me. Perhaps with time, Erin and I can reach a point where she'll consider me her mom, too, and she'll tell me. Until then, I can be patient. She is going to be around awhile, right?"

If Jayden hadn't already made that decision, he would've been left slack-jawed at the implied message his mom was delivering. Instead, he gave her a gentle squeeze. "Yes, Mom, I think she will be—that's what I'm hoping for, at least. I love that you've welcomed her without judgment." Jayden smiled.

Yes, his parents were aware of his lifestyle even though they were not part of it. Jayden had never been able to keep secrets from Jillian, and in return, she'd always supported her son, no matter what. He'd told his mother everything he could about Erin without giving away the bits that were Erin's story to tell, and he appreciated her subtlety with Erin now. In fact, it was Jillian who had suggested the private investigator when Jayden had gotten frustrated with dead ends during the search for Woody.

He kept a gentle grip on his mother, and they turned to watch father and daughter reunite. The duo had stopped hugging fiercely, but they still had a grip on each other, much like he and Jillian did. Tears were flowing. Seeing them side-by-side, the family resemblance was uncanny. Woody's hair was greying, but traces of the crimson fire that cascaded from Erin's scalp still lingered in his beard and mustache, and their eyes were a perfect match.

"Oh, God, Catherine, you had me so worried, baby girl. You just vanished and I couldn't find you and I tried everything and—" Woody was spilling his heart out, fat tears rolling down his cheeks.

"Shh, Da," Erin consoled him. "I know I worried you, and I'm so sorry. It was just—I needed to get away from my old life and make sure it couldn't follow me."

Jayden could see the shame in her eyes while she struggled to find a way to apologize.

"Well, I guess it doesn't matter now. I've got my Cat back, and look at you! What a beautiful woman you've become. You're the spitting image of your Ma, God rest her soul." He smiled at her.

"Da, there's someone I want you to meet," she murmured while reaching out for Jayden. He took her hand and let her pull him in. "Da, this is Jayden, the love of my life. Jayden, this is my father, Woody O'Chancey."

Jayden offered his hand, which Woody took in a firm grip. "Nice to finally put a face to the voice, son."

Erin shot Jayden a 'we'll be talking, mister' look.

Woody went on, "I don't know why I've had to wonder if my *iníon* was alive or dead for so long; don't know if I want to know at this point. However, young man, I do know you've brought my girl back to me—for that I will be forever indebted to you."

"Thank you, sir."

Erin jumped a little in his embrace. His mouth quirked at the corner in response to her reaction, but it was understandable. Never before had she heard him acknowledge another person with that level of respect.

"I only did what I felt was right in the situation. Your daughter is my whole world, sir, and I'd do anything for her." Next to him, Erin gasped. While maintaining eye contact with Woody, he was able to feather a light kiss across her forehead before silence bore down on the small group.

Woody eyed Jayden for several moments, and then startled them all when he clapped his hands together. "So," he boomed, "something smells delicious, and I was promised a home-cooked meal. When do we eat?"

The tension seemed to melt away while everyone laughed at this question.

Jillian soon took charge. "It's ready, Woody," she promised, hooking her arm in his and starting to lead him back to the dining room. "I just need to bring the dishes out to the table. Why don't you boys seat yourselves? Erin, can you give me a hand?"

Jayden's beautiful girl smiled. "I'd love to, Jillian! Just tell me what to do, and I'm on it."

He couldn't resist a hidden swat to her ass when she walked away from him. She giggled in response.

Yep; slow, pleasurable death coming right up.

ഐଔരଔ

CHAPTER THIRTY-FOUR
A Divine Life

ഐଔരଔ

Dinner had been delicious. Jillian was a fantastic cook, and Erin was planning to get together with her to learn some of Jayden's favorites. She'd promised to call Jillian in the coming week to set up their next visit. Woody was going to start working on the Masterson's ranch, and therefore would be staying in Texas, so they'd have plenty of time for catching up. Everyone seemed to understand that Jayden and Erin were celebrating something special and needed privacy.

Both Jayden and Erin had spent most of the night blushing the color of tomatoes while their parents took turns regaling the group with childhood stories. They'd learned some very interesting things about each other's younger years over the course of the evening.

Erin's Da had sat next to her and reached out to touch her throughout dinner: patting her hand and squeezing her shoulder. She guessed that he was just assuring himself that she was real, and she felt bad that she hadn't tried to contact him herself. Jayden couldn't have touched her heart any deeper than he had with this gesture. He'd given Erin her daddy back.

The evening had been long and tiring, but Erin had loved every minute of it. Sad though it was, the time had come for them to gather at the front door and say their goodbyes. Jayden closed the door and turned around to face her. "Just what are you so happy about?" He quirked his eyebrow at her playfully.

On impulse, she threw her arms in the air and started spinning around. "Everything!" Her eyes clenched tight, Erin smelled his cologne when he scooped her up in his arms and continued spinning her around. He slowed down and set Erin on her slippered feet, keeping a grip on her so she didn't fall from the dizziness.

Raising her eyes up to meet his dark brown ones, the dizziness morphed into longing and need. His lips were on hers in a matter of seconds. They teased, licked, and kissed for several minutes, enjoying the peaceful bubble around them.

"You promise you're happy right now?" Jayden whispered while resting his forehead against hers.

She nuzzled her nose against his chin. "Very," she whispered back.

"Mm," he moaned when her nuzzling turned into nips along his jaw. "I hope you aren't too tired for one more surprise, sweet girl." His eyes twinkled.

Erin faked a big stretch and yawn and tried to put on a bored face. "I guess I can handle one more, if I must." She sighed.

"Well, I wouldn't want to put you out or anything," he grumbled with mock disdain.

"Please, Jayden." Erin bounced in place to show her excitement. "I can't imagine what more you could surprise me with, but I can't wait!" The bouncing had jarred her bladder, and she stopped her movements. "But I have to pee first!" she blurted before running off to the bathroom. His answering laughter followed her, not cutting off until she closed the door.

When she came back out a few minutes later, Jayden was gone. Erin walked around, poking her head into the living room, the dining room, and then the kitchen.

"Jayden?" she called out. There was no answer.

Since she was in the kitchen, Erin opted to get a glass of water and wait for Jayden to come back, assuming he'd ducked into one of the other bathrooms as well. Sipping the water, she turned her attention to the picture window overlooking the backyard. It was dark, the sun having set about an hour before, but there was a soft flickering glow off in the distance. Curious, she called out to Jayden one more time, and when met with silence, she put her glass down and headed toward the French doors that led out back. Her eyes were focused on the far away glow when her hand reached for the doorknob.

A sharp sting radiated up through her finger, and Erin looked down to see that she'd grabbed a single rose, which had been attached to the handle. Using care, she collected the flower and noticed the door was also ajar. Erin lifted the red bloom to her nose and inhaled its light fragrance while stepping into the night. Thanks to the full moon, it was brighter than she would have expected.

On the wooden patio table, she could see another single red rose lying across its surface. Erin picked that up also, and then looked around. "Jayden?" she called out again. A few more steps forward brought her to the edge of the wide wraparound porch. She glanced down to watch her footing while she descended, and she found another rose lying across the step. When she stooped to pick it up, she noticed the trail: red roses had been tossed every couple of feet to make a path across the grass.

Erin felt her heart flutter, and her excitement level spiked. She didn't know what he was up to; but his games were always fun, and she was ready to play.

Heading off along the trail, she made sure to pick up each rose she came across. The path wound around the pool, which was filled with floating tea lights. The candle's presence explained the flickering glow she'd noticed from the window. It was a mesmerizing sight, and she paused to appreciate it and wonder how he'd set this all up so fast. Then she recalled Jillian informing Jayden that everything was good to go. She'd blown off the comment at the time, not understanding its significance. His mother must be in on whatever Jayden was up to.

While she studied the pool, romantic music began floating on the air. Erin glanced around, trying to decide from which direction it was coming. Beyond the pool and deck, the trees thickened, and the yard was pitch black. She clutched the dozen roses she'd gathered against her chest and peered into the darkness.

"Jayden!" Erin called. "Are you out here?"

Light exploded before her eyes. Erin blinked rapidly while they adjusted. Then her vision came into focus on a gazebo covered in tiny twinkling lights about ten feet away. Standing on the steps and leaning against the rail, was Jayden, and the look on his face was smoldering.

His rich voice extended across the distance between them, wrapping around her and enfolding her in pure desire. "May I please have this dance, my beautiful Erin?" He held out a single rose toward her.

Somehow, her feet cooperated before her mind could catch up, carrying her forward to him—to her love. He brought her to a halt at the bottom of the gazebo steps by extending the rose to touch her forehead. Her eyes drifted closed when he began to stroke the satin petals across her face. Caressing the side of her jaw, he let the flower curve under her chin, coaxing her head up with light strokes of the bloom. She lifted her face in response and opened her eyes when she felt his breath on her.

Jayden's face was mere inches away, and his lips hovered over Erin's lips. He closed the distance, and time froze while she was kissed with absolute thoroughness. When they had to part to allow in fresh air, she realized Jayden had moved them up into the gazebo, and that they were dancing.

One song faded into another while he continued gliding Erin back and forth in slow circles. Erin had never learned to dance, but with Jayden leading, it was effortless. He twirled her around and around until they made their way to the far side of the gazebo. Jayden stilled their motions in front of a table set with an empty vase, a bottle of wine in an ice bucket, two crystal glasses, and a flat, long box embossed with a fine jeweler's logo. *Her new collar?*

Erin was speechless while he took the roses from her arms and deposited them into the vase, where they fanned out to fill the space. Then he lifted the bottle from the bucket; Erin was awed to discover that he'd remembered her preference after all that time. He filled the glasses and returned the bottle to the ice. Lifting the glasses, Jayden offered one to her. "Ice wine, sweet girl?"

She continued to gape at him. He was pulling out all the stops to replace her collar, and her mind was buzzing.

"I do believe I owe you this. If memory serves me right, I didn't allow you to enjoy your glass the night we met." His smile was soft and loving.

Erin took the glass and raised it to her nose to inhale the sweet fragrance. "Why, Mr. Masterson, are you trying to get me drunk so you can have your wicked way with me?" she asked, playing coy.

His answering smirk should've been illegal for the havoc it wreaked upon her body. "Why, Ms. O'Chancey, you know I can have my wicked way with you any time I want."

Erin gulped.

"However, my intentions are nothing but honest, Ms. O'Chancey." He lifted the box from the table and knelt before Erin.

What was he doing? Oh, God. Oh, God! Erin held her breath while he lifted those chocolate eyes to hers.

"Catherine Eilene O'Chancey, your servitude has been the most surreal experience in my existence, but it is nothing compared to the depth of love that has blossomed in my heart for you. It would be a great honor if you would agree to stay at my side for the rest of our lives." His eyes held a pleading look while he lifted the lid of the box.

Sitting in the middle of the jeweler's box was a square-cut, black diamond in a platinum setting. The upper part of the band that held the stone had been crafted into Celtic eternity knots. Jayden lifted the ring out of its velvet nest, setting the box on the table. Taking her hand in his, he positioned the exquisite piece of jewelry at the end of her left ring finger.

"Before you answer, let me explain that I want both lives with you. I want Catherine to kneel at my feet, and I need Erin to sleep in my arms. Tell me if I'm wrong, but I believe that much like I need to dominate, your submissive nature won't be ignored. I want to nurture your strength and independence, Erin. The Dom in me is willing to share the helm with the man that wants to be your partner. *A rúnsearc,* will you marry me?"

She still hadn't taken a breath, but she did now: a deep, shaky breath that stuttered with her erratic heartbeat.

"Catherine, Erin, please say you will accept this token as a symbol our unbreakable bond, not only as Master and submissive, but also soul mates and lovers."

A lone tear fell free and trickled down her cheek. "Jayden, to serve you has always been divine, but to be your wife would be the greatest pleasure I could ever know. Aye, I will marry you!"

Jayden slid the eternity diamond onto her finger before rising and scooping her up in his arms, heading for the house—and the bedroom.

The ice wine was left untouched.

❦

FIN

❦

Now an excerpt from Surreal, Book Three of The Divine Trilogy

ಬಂಡಿ

CHAPTER ONE

ಬಂಡಿ

New age music reverberated around Catherine and her Master. The sound blended with the submissive's soft echoing moans while Master teased her flesh with a Wartenberg wheel.

He'd turned the thermostat down so that the playroom was frigid—to Catherine, at least. The woman didn't have a stitch of material to cover her body, and her Master was playing mind games with her with his attire, which was tight, leather, and black. Just the sight of him had started the boiling heat within her. Combating that warmth was the cool air, which drew her nipples into hardened buds, making Catherine more

359

than aware of the metal that pierced them. The inconspicuous wheel rolling over her tender flesh soon became maddening.

Master had left her eyes uncovered, explaining while he'd bound her legs to the spreader bar and her wrists to the fur-lined cuffs dangling from the ceiling, that he wanted his slut to see everything tonight.

Catherine's eyes were wide open, watching him move around her. He was bringing her skin to sizzling life with the cat o' nine tails. Sir Jonathan had suggested it as an interim tool until the couple could begin their private lessons with him. Wielded much like a flogger, it delivered the stinging bite of a whip, and as such, was a perfect beginning compromise for the submissive and her Master.

The coolness of the room had been forgotten by the needy woman almost as soon as Master had started flailing her. Delivered with a steady, controlled hand, the leather *thwapping* against her skin warmed it so that the cold air became a welcome thing, keeping her balanced and comfortable. Master had not taken up the wheel until her whole body was striped pink and white, with the exception of her breasts—they'd been spared, and ached because of it.

Bound and spread for her Master's pleasure, Catherine had kept her eyes lowered until he told her to do otherwise. When she raised her emerald orbs at his command, she'd found him mere inches away, his own brown eyes dark with desire. She didn't dream of resisting when he pressed his lips to hers; she welcomed him in, crying out in surprise when he ran the spiked wheel over her nipple the first time.

Another twenty minutes passed in which he teased her breasts with the little wheel. She continued to assure him that she was "green," still eager and enjoying herself. Master was being cautious of her healing nipples, and for that she was grateful. Yet, part of her wanted to ask him for more. Her nipples throbbed, desiring to be pulled and twisted despite the low, constant ache that had been with her since Sir Landon had run the cold steel through them a few weeks before.

"There. I think you are prepared." Master's strong hands stroked her flesh with a tenderness that made goose bumps erupt up and down Catherine's arms and legs. Slipping his fingers inside her slick folds, he filled her, creating a firm pressure, and then stilled and continued, "Always so wet and willing for my touch—my whims. You're a good little slut, aren't you?"

Catherine had enough of her wits about her to not fall for his trick. She'd not been given permission to speak; therefore, she didn't. However, the submissive didn't fight the lustful moan that slipped from her lips when Master dragged his fingers from her heat with an agonizing slowness, just to cram them back into her.

Bestowing a proud smile on Catherine, Master kissed her rough and quick. "Yes, you are, my *cailin maith.* As much as I would love to fill that cunt with my cock, we would both come too soon, and that would ruin my plans for later."

The submissive whimpered when her Master took his touch away, leaving her bereft and wanting. Her heart jumped at the new endearment he'd taken to using. She loved being his "good girl." Every part of her felt alive and alert for any bit of friction she could get. Catherine fought the urge to plead for an orgasm, savoring his gentle attentions instead while he undid her cuffs. He rubbed each of her wrists and ankles when the restraints came off.

"Your costume for tonight is hanging in the en suite. You have twenty minutes to freshen up, dress, and meet me in the foyer. Do not touch that pussy. I assure you, Catherine, that if you wash away the essence I worked so hard to get out of you, you will not enjoy the punishment. Do you understand? You may speak."

"Aye, Master."

Master beamed at her, and she straightened her posture. There wasn't much room to adjust, but Catherine relished giving him the closest thing to perfection as she was capable. With a searing kiss that left her lips puffy, he exited the room in a cloud of commanding confidence.

Catherine was slick and breathless upon his departure. She allowed herself a few moments to calm her breathing and center her focus before following him out of the playroom. Curiosity drew her toward the submissive's room. They'd discussed costumes for Dungeon and Dreams' Halloween bash just once; Catherine had told him that she trusted his decision and would wear anything he chose with pride.

Now she was giddy with anticipation, wondering what he might have selected. Would he have her in something cute and frilly, or would he be the stereotypical male who preferred the risqué: naughty nurse, French maid, school girl—the possibilities were endless.

Arriving at the bedroom door, she paused, fingering the black diamond adorning her left hand. No matter what he'd chosen, she knew she could pull it off if Master believed she could. He would never humiliate her more than she was comfortable with. With that thought, Catherine turned the knob and walked into the room.

Waiting on the bed were two things, and both were made of metal.

❖❖❖

A little bit nervous and a whole lot excited, Jayden paced the foyer. He couldn't wait to see Catherine on display for him. Any normal person might think it madness that Jayden wanted to take his jewel out into a public setting in so little, but it was pride that drove the Dom, not insanity.

His close friends knew of Catherine's latest body modifications, but this would be the first time the couple had gone to the club since they had been done. What better way to show them off than to put her on display in a "cage" with himself as the "jailer"? Jayden had known his black leather outfit would arouse his slut, hence the reason he'd worn it to play with her, preparing her to wear the custom-made dress.

A telltale clack of heels prompted him to move to the foot of the stairs. He looked up, fixing his stare on Catherine while she descended. *Perhaps the outfit was a bad idea after all,* he thought with amusement while taking her in. So seductive was she that Jayden wanted to ravage her right then and there, and he had the sudden feeling that the night was going to be a long one.

Catherine's small feet were enclosed in black, patent leather stilettos. When she reached the landing and spun for him, he could see the chain-work that ran up the back of the heel. He allowed his eyes to follow the curve of her strong calf and continue up her body. Held up by spaghetti straps, there wasn't much to the dress; lightweight lengths of chain had been welded together to weave the garment, which hung to her mid-thigh. Approximate two-inch spaces between each length left nothing to the imagination. Her tattoo was on full display, as were her emerald J's and smooth cunt. As she twirled, the light from the overhead chandelier refracted off her black diamond.

"You look amazing, Jewel. Please kneel."

Without a word, Catherine took her place at his feet, her arms locking behind her back in perfect position. Jayden took the collar from his pocket and leaned forward. "Your servitude is surreal, Catherine," he murmured while buckling her leather play collar around her neck. "You may speak."

"To serve you is always divine, Master."

He smiled. "I expect that you will be on your best behavior tonight, slut. You will speak only when given permission, and I don't want you making eye contact with anyone but me unless otherwise directed. Do you understand?"

Jayden moved around her with slow, sure steps, waiting for her reply. It didn't come. "*Cailin maith,* you may answer."

"Aye, Master. This girl knows her place for tonight and looks forward to making her Master proud." Her voice was breathy, and the Dom reveled in the knowledge that he had done that to her.

"That you do, my jewel. Rise, and show me the rest of your costume."

Catherine's breath caught at his words, but she did as requested. Standing before turning around, his submissive bent at the waist and grabbed her ankles with a muffled groan. Jayden's face broke out in a mischievous grin when he eyed the steel sunburst, whose rays grew from the end of what he knew to be a rather large plug. The rays extended from the center, like hands, so that the custom accessory cupped her firm cheeks.

"Beautiful. Let us be on our way. I'll be driving tonight because Micah requested the evening off. You have no objections to the Wraith, do you?" Jayden asked while snapping her leash into place on the collar and helping her into a dress coat.

The question was rhetorical; Jayden didn't expect an answer because it wasn't her decision to make. It was his.

෨෬

Surreal – Coming 2014
෨෬

About the Author

R.E. Hargrave is a fledgling author who has always been a lover of books and now looks forward to the chance to give something back to the literary community. She lives on the outskirts of Dallas, TX with her husband and three children.

෪ාශ්

෪ාශ්

Her works:

Sugar & Spice, a novella
Haunted Raine, a novella
To Serve is Divine, Book One in The Divine Trilogy

www.rehargrave.com

R.E. Hargrave

79586470R00204

Made in the USA
Lexington, KY
24 January 2018